KU-756-033

TALES OF AMBERGROVE
RANGER'S ODYSSEY
DRAGONWOLF TRILOGY BOOK ONE

H. T. MARTINEAU

authorHOUSE®

AuthorHouse™
1663 Liberty Drive
Bloomington, IN 47403
www.authorhouse.com
Phone: 833-262-8899

© 2020 H. T. Martineau. All rights reserved.

No part of this book may be reproduced, stored in a retrieval system, or
transmitted by any means without the written permission of the author.

First published by AuthorHouse 10/10/2020
This edition published by AuthorHouse 08/06/2021

ISBN: 978-1-6655-0203-0 (sc)
ISBN: 978-1-6655-0202-3 (hc)
ISBN: 978-1-6655-0204-7 (e)

Library of Congress Control Number: 2020918900

Print information available on the last page.

This book is printed on acid-free paper.

Because of the dynamic nature of the Internet, any web addresses or links contained in
this book may have changed since publication and may no longer be valid. The views
expressed in this work are solely those of the author and do not necessarily reflect the
views of the publisher, and the publisher hereby disclaims any responsibility for them.

For years, my husband has tried to teach me
not to lose sight of the things I love
because I don't have time for them, or I think I'm not good enough.
If you make the time for the things you love,
who you are and what you do will always be good enough.

This is for you, dear Reader.
You are always good enough.

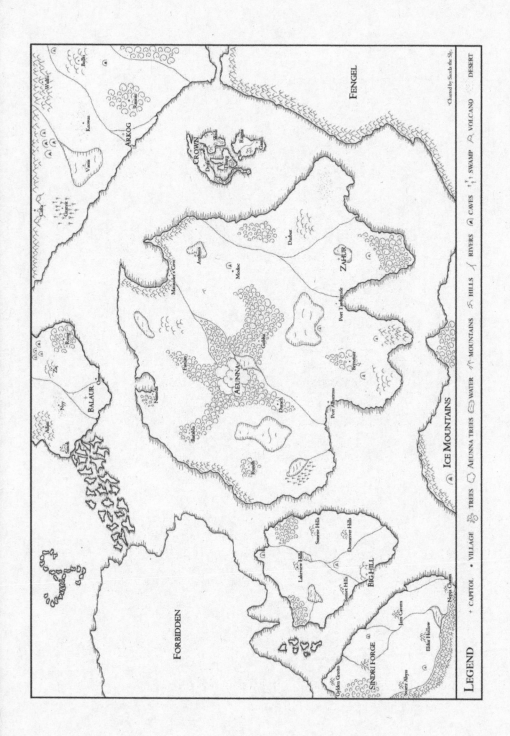

FENGEL

CROWN

ARKOG

ZAHUR

BALAUR

FORBIDDEN

SINDRI FORGE

BIG HILL

ICE MOUNTAINS

'Charted by Saindi the Sly.

LEGEND   + CAPITOL   • VILLAGE   ☆ TREES   ◈ AEUNNA TREES   ≈ WATER   ⋀ MOUNTAINS   ⌇ HILLS   ⌇ RIVERS   ⊙ CAVES   ⌇ SWAMP   ⌂ VOLCANO   ⠿ DESERT   ⊙ ICE MOUNTAINS

Contents

CHAPTER ONE

ROLE-PLAYING GAME

Danag ran as fast as she could through the forest. It wouldn't be long before the goblins caught up with her, and she was outnumbered. Even Dalzi had fallen into a trap, so there was no one left to help her.

Once she had ventured deep into the forest, she turned and quietly backed away, listening intently. She heard a rustle to her left, pulled her bowstring back, and shot once. Twice. The goblin crumpled to the ground. The next one she didn't hear. She drew her sword as it charged her, then swung and missed. Swung and missed. Swung and hit her own leg.

"Come on!" she shouted, swinging again. This time she got him.

She was able to pick off the goblins one at a time—until the leader arrived. Glancing quickly around her, she saw one of the goblins' traps waiting to be sprung. In a matter of moments, the leader of the goblins was dangling in the air by his ankle. Danag stood, bow taut, as the other goblins arrived, circled her, and surrendered to save their leader. The quest was won.

"Great job, Mara!" A wide grin spread behind Toren Green's russet beard as he tousled his daughter's hair.

"Are we all back now, or does she have to actually free us before we can move on?" Kara asked.

Kara was Toren's youngest daughter. He had a third, the eldest, but she never came with them to the dungeon. Mara, Kara, and Toren sat together on a long, maroon couch. They each had trays of dice in their laps and eager looks on their faces. Once a month, Toren brought his younger daughters to Jim the Dungeon Master's house to play DUNGEONS & DRAGONS. They affectionately called Jim's living room the dungeon. The dragon came when they played late into the night and Jim lit his fireplace.

Mara snapped back to reality and glanced around the room. Tapestries were hung around the walls to emulate a forest. Jim's wife and son sat on a brown loveseat next to the couch. Jim sat across from them at a folding table, which was strewn with manuals, dice sets, and markers.

Toren glanced across the room at the grumpy man behind the table. "What do you say, Dungeon Master?" he asked.

Jim sighed and scratched his chin for a moment before turning to Mara and nodding curtly. "Now—I suppose this is the best time for birthday cake and presents," he replied, grinning.

This was a special game day because they were gathered to celebrate Mara's sixteenth birthday. When her dad had asked her what she wanted to do for her birthday, there was only one possible answer. Here they were, among friends who were like family. Mara's older sister, Sara, had gone out to a movie with friends. Her mother had scheduled a selling party for her current pyramid scheme, wanting the girls to be out of the way for her to work. The current product was Lovely Lights, a do it yourself highlight and lowlight hair tool.

Mara grinned back at Jim. She was happy to be right where she was. Whereas Sara was more like their mother, Mara was like her father. Kara was a little bit of both, excited about swords and dragons while also admiring her pink painted nails. Mara loved her little sister, so much that even though she despised pink and all pink things, she had accepted and immediately worn the little pink, purple, and sky-blue friendship bracelet her sister had given her as her first birthday present of the morning.

"Yes, it's a perfect time for cake!" Mara agreed, standing and placing her dice tray on the coffee table.

"Okay, okay. Let us get it all set up first," said Alaina, Jim's wife, standing and beckoning for the men to follow.

Jim and Alaina's son, Johnny, was just starting to get antsy when their parents called them into the kitchen. Johnny and Kara were both fourteen, but they sure did have some growing up to do. As soon as they heard Alaina's call, Johnny and Kara ran, tripping over each other, into the kitchen. Mara strode in close behind them, hearing her sister's squeal of delight.

When Mara saw the state of the kitchen, she squealed too. There were Celtic knot streamers hanging all around the room and presents, each wrapped in bright colors, stacked on the table. The cake, however, was the main spectacle. It was crafted into mountains on one side with a forest and a stream on the other. At the peak of one mountain was a deep green dragon, and by the stream were their D&D characters—protecting a water nymph from some wolves.

They all let her stare at the cake for a moment, then she saw a flash as Jim took a picture with his old-fashioned Polaroid instant camera. Mara stared as Alaina began to explain parts of the extravagant cake to an excited Kara.

"Jim carved and painted our characters, the wolves, and the dragon up top. You know how good he is with wood. There's plastic bases on them. The nymph was done with a toothpick. Um ... the mountains were done by freezing the cake and cutting it, then layering the pieces into pyramids. I just bought the trees."

Kara was stammering about the work and the craftsmanship and was already making requests for her own birthday cake, but Mara just gaped at Alaina, unable to believe that something so wonderful was made just for her.

"Presents first!" Johnny cried.

He stuffed a big, green box into Mara's hands. That was that. Mara hated opening presents, so she always ripped them open quickly and without ceremony. In a few seconds, she held a bright red shirt depicting a fearsome red dragon fighting a tiny knight. She thanked Johnny quietly before picking up the next present. From Jim and Alaina was a deep green velvet cloak. Mara immediately threw it on and exclaimed, "It has pockets!"

Last was from her dad. This one was accompanied by a note. *Parents need things to pass down. These are mine to pass down to you, now that you're old enough. One is my first and now your first. The other was my family's and now a token of family for you.* Raising an eyebrow, Mara opened the little package. The first present was a small dagger. It was simple and short with a wooden hilt dyed blue.

"That was my first dagger," Toren told her.

The other thing was a bracelet, some kind of bangle or cuff. It was a silvery metal and was embossed with an intricate Celtic knot with a tree in the center—though it wasn't like any tree Mara had ever seen.

"That's been passed down as long as I can remember. I've been keeping it safe for you, for when you were ready," Toren told her, gently pushing a fiery wisp of orange hair back from her cheek. Mara winded her father with a tight hug and muffled thanks before sliding the bracelet on her left wrist—it fit perfectly next to Kara's friendship bracelet—and putting her dagger in one of her cloak pockets.

Overwhelmed with joy, Mara allowed her sister to steer her back over to the cake. Alaina brought out plates, forks, and gallon tub of fudge swirl ice cream. Jim followed suit with a knife and dishcloth. After Jim had taken all of the figurines off of the cake, swiped the icing off, and put them in a little velvet bag, Mara tucked the figures away in her cloak pocket.

When everyone had a sizeable piece of cake and two large scoops of ice cream, they all headed back into the dungeon to continue the game. Jim sat his cake down and started the fire before taking his seat, so Mara and Kara took their cake, grabbed their dice trays, and plopped down by the fireplace.

"You have just taken out all of the undead rats in the room Johnny foolishly barged into. The scroll is still glowing on the table and the chest in the corner is still rattling," Jim announced. He picked up his little laser pointer to show everyone what he meant.

"Alaina, it's your turn, I think," Jim continued.

"Well, I'm gonna go for the chest! It must have something good in it!" his wife mused.

Mara looked at her, an expression of mild frustration on her face. "You should investigate first. I think it's a Mimic."

Alaina rolled for perception and got a nineteen, whooping and looking at her husband. Jim groaned and sighed, glaring at Mara. "It's a Mimic. You definitely just saved Alaina here. Again. What are you going to do Toren?" he asked, turning to the next player.

Toren turned solemnly to his daughter, ignoring Jim. "It's a good thing, being observant," he said. "You need to know what's going on around you. You need to be quick to survive."

Mara felt a chill rush through her. *Where did that come from?* she thought. Why did it sound like he was talking about her survival and not Danag's?

Toren seemed to have realized his mistake and added, "Your character needs to."

They played for a few hours before Mara got sleepy. Near midnight her eyes drooped, and she was losing track of the conversation. As she looked into the fire, she caught snippets of what was going on, mesmerized by the dancing flames.

"Right, so, Mom, you're here ..."

"Toren, you roll for it..."

"Dad, you got this, or should I help?"

"Mara—oh, she's asleep. Toren, are you okay?"

Toren stared at his middle daughter, his eyes overbright. Mara's eyes fluttered closed, and calm sleep took her, blanketed in the warmth of the fire.

When Mara woke, the room was pitch black but for the embers of the dying fire. She stirred, expecting to feel stiff from laying on the floor. Strangely, she found herself lying on her back on a soft bed. She blinked rapidly, panicking and trying to get her eyes to adjust. Just then, she heard shuffling footsteps at the foot of the bed. Someone groaned. For a moment, the fire was blocked by a bulky figure. She heard a rustling sound as the fire came alive.

The bulk moved to the side of the fireplace, and Mara could see it was a man. He turned and looked straight into her glistening, wide eyes.

"Freya!" the man called. "She's awake!"

Mara couldn't help but be frightened. Where was her dad and why had he left her here? Where was Kara? Was this some kind of birthday prank? She clutched onto the covers as the man stepped toward her, but when she looked into his eyes they had softened, and when he spoke his voice was gentle.

"You mustn't fear me. I swear I'll not harm you," he said soothingly. "My name is Tederen."

Mara remained silent. What was she supposed to say?

"Freya, you'd better come in here!" the man, Tederen, called again. "I think she's afraid of me."

A stout woman strode into the room. "Well of course she's afraid, you dolt!" she fumed. "She's in a strange place with a man she's never seen—and he forgot to open the curtains this morning!"

There was a clink and a sudden burst of light as the woman flung the curtains open. Mara's eyes took a moment to adjust, but when they did, she was even more afraid. She pulled the covers up tightly to her chin—as if they would protect her—and bit her lip to keep from shrieking.

The room was quite small with the bed, bedside table, hearth, and a wooden rocker all that was inside it but the three of them. Mara realized looking at the hearth that it wasn't for a fire. Piled in the bed of the fireplace were glowing stones. They had dimmed again once the curtains were opened. Everything around her was so strange, so unreal. What frightened her most was looking at the man. He had a great, curling, red beard, grey eyes, and a shiny bald head revealing greenish skin. *Green skin.* She blinked.

"Now," the woman crooned. "Isn't that better?"

Mara turned to stare at her. So many questions swirled through her mind, but she just couldn't form the words. Why was she there? Where was her dad? Where was her sister? What was *wrong* with that guy?

"Oh! Poor dear!" Freya plopped herself down on the edge of the bed and pulled a kerchief out of the pocket of her dress. The woman looked friendly enough. She had long, greying hair pulled up in a loose bun, and her dress was a muted brown. It made Mara think of a pleasant, motherly hedgehog. The woman turned to the man and ordered, "Tederen, go get Cora. Tell her Toren's daughter has just woken up."

At this, Mara found her voice. As Tederen left the room, Mara sat bolt upright and rounded on the woman.

"What about my father? Who told you who he was? Why isn't he here? Where's my sister? What's going on? What—"

"There, there. Calm down, poor soul." The woman stood up and gently placed her hands on Mara's shoulders.

"No, I will not calm down! I want to know where I am! Where is my dad?" She was shouting right into the poor woman's face, but she didn't care.

Mara couldn't handle another minute in bed, and she was frustrated at the woman's lack of answers, no matter how pleasant she was, so she flung herself out of the bed and began to look around the room. The room was rounded but not a perfect circle. The walls were wooden and seemed to be one solid piece all the way around. As Mara walked around, she noticed there were no outlets nor anything at all electrical. A lone candle sat on the table next to the bed. The bed itself filled most of the room, and Freya sat quietly there while Mara looked around. Mara peeked through the curtains the woman had flung open and staggered, clutching the frame for support.

They had to be over a hundred feet from the ground. The room appeared to be within a tree or tree branch. There were rope bridges extended across to all the nearby trees and she could see little windows throughout the entire forest. *How is it possible that all the trees are like skyscrapers?* Mara thought, the panic rising again. *Where am I? What . . .*

She dimly heard a shout as she crumpled to the floor.

Tederen found Mara on the floor a little while later. Freya hadn't been able to lift her up, so Tederen hauled her onto the bed when he came back in. When Mara came to, she heard the woman yelling at the man.

"What were you thinking? If you hadn't scared the poor girl the moment she woke . . ."

"Yes, dear," he murmured. Mara could hear the amusement in his voice. Sure enough, when she peeked at the two of them, the old man was smiling under the woman's scathing gaze. Mara grinned despite herself and closed her eyes again.

"Ah, seems like our lady is awake."

When Mara opened her eyes a moment later, the man was leaning over her once again. Freya glared at him and pushed him back with surprising force for her small frame, shouting, "I just told you to stop scaring that girl. You are old enough to know better!"

Tederen rubbed his arm and gave Freya a sly look. "Well, I'm not near as old as you, honeydew," he crooned.

Mara sat up slowly and rubbed her face. "Man, you fight like an old, married couple," she ventured.

They exchanged looks. "That's because we are," the pair answered in unison.

Freya furtively stepped toward the bed as Tederen's face fell. "You should have known that," he whispered. Was that anger in his voice? "You should have— You would have— You ..."

"It's not her fault," Freya told him softly.

Mara, suddenly alert and defensive, asked, "What's not my fault? What are you talking about? Why—" Realization hit her like a slap to the face. "You mentioned my dad before. You know him."

They both nodded. Freya looked expectantly at her husband. With a sigh, Tederen sank onto the bed, this time at the edge, just out of Freya's reach. "I know your father because he's my nephew. I'm your great uncle, Mara."

"Wait..." Mara began slowly, "Tederen? ... Teddy? Uncle Teddy? Is that what my dad called you?"

"You've heard about me?" he gasped, eyes darting to his wife.

Mara smiled inwardly and fiddled with the sheets. "Dad used to tell me a lot of stories about his Uncle Teddy. Every time I would mess up, he would ask me what I learned and say, 'It's like my Uncle Teddy always said: it's only a mistake if you don't learn something.'"

When she looked back up, she saw the old man's eyes glistening, and a tear cascaded into his russet beard—red just like her dad's. "It broke my heart when Tor left," he whispered.

"Now, what do you mean, 'he left?'" she asked, crossing her arms. "When was my dad here? Where exactly *is* here anyway?"

The old man took a deep breath. "Ambergrove."

"What?"

"This place is called Aeunna, Mara," he explained. "It is the capitol of the forest dwarf civilization in Ambergrove." He paused expectantly, but Mara just listened. "Ambergrove is its own world, separate from your Earth but connected in its own way. Your father was born in Ambergrove, and for a brief time he was our Ranger—the leader of our kind." Teddy sighed deeply.

"You say 'our kind.'" Mara ventured quietly, leaning forward, "Does that mean my dad is a ... dwarf? Dwarves are real? He's kind of tall for a dwarf ..."

Teddy chuckled, rubbing his nape awkwardly. "That's a common mistake in your world. So——"

"Wait, what do you mean by *my* world?" Mara asked. She was frightened again. She noticed he was wearing the kinds of clothes she only ever saw at a Ren Faire. Either this man—her uncle—was insane, or she was very far from home.

Freya got up and went over to the table, pulling out a locket with a J encrusted in emeralds on one side. She brought it over and showed it to Mara, opening the locket to reveal yellowed pictures of a man and woman. "I'm from Earth, too," the woman told Mara. "My mother was from Ambergrove. Those with Ambergrovian blood have the chance to choose to come here on their sixteenth birthday. Just like you did, Mara."

"But I didn't choose!" Mara protested. "I didn't! I just woke up here!"

"What were you doing for your birthday, Mara?" Teddy asked.

Mara was flustered. She was confused, annoyed, and overwhelmed. "I was playing Dungeons & Dragons with my family! My dad, who's perfectly normal, and my little sister," she snapped, rubbing her face in exasperation.

They were both silent for a moment. Then Freya said, "That was your choice, Mara. You love what you consider medieval cultures and fantasy worlds. You may not have announced that you were coming to Ambergrove, but it's what your soul wanted."

"Okay, fine. Maybe I didn't say I wanted to come here, but my dad played D&D with me, so that should mean that he wanted to be here, too! None of this makes any sense!" she shouted.

Teddy's voice was suddenly dark. "He did want to be here. This village—this entire world—was your father's blood. It was his heart. Then his heart was stolen."

"S-stolen?" Mara asked, hugging herself to keep it together.

"That's harsh, Ted," Freya whispered, laying a hand on his arm. "He fell in love. He would have gone anywhere with her. He did go anywhere with her."

Mara could feel the heat on her face. "One of you had better start making sense," she commanded.

"Your father was once our Ranger. The Ranger is the leader of all forest dwarves," Teddy explained. "He fell in love with your mother, and when she decided she wanted to go to Earth, he had to go with her or lose her forever. Their relationship was new. Their love was still young and warm. He chose to go."

"He did not regret his decision," Freya told Mara, placing a hand reassuringly on Mara's leg. Mara stared disbelievingly at the woman. Freya pulled an envelope out of her dress pocket, and Mara could see Freya's name written on the envelope in a familiar scrawl. Freya explained, "In this letter, he writes about what he lost ... and what he gained. He gained you. Your sisters. He allowed his line, the line of Rangers, to continue. He was able to experience good moments with the bad, and he would not change that decision. That's all you need to know for now." She tucked the letter back into her pocket.

Teddy looked at Mara, a warm expression on his face. "How is this all sitting with you?" he asked.

She thought for a moment, trying to process what they'd said. Mara's heart sank. "Wait ... you said forever. You said he had to go, or he would lose her forever." Mara's eyes filled with tears and hear voice shook as she continued, "Does that mean he's never coming back? That I'm never going home?"

Teddy and Freya exchanged glances. Freya softly placed a hand on Mara's cheek before whispering, "It's true, Mara. You are here forever. Ambergrove is a different world. You ... you can never see your dad again or return to Earth. This is your home now."

Mara's lip quivered as she flung herself down to the bed and buried her face in the pillow. *Never.* She would never see her dad again. She would never see Kara. She hadn't even been able to say goodbye.

She wailed, and they let her cry without interruption. Freya rubbed and patted Mara's back, as if she were soothing a toddler. She knew what Mara was feeling. The loss at first would outweigh the gain. After some time, Mara calmed down and sat up, sniffling and breathing deeply to compose herself.

"I'm sure it'll all sink in sooner or later," she murmured, exhaling sharply, wiping her eyes, and rubbing her temples before putting on a brave face. She paused and turned to Teddy, continuing, "but ... you said my father allowed the line to continue. Wh ... What does that make me?"

Teddy smiled and put a hand on her shoulder. "That makes you the rightful Ranger, Mara. Once you prove yourself."

"Prove myself?"

"Yes, Mara. Your arrival has been foretold, but any Ranger must still prove their worth. That is for tomorrow. You don't need to worry about anything now. Today ..."

Mara looked up at him timidly, waiting for more unwelcome, unbelievable news.

Freya asked, "When's the last time you had something to eat?"

Seemingly in response, Mara's stomach grumbled. Her last meal seemed so long ago. That night seemed so far away, and it was. So very far.

Freya put her hand on Mara's shoulder. "Let's get you something to eat, dear," she said softly.

They both smiled at Mara, and she smiled back, sniffling. She would have to take some time to think about her loss and her fear. As her stomach grumbled again, she was more interested to see what this world called food.

It was the sweetest fruit she'd ever tasted. The fruit was a similar shape to a strawberry, though, instead of being rosy with green leaves, it had an emerald skin and a yellow heart. It was a fusion of all the fruits Mara had ever loved, but she couldn't put her finger on an exact flavor. As she filled her face, Teddy began to chuckle. "Slow down, Mara. You can have too much of a good thing."

Mara swallowed and smacked her lips. "What do you mean?" she asked, popping a large berry in her mouth.

"These are anamberries. They're magical berries that taste like your favorite fruits. They're wonderful and filling, but they're *soul* berries. If you have too much of something you love, your anam—your soul—will be overwhelmed and you'll die."

Mara stopped chewing and stared wide-eyed at Teddy. *Smack.* Freya was behind him, towel in hand, her every muscle quivering with fury. She scolded him, emphasizing with a whip of the towel, "Stop. Scaring. That. Girl."

"I wasn't!" he protested. "It's the truth! Anam means soul and—ow— and they do actually—"

"Yes, I know that, dear," Freya said in an impossibly sweet voice, pausing her attack. "Yes, but there were so many other ways you could have said that to her that wouldn't make her think she was *dying* while she was eating them!"

Freya gave Teddy one more smack for good measure. The only reason her manner was amusing and not concerning was because Mara and her sisters knew the towel whip all too well. They had frequently played with their dad, chasing each other around the house and whipping each other with towels, laughing. It stung some, but it wasn't intended to harm Teddy— not really. Freya turned to Mara, who looked back at the anamberries with an expression of ultimate betrayal.

"C-can I eat these?" she asked.

"Yes, dear. What Teddy said is true, but you'd have to eat a whole bush full before getting so much as a stomachache." Freya glared over at her husband again, and he sheepishly scratched his bald head.

Mara slowly resumed her meal, looking around her. She was in the same tree branch, just further down. It seemed to be the couple's kitchen and dining room in one area. The room appeared like a rustic cabin. The furniture was natural wood lashed together. There were four chairs, a table, counters, and cabinets all made from logs and bark. Mara finished her handful of berries and looked around her for other food.

"No stove in this house," Freya chuckled, guessing, no doubt, from her own first thoughts when she'd arrived.

"We have community dinners, Mara. You'll have a real meal later this evening," Teddy offered. "Come to think of it, we should probably head out and meet some of the village—if you're up for it, that is."

"It's as good a time as any." Mara sighed.

Teddy clapped her on the shoulder and Freya gathered some berries to go. Then they ushered Mara toward a side door as Freya muttered about getting her some proper clothes before taking her to meet new people.

CHAPTER TWO

RANGERLING

When Mara stepped onto the rope bridge connecting her aunt and uncle's house to the upper village, she looked every bit an Ambergrovian native. Freya had given Mara some soft pants in a deep green, knee-high chocolate boots, and a dingy, tan shirt that had sleeves to the elbow and lacing between the neck and chest. To top it off, Teddy had braided her hair—in a surprisingly delicate and intricate pattern. Teddy boasted this perfect braid to his wife as they led Mara across to the village.

Crossing the bridge, Mara looked out at the forest around her. There was a spiral staircase going up each tree, with doors spaced evenly up the trunk and branches. Rope bridges cascaded throughout the forest, networking every tree to the village tree at the center. The village tree itself was massive, more than double the girth of all the other trees. Looking around at this network, something dawned on Mara.

"T-Tederen?" she asked uncertainly.

"Teddy—Uncle Teddy. Yes?"

"How can a civilization that's all about nature be okay doing this to trees? And how are they even alive with so many holes in them?"

"Ah, now that's a simple one." He chuckled. "These are Aeunna trees. They were given to us by Aeun, the goddess of nature. These trees grow large and hollow for our use. The pegs for the stairways are natural branches. The only real modifications we make are to add doors to our homes and to string the bridges from tree to tree."

Mara marveled at this as she neared the village tree. There were people waiting for them on the other side of the bridge. One was an ancient woman, grey and hunched. One was a tall, middle-aged man with a hunter green beard, and one was a heavily tattooed young woman with red hair all spiked up like flames. They all wore pale green robes and little circlets of leaves. When Mara got to them, it was the man who first introduced himself with a bow.

"Welcome, young Mara. My name is Aengar the Green." He gestured to the elderly woman and the young woman, respectively. "This is Rhodi the Wise and Cora the Marked." They each bowed in turn. He continued, "We are the elder council of Aeunna. We are pleased to finally meet the child of Toren." Aengar reached out his hand to shake hers, and she shook it numbly.

The others made space for Mara as she stepped off the bridge. Rhodi greeted her with a smile, clasping Mara's hand in hers and patting it softly with her other hand. *How can this woman still be alive?* Mara wondered, feeling the loose skin shifting as Rhodi patted her hand. She looked older than anyone Mara had ever heard of, but she saw a twinkle in the old woman's eye. "I've still got a few years left in me, young one," Rhodi said, making Mara's face flush.

Cora stepped up and nudged Mara's shoulder. "Full-blooded forest dwarves are more like trees than people. Got the lifespan of an oak, this one." She grinned and winked at Mara, who smiled back.

Teddy strode over and wrapped an arm around Cora's shoulder. "Cora here is the youngest member of the elder council in history. Not really sure she could be called an *elder*, but..."

Cora deftly slipped out of his grip and gave him a playful punch on the shoulder, saying "Yeah, well *you* certainly could!"

Teddy opened his mouth as if to argue, then shrugged in acceptance and continued, "I train the warriors here. Cora was my best fighter—she became the youngest elder due to her prowess in battle."

Cora shrugged and her emerald eyes twinkled. "I like knocking cocky boys down a peg. I could teach you to—"

"Alright," Aengar interrupted, "It's about time for us to be heading down to the feast. Will you walk with us, Mara?" He beckoned to Mara and shot Cora a disapproving glance.

As Mara grudgingly followed the grumpy man, Teddy walked over to Rhodi and offered her his arm. They all headed down the stairs, Teddy and

Rhodi setting the pace. On the way down, Freya strode forward to walk with Aengar, and he and the woman discussed Aeunna's medicine stores. Freya was the head medicine woman, and she was concerned they would need particular herbs before they were out of season. She was requesting a troupe of apprentices be sent to gather it. Mara was glad to have the chance to talk to Cora. She was awed by the youngest elder and wanted to ask her about being a warrior, about spending so much time with her uncle growing up, and about life in Ambergrove. Mara wondered if this had been the woman Teddy was going to go get when she first awoke. Surely, she was. Cora seemed like someone Mara could really talk to—if she only had the nerve. She didn't have the nerve. Instead, Mara asked Cora about her tattoos.

Cora was used to the awe that came with being the Marked Warrior and she never tired of talking about it. There were flesh artists—people those from Earth called tattooists—all over Ambergrove. Cora's Marks covered her journey as a warrior. There were knots and whorls from each culture she had visited. The mining dwarves had more angular symbols than their forest kin. Each human village had been inspired by an ancient civilization from Earth—Mara recognized Egyptian hieroglyphs, Native American totems, and Ancient Greek figures, among others. Cora had also received a burrobear from the gnomekin, a crystalline shard from the Ice Mountains, a sea serpent from the sea elves, and two special gifts. One was a dragon's breath triskelion from the isles of the gods. She had received this after befriending every type of dragon in Ambergrove. The other was a brand from the giant lands. Many of these Marks she had received immediately after her great deeds in these lands, which was also how she had earned her place on the elder council. She had fought a terror in every land and won. Every land except the forbidden lands—even she had not wanted to disturb the evil there. This she told to Mara, and all it did was raise more questions. Cora could see this in her eyes and chuckled.

"Later, I will explain all this to you Mara. Today is not the day."

"Why do people keep saying that to me?" Mara muttered.

When they reached the base of the tree, Mara was surprised to see the forest floor filled with people. She hadn't looked down as they'd descended the village tree, because she didn't want to scare herself, and also because she was so enamored with Cora's stories. She figured the forest dwarf village would be large, but this was so much more. There were hundreds of people sitting at long banquet tables lining the forest floor. It took her a moment to see them, because their skin, hair, and clothes were all greens, browns, and rusty oranges—colors of the forest. Past the crowds, at the end of the long banquet tables, there was a raised dais for the elder council, for Teddy and Freya and, it seemed, for Mara herself.

As they walked past the full tables to the dais, Mara felt rather than heard the attention on her. There were scattered whispers of "Is that her?" and "By Aeun, she looks just like him!" among other less-than-savory comments. Had everyone known her dad? Why were she and the others heading up to the dais with the elder council? After what seemed like a lifetime of murmurs—which Mara tried with all her might to blot out— they reached the dais. Teddy guided Rhodi to a seat on the end, pulled out a chair for Freya, then placed himself next to his wife. With a wink and a nudge, Cora left Mara to sit next to Teddy. There were two seats left. As Mara went to sit next to Cora, Aengar held her back and motioned for her to stand beside him instead. He had centered himself before all the banquet tables and was holding something that looked like a twig.

"Good evening, brothers and sisters." Aengar hadn't raised his voice, but somehow his voice was echoing throughout the forest. *He's using that twig as a microphone,* Mara marveled. She shook off her amazement and focused her attention on Aengar.

"Today is a joyous day and a trying one. First, I will lay all your speculations to rest. This young lady beside me *is* in fact the daughter of Toren and rangerling of Aeunna."

There were scattered whispers and applause. Mara tried to make herself small. She didn't like all the eyes on her, all the murmuring and the judgement. What exactly was a rangerling? Why hadn't her dad told her about any of this? Mara let out a slow, deep breath to calm herself, but no one seemed to notice her panic.

Aengar continued, "She is new to our world. She has just arrived from Earth. She has not been tried. She will be tested soon, and her trial will begin, but for now, take heart. Toren has sent a letter with her for the elder council." Aengar pulled the letter from his robe and held it up. "He believes she is ready. He believes that she will be a model Ranger and will be the one to lead our world back to the light. Give her time. Give her space. As the tree grows, so will she. She will make her father proud; I have no doubt."

At this, the scattered applause and periodic cheers grew into a roar. Mara felt sick. So much of that speech made no sense to her. She was so unsure, so confused, uncomfortable standing in front of all those people who seemed to know so much about her. Aengar said she'd make her father proud, but she wasn't sure she would. *Wouldn't he have told me about this if he believed in me?* she asked herself. *Why didn't he give me the chance to ask?* Aengar raised his hand and, as he slowly lowered it, the conversation quieted and disappeared.

"Now, let us show Mara how the forest dwarves eat their evening meal!" he announced.

A gong sounded from behind the dais. Mara turned around and noticed a stone building for the first time. There were little, furry creatures pouring out of it, carrying trays of meats, bowls of fruits and vegetables, and platters of various cheeses. Others carried pitchers. Mara watched them file out to every table and begin distributing their treasures. Aengar stood next to Mara for a moment, allowing her to take it all in.

They might have seemed like little bears if it weren't for the aprons they wore and the opposable thumbs they used to carry their goods. As a large, brown one clambered closer to her, Mara resisted the urge to pet it, wondering, *Are they friendly? Are they pets or are they people?* The creature came nearer to her and gave a low bow. When he spoke his voice was deep, like that of a bear, and much deeper than she might have expected from a creature of that size.

"Greetings, miss," he rumbled. "My name is Mapleleaf. My people are of bearkin, but we have long served the kind leaders of Aeunna. We hope to one day add you to that number."

Mara couldn't form a response, so she just smiled and nodded at the little creature.

"Please, miss, have a seat and enjoy your meal. Should you wish to learn more about bearkin, visit me in the kitchens any time."

"Thank you, Mapleleaf," she managed.

He gave her a small nod, then the bearkin around him ushered her to her seat and offered her the most delicious looking food she could imagine. She accepted a small portion of each dish, thanked each bearkin, and began her first evening meal in Aeunna.

Mara leaned back and stretched her full stomach. If every supper was that tasty, she wouldn't have to worry about food in Ambergrove. She had savored every bite and lost herself in the taste, so when her plate was empty and she noticed the rest of the table patiently waiting, she turned crimson. She looked around her, gaping at her audience. She swallowed her mouthful in one half-chewed gulp and leaned toward Aengar.

"Um ... Aengar ... why is everyone looking at me?"

"It is our custom that no one has their sweets until everyone has finished their supper."

"Wha—"

"They're waiting for dessert, Mara," Cora cut in. "We don't have dessert until everyone finishes their vegetables."

The gong sounded again. The bearkin flooded out of the stone building—this time with identical steaming pans. Mara recognized Mapleleaf this time. *He must be the one who brings food to the dais.* He nodded at Mara as he deposited a slice of warm pie on her plate. She recognized it immediately.

"We've found this is the most economical way to ensure everyone is happy with their sweets," Mapleleaf explained.

The smell of the anamberries was irresistible, but Mara had so many questions for Mapleleaf. "Excuse me," she began as he made to leave the dais. Mapleleaf turned. "I just wanted to thank you for the food. Could you tell whoever makes it that it was amazing?"

"Thank you, miss. We all had a hand in it, but I will pass your gratitude along to the bearkin."

"I know I have a lot to learn, but I would like to learn what you can teach me about your people whenever I can." The small creature smiled warmly. Mara continued, "You said to look for you in the kitchens. Why is that? Surely you do more than cook?"

"Yes, we do. We do much to help your kin. I will tell you all about that when we speak, but I will answer your first question now. Your Teddy oversees the training of hunters and warriors in Aeunna. His woman is in charge of medicine. I am in charge of food. I leave the kitchens, but that is where I am most often found."

"Thank you," Mara repeated. "Please finish what you were doing. I will come to see you soon."

Mapleleaf bowed and headed off with the empty tray tucked under his arm. Mara quickly ate her anamberry pie, conscious of those around her this time. It wasn't long before everyone was finished. When Mara looked up, she saw they were all looking expectantly up at the table again, but this time it wasn't in her direction—Rhodi had a few bites left of her pie.

Once the old woman had finished, Teddy stood and helped her up. He led her to the spot where Aengar had stood to address the village and remained beside her. Aengar passed her the strange twig, and the entire forest seemed to go silent.

"Young ones," Rhodi began, for everyone was young to her, "I am sure you are ready to sleep now, with the bearkins' wonderful pie filling your bellies, so I will leave you with just one announcement. Tederen will bring the rangerling to the Oracle at dawn tomorrow so she can learn her heritage, our heart, and what her Ranger trial will be. Dawn will smile anew in Aeunna. For now, head to your homes and rest well. By this time tomorrow, we will surely have a grand announcement."

Rhodi gestured to the crowd, and everyone began to disperse, climbing back up the pegs of the village tree and crossing various bridges to their own homes. Only Mara did not move. What exactly was she supposed to do?

Cora hung an arm over her shoulder, still planted in the seat next to her. "Don't you worry none, rangerling. It'll all work out, I promise. Aeunna is in your blood."

"What does that even mean?" Mara asked her.

"What do you mean?" Cora replied.

"What's a rangerling? People keep calling me that."

Teddy and Freya stepped up behind Cora, and Teddy cleared his throat to explain. "The leader of the forest dwarves is called the Ranger. Any child of the Ranger is called a rangerling. Think foundling or youngling."

"Okay, I guess that makes sense," Mara muttered, avoiding his gaze.

Freya walked over and placed a hand on Mara's shoulder comfortingly. "You'll learn," she said. "It'll take some time to adjust, but you'll get there."

"Now, aren't you ready to head home to bed?" Teddy asked.

Freya leered disapprovingly at her husband. "You are not going to make this girl spend the night here alone!" she told him. After narrowing her eyes at Teddy, she turned back to Mara. "Come with us back to our home for tonight. You can stay there until you're ready to go to yours."

Mara wondered apprehensively what her own home might be and where, but there had been enough mysteries for the day, so she just nodded. As she headed up the pegs, across the bridge, and to that room she'd woken in that morning, she couldn't help but wonder what it all meant. What if they were wrong? What was her dad doing? How was her sister faring? … And who would she be the next time she woke?

CHAPTER THREE

THE ORACLE

Mara's eyes fluttered open. She looked around and was somewhat relieved to discover she was in the same room from the night before. Relief turned to nervousness. What would the day hold? What was she supposed to do? She really was in another world. She didn't want to oversleep, but she wasn't sure what time it even was, so she got up, put on the clothes she had worn to supper, and opened the bedroom door.

It was still dark, but she saw the faint hint of light through the massive tree's canopy. If dawn came around the time it did at home, it was probably six or seven in the morning. She stepped out and looked around her. Down the branch was the kitchen. Further down was probably Teddy and Freya's room. Mara didn't want to overstep by raiding the kitchen without permission, but she was starting to get hungry. There wasn't any harm in looking.

She pushed open the kitchen door and found Teddy sitting at the counter. "Well, good morning there, sunshine!" he called. "Finally decide to join the living?" Seeing the shock and remorse on her face, Teddy chuckled and continued, "Now settle down. Freya won't be up for a while yet. You haven't overslept any. I'm just on a warrior's schedule, so I'm up before the birds." He patted the seat next to him.

Mara sat. She noticed a bowl of muffins on the counter, and Teddy saw her look of longing.

"You can have as many as you want, Mara." Teddy chuckled. "But I would advise you to take it slow. Freya's muffins are packed with protein and fiber. There's enough in one muffin to tide you over for most of the morning."

Mara took a muffin and thanked him. When she bit into it, she was surprised to find a familiar taste. Her eyes widened as she thought, *This must be a dream. It just has to be.*

"These … these are—" she began.

"Yes, those should be familiar," Teddy replied, smirking.

"But how?"

"Those were never your da's muffins, Mara."

She just looked at him, her grey eyes clouded. How did he know her dad used to make muffins just like these?

"Freya has been making those for decades. She taught him how to make them when he was little. Before he went away to Earth, she gave him a talk. She said that at least one of his little ones would be back one day, and they would need something familiar to ground them when they got here. She sure does think of everything, doesn't she?"

Mara nodded. She'd taken an extra-large mouthful in the middle of his little speech to hold the emotions back. How was Freya so kind? How could her dad have left here? Why had he never told her about any of this—so she could have asked him? As she chewed, the tears abated. Teddy sat and let her eat her muffin in peace while he munched on his own. He offered her some water as she ate, and she took it, thanked him, and kept eating.

Once she finished her muffin, Teddy covered the remaining muffins with a cloth and poured some of the cool water into two pouches. He attached one to his own belt, then he offered her the other and asked, "Are you ready to face the day?"

"As ready as I can be," she muttered, attaching the skein to her belt.

Teddy smiled. "First, we'll be heading up to the highest rooms in the village tree to see the Oracle, so at least you don't have to worry all day about that."

"She's supposed to tell me about my past?"

"Aye, and your future. The Oracle gives the rangerling their quest to prove they can be a Ranger. She also will tell you how you will fit into Ambergrove's future. Nah—don't ask me," he finished, seeing she was opening her mouth to speak.

"She'll tell me. Okay. Will … will you come with me at least?"

"It can be hard to face such uncertainty on your own."

"So … you will?"

"I will come as far as the door. I am forbidden to enter the Oracle's sanctuary unless she invites me herself, but I will be waiting for you just outside."

"Thank you, Teddy."

She tried to mask her relief as he gave her a reassuring smile, clapped her shoulder, and headed out the kitchen door. Teddy pulled the door closed, and they took their time walking up to the Oracle's home.

"Will you tell me what my dad was like?" Mara asked, eyes intently focused on her boots.

"What do you mean?"

"Well, who was he before …"

"Before he left?"

"Yeah. Before he left, before he met my mom, before he grew up—when you knew him."

Teddy paused for a moment. They'd reached the rope bridge, so he motioned for her to head out in front of him before beginning. "I am older than my sister, your grandmother. Our parents died when we were young, so I ended up raising Gaele when I was about your age. She took their losses hard and she didn't want to listen to me, so she spent a lot of her time in the village tree instead. I didn't watch her as much as I should have. Freya had recently arrived in Aeunna and I was … distracted."

Teddy walked silently for a moment, causing Mara to pause and turn around to him. She smiled. "Please, go on," she urged.

"Well … after some time … Gaele ran away. My sister wandered for a while and ended up with a human. She didn't love him, and he didn't love her. They only saw each other a few times, but it was enough to make Toren. Freya helped her through the pregnancy as best she could. She had been interested in the herbalist crafts before coming to Ambergrove, so she had some skill. It was her help in birthing your father that earned her the position as medicine woman of Aeunna. She was assisting the old medicine man at the time."

They reached the end of the rope bridge, so Teddy motioned for her to continue up the pegs of the village tree. Mara paused at the end of the bridge and asked quietly, "So does that mean she had trouble?"

Teddy's eyes grew distant, "Oh, yes ..."

"That bad?"

"No, what was bad was ... after." Teddy sighed.

"After?"

Teddy gestured the pegs again, so Mara turned and began to ascend the village tree as he continued, "Gaele had not gotten over her rebellion. Especially since she had birthed a child in chaos. She named him Toren after the god of chaos, hoping that he would be a troublemaker."

"There's a god of chaos?" Mara asked incredulously.

"Yes," Teddy answered, in equal surprise. "There are many gods and goddesses in Ambergrove."

"Huh. Wow, okay then." Mara shook her head. She should have realized that if there was a goddess of the forest dwarves, there were probably many more. Though, to be fair, she'd been too overwhelmed yesterday to think of much else. Looking up at the many pegs ahead to the Oracle, she figured she would end up overwhelmed today too.

"Anyway," Teddy continued, "she wanted your father to turn out bad because of his name. It had the opposite effect, mostly because I made a point to be present in his life. I didn't want his future ruined by her pain, so I took him whenever I could. He was a good boy. He was raised by many of the forest dwarves, and he learned quickly. He smiled all the time, he played in the forest with the bearkin cubs, and he tried his hand at everything. As he grew older, he learned to hunt and to cook. He learned about herbs, and he learned about the world. He loved everything about this place. Soon enough, he went through a trial and became the Ranger."

"Why did he become the Ranger and not you?"

"I didn't want it. I'm a simple man, Mara, and I like the responsibilities I have just fine." He sighed. "When my parents died, I had the elder council reinstated until another leader could be found somehow. Until your father became old enough for his Ranger trial. Much to Gaele's dismay ..." he trailed off.

"You said it was worse after?" Mara asked quietly, stopping and turning to look at him, nearly whipping him with her braid. "What happened to my grandmother?"

Teddy sighed again and scratched his beard. "She let me take Toren, but she was always ... dark. She wanted chaos and destruction. She left Aeunna before Toren's Ranger trial, and we haven't heard from her since. I can only assume she perished in the search of chaos."

Mara had never seen such a sad and lost look before. Teddy wiped his face and continued, "I hope she's dead. It would be a mercy. Otherwise, what manner of monster would she be after this?"

Mara turned wordlessly and continued up the pegs. There was so much she didn't know about her family. It seemed her life thus far had been a lie. What more would she learn by the time this trial business was done? They stepped off the final pegs and reached a platform at the top of the tree with a single small hut at the center. They had made it to the Oracle's sanctuary.

"I'll tell you more once you've finished here," Teddy told her. "Don't be afraid. The Oracle will help. I'll be right out here waiting for you."

He smiled and gave her a quick hug. She had not been expecting such a show of affection, but she was happy to reciprocate. She squeezed him tight and closed her eyes, thinking of her dad, wishing she was enveloped in the safety of his embrace. Then, she took a deep breath, walked up to the Oracle's door, and rapped three of the most diffident knocks ever heard.

The door creaked open, and Mara heard a soft voice from deep within. "Enter, daughter of Toren, if you would become a Ranger."

Mara held her breath and stepped over the threshold. The door snapped shut behind her. She shivered, trying to force out her fear. When she looked around her, she was surprised to discover the room was normal. There were various tapestries on the walls, but otherwise there was no decoration. There was a small table in the center of the room with a doily and tea set centered on it and a large chair behind. Before this moment, Rhodi was ten times more ancient than anyone Mara had ever seen. Now, even Rhodi seemed young by comparison. The Oracle was sitting in a poofy, brown armchair, and she looked like she would crumble into a pile of bones at any moment.

She had long, white hair that was braided down one side and trailed across the floor and past the table. Her eyes were closed, but she seemed to be smiling at Mara all the same.

"Please come forward, my child, and have a seat," the Oracle whispered.

Mara looked around. Seeing no other chair, she sat down on the floor near the Oracle and crossed her legs. "Thank you for welcoming me into your home," she said. After a pause, during which Mara wondered if the woman was still awake, she pressed, "Would you like me to get anything for you?"

"Ah, yes," the Oracle breathed. "Why don't you pour some tea?"

Mara had never been introduced to tea so, while she believed the pouring to be a basic concept, she wasn't sure if there was a wrong way to do it. One of Sara's friends had yelled at her once for pouring soda wrong and wasting the carbonation. She didn't want to make that mistake again. Apprehensively, she picked up the floral teapot from the table in front of her and poured some tea into a cup. She noticed there were other containers on the table, so she asked, "Would you like ... anything else ... in your tea?"

"I see you haven't had tea before." The Oracle chuckled. "Tea comes with sugar and either cream or lemon. This one comes with cream. Please give me one scoop of each. Be sure to get some tea for yourself. You'll like it."

Mara did as she asked and tried to stir out the lumps of sugar. Not wanting to reject the offer, but not knowing how to prepare her own tea, Mara simply made two identical cups. When she turned to hand the tea to the Oracle, she was startled to see that the old woman was sitting up in her chair with her eyes wide open. Not that it seemed to matter—her eyes were swirls of stormy clouds. Startled, Mara splashed some of the tea on herself.

"Oh, I'm so sorry!" She squeaked. "I didn't mean to make a mess, I just—"

"You were surprised because you thought I was decomposing into that chair?" The Oracle squinted one eye at Mara, then burst into soft cackles. "Girl, there hasn't been a single person sent up to speak to me who hasn't left with tea all down their front! It's one of life's little pleasures ..." She sank back into her chair before adding, "Now, may I please have my tea?"

Mara looked at the spilled tea and picked up the cup she'd made for herself instead, handing it to the Oracle and meeting another reproachful gaze. The woman cackled again, accepted the tea, and took a sip.

"Mmm ... tastes like you made your tea just like mine."

"Well, I haven't had tea before, so I wasn't sure what to—" Mara paused. She'd realized she just told the Oracle she'd given her the wrong tea.

"Hah! Just as well you kept the spilled one. There's less waste if you decide you don't like it! Now ... take a sip and see."

Mara took a tiny sip and was surprised at the taste. It was sweet and almost floral, but there was a hint of toastiness to it also. It was good. "What is this?" she asked the Oracle.

"Ah, it is an Aeunnan version of oolong. It's quite tasty—and good for you also. Oolong tea is one of my better-known aging secrets." She winked at Mara. "Now, it's about time we got started. What do you want to know?"

Mara thought for a moment, quietly sipping her tea, then began, "Well, I had figured this would mostly just be you telling me what I'm supposed to do. I heard about the Ranger, being the Ranger, and some sort of test to prove that I'm worthy. I'm not sure that I am, so ... I guess I want to know if you could tell me who I am? What do I have to do with this world?"

"Good question," the Oracle began, "and what a story it is." She sipped her tea and settled back into her chair.

"The story of this world is a long one, and your family plays a large role in its future. You see, Ambergrove—as you will know it—is a corrupted place. Brother fights brother. People strive for advancements and power to which they weren't born. Wedges have been driven between all the races of our world. It began long ago, when the first descendants of Ambergrove returned to our lands from Earth." The Oracle sipped her tea.

Mara looked down into her own tea and asked, "But why would people be allowed to come here if they were ruining the land?"

"It is the nature of Ambergrove to believe in the good of others. We believed that our family warmth and acceptance would be enough. Ultimately, it was humans from Earth who started the first cities, to create a kingdom that would rule over the others. Those cities are lost now. None travel over there because the place was overrun with evil."

"What does this have to do with me?"

"Well, according to Aeun, one day the Ranger of the forest dwarves would go to Earth. One of his children would return and would lead all of Ambergrove into a new age of peace and unity."

Mara felt sick.

"That person is you, Mara," the Oracle said gently.

Mara shook her head, slowly at first then more fervently.

"You cannot deny prophecy, Mara."

"Yeah, I can. My dad is a teddy bear. He's not a ruler of anyone, and I'm not strong. I'm fifteen, and just the other day I was so afraid my character was going to die that I spent twenty minutes running firing arrows backwards and even jumped when it was all over." She set her tea back on the table and shook her head some more, frowning.

The Oracle set her own tea on the table and leaned toward Mara, her body creaking. "You're sixteen, Mara. It's not much more, but you're growing. You are the daughter of Aeunna's fairest leader. He led; he didn't rule—and so will you. You may have backed away from danger, but you kept fighting. You persevered. That shows strength."

Mara crossed her arms, and her frown deepened. The Oracle sighed and continued, "Well, the good thing about prophecy is that you don't have to believe it for it to be true. Your people believe in you. Think about that."

Mara thought about the angry whispers she'd heard as she had walked up to the dais the night before. A lot of people didn't believe in her. They didn't know her, and she didn't know them. "They're not my people," she said defiantly.

"They are your people," the Oracle replied patiently. "This entire forest grew from a single tree. You are a branch on that tree, and it connects you to all forest dwarves, past, present, and future. You cannot change that. Your only choice is whether to help them rise or to let them fall." The ancient woman gave Mara another piercing look and sipped her tea.

Mara stared into her tea. What would her dad want her to do? What was the right thing to do? One thing she did know—whatever leader she might be, it would be wrong to turn her back on people who needed someone, even if that someone wasn't her.

"Okay."

"What was that, dear?"

"Okay," Mara repeated. She sighed heavily. "I don't know if what you say is true, but I know that my dad would want me to do the right thing. Helping is the right thing." She took a sip of her tea, and it made her feel surprisingly steadied. She took a deep breath and set the teacup on the table, looking into the Oracle's stormy eyes. "What do I need to do?"

"Ah, that is going to require strength." The Oracle took one last sip of her tea and grasped Mara's hands in hers. She continued seriously, "In order to become a Ranger, you must win the loyalty of three companions and complete a task set for you by Aeun."

"What does that mean?" Mara asked, brows furrowed.

"You must sail to the isles of the gods beyond the Dragon's Teeth. Find Aeun on her forest island and she will tell you your task."

Mara was confused—and she was starting to feel sick again. "The gods have islands?"

"Yes. They each have their own sanctuaries at the end of the world."

"What's the Dragon's Teeth?"

"The Dragon's Teeth make up a sharp rock barrier between the gods and the rest of Ambergrove. You will need specific companions to complete this quest."

Mara paused for a moment before replying, "Three of them, you said? And I have to win them? How do I do that?"

"The first will be easy. You need a wise warrior of the forest dwarves."

Mara agreed that might be easy. She knew at least one warrior who would be willing to help her. "And the others?"

"The second you will find among the gnomekin. You must find someone who knows the earth and its mysteries—someone grounded."

Mara blinked. She didn't even know there were gnomes in this world, but she wasn't sure why she was surprised. "And the last?"

"Ah, this will be the most difficult. In order to sail through treacherous lands, you will need an expert wayfinder. A man with the skills needed to make it through the Dragon's Teeth can only be a sea elf."

Hadn't Cora mentioned elves when she talked about her tattoos? But what was a sea elf? Why would getting him be the most difficult? Mara's fears ran away with her. She barely heard the Oracle as she continued, "You must complete a test to earn the services of each of your three companions. This task will be set for you after you reach their lands, and failure will mean more than the loss of Aeunna."

"Wh … what? I'm sorry, what did you say?" Something in that last bit had snapped Mara to reality.

"Each companion is accompanied by a test," the Oracle repeated. "You must complete this test to gain their services. However, if you fail, survival is not likely. These tests will stretch you to your limits. The only way to survive them is to prove you are worthy."

Mara stared into those cloudy eyes. In them, she saw pain and loss. She saw danger. She saw uncertainty. Fear. It seeped into her like water into a sponge. She began to shiver. She couldn't do this. She would die. She had no idea what to do. Surely, she was the wrong person. Surely. She felt a sharp pain on her cheek. The Oracle had slapped her—with surprising force.

"Better?" she asked, rubbing Mara's cheek where she'd just slapped. "You don't have time to process this now. Your loving uncle is waiting outside to take you to begin your training. And he still has to finish telling you about your family, besides." The Oracle got up slowly and shuffled to the other room. How had the Oracle known what she and Teddy were talking about? Mara got up in a daze and walked to the doorway.

The Oracle came back with a small chest, smiling at Mara. "I still have some secrets and treasures young Toren bade me keep for now, but these items will help you on your quest—in one way or another. They traveled here with you from Earth. They will hold your memories from there close to your heart and they will bind you to Aeunna. Take them." She handed Mara the chest, and Mara went back to her seat to open it.

There were many things inside. First, a small pouch with the meticulously carved and painted figures from her birthday cake. Beside that, the dagger her father had given her for her birthday—the one he'd said was his first dagger. Next, the silver cuff her dad had given her for her birthday—the present he'd said was a family heirloom. Looking at it again, she realized the tree embossed at the center was an Aeunna tree. *His family heirloom was from Aeunna.* Finally, wrapped perfectly at the bottom, as if it had never been worn, was the little friendship bracelet she'd gotten from Kara. Gingerly, Mara picked it up and softly ran a finger along the intricate pattern. At that moment, finally, the tears began to fall.

CHAPTER FOUR

THE HUMAN AND THE DWARF

When Mara opened the Oracle's door, she had the velvet bag tied to her belt next to her water pouch and the dagger slipped through on the opposite side. The silver cuff and the little, pink friendship bracelet she'd returned to her left wrist. She thanked the Oracle one last time before closing the door behind her. Teddy was sitting at the edge of the platform, looking out at the forest. At the creak of the door closing, he turned.

Mara's distress was plain. Teddy stood and stepped toward her cautiously. "You alright there, lass?" he asked. "You look a bit pale." He gave her a gentle hug and a pat on the back.

Mara smiled, but it didn't reach her eyes. "I'm alright, Teddy. It's just a lot to take in. The Oracle said that I wasn't supposed to talk about my Ranger trial until our evening meal. Aengar will announce it to all Aeunna then."

"That is customary," Teddy told her.

"If you say so. I just hope it all works out," Mara whispered.

"It will. I truly believe that. Truly." Teddy placed his hands on her shoulders and made her look at him, staring deeply into her eyes. "Truly."

"Thanks, Teddy." She smiled up at him again, realizing that, with her dad so far away, his support made her feel safe.

Teddy cleared his throat awkwardly. "Now, Mara, are you ready to hit the training grounds?"

"I'm sure I will be by the time we get down there," she said with a sigh.

Teddy chuckled, gave her another pat on the back, and they headed off the platform to begin the long trek down the village tree. "Would you like to hear more about your dad as we walk?" he asked. Mara nodded, so he continued, "Where did I leave off before you went in to see the Oracle?"

"You were just talking about Dad becoming the Ranger."

"Ah. Well … okay. So … Toren met your mother on his Ranger trial," Teddy began. "For his trial, your dad had to find a human companion and travel deep into the earth near Modoc—a human town—to complete Paeor's game. Paeor is our trickster god. His game involved luring children and young warriors deep into the earth to a series of traps, beyond which was meant to be a treasure that would grant all of their greatest wishes."

"He sounds like a fun guy," Mara said wryly.

"Oh, yes, it goes just about as well as you'd think. According to the Oracle, a clear-headed human and a young Ranger would be able to find the traps and the right way through the deep, and finally be able to outwit the trickster and free the innocent. Well, your dad got his companion, went into the game, and had made it to the end when Paeor demanded they solve a riddle. He told them if they completed the riddle, they would be freed and the deep would be closed forever. The human knew better than to guess, for there could be no correct answer where a trickster was involved. He advised your father so, and Toren gave this answer to Paeor. The god became irate at losing the game. Paeor snapped his fingers and lit Toren's companion on fire. Distraught and unsure what else to do, Toren fought Paeor."

"He fought a *god*?" Mara asked.

"Yes, he did. But he didn't last long. Injured and losing, he asked Aeun for help. She appeared with Maonna and Daeda—our mother goddess and father god—and together they took Paeor back to their isles, closing the deep and giving Toren a badger token to prove his victory over Paeor."

Teddy paused, looking at Mara's clouded eyes as she wiped her face. She told him she was alright, waved a hand impatiently, and asked if he would continue. "It's horrible that a god could be so fickle with so many people's lives. Especially that man who was helping. But … if his Ranger trial was over, how did he meet my mom while he was on it?" she asked.

"Your mother was indirectly involved with the whole thing. The human who helped your dad complete his trial was named Dakota. He was your grandfather—your mother's father."

"What?" Mara shouted. She stumbled on the pegs and nearly fell. Teddy caught her and steadied her.

"Easy there, lass!" he called, alarmed.

Mara sat on the nearest peg and looked at the ground. It was so far away. If she'd fallen, she wouldn't be getting back up. Just like her grandfather. When she spoke, her voice was shaky. "I guess I never thought about what happened to my grandparents. I just assumed they died of old age or sickness or something. Lit on fire …" she trailed off, choking up.

Teddy nervously rubbed his green scalp. "I guess I shouldn't have told you that …" He winced and patted her back. "If it helps at all, your grandpa was a hero amongst humans and forest dwarves alike. He helped to save many people. So many."

"Yeah?"

"Yeah. Including your dad. He sacrificed himself so your dad could be successful. He knew he wouldn't make it back, and he went anyway."

Mara smiled. It was good to know that her grandfather had been a good person, even if he had died so horribly. She saw an annoyed look on Teddy's face. "What is it?" she asked.

"Well … there was one person who didn't think so. Kenda."

"Of course not," Mara said dryly. Mara had never really gotten along with her mother. Her friends at school had always said that Kenda fit a particular motherly stereotype—and not the good kind. Mara agreed. She cared more about her manicure than her marriage. The only one of her children Kenda liked was Sara, because her eldest daughter was made in her image. She hated most things others would treasure, so Mara wasn't surprised the woman had a negative opinion of heroism as well.

"Let me guess." Mara glared into Teddy's eyes. "She blamed him for my grandfather's death and demanded that he support her, since obviously it was all his fault?"

Teddy smirked. "Close enough."

Mara nodded and stood to continue the descent—this time striding to exhaust her emotions. Teddy was right behind her. "Tell me how they went from that to Earth," she called back.

"Ah, well …" Teddy launched into a long story with many asides. Toren brought Kenda back to Aeunna, and Teddy had taken her in as well. She was very needy, but she never seemed to show that side to Toren. She made sure he always saw her put together, proper, and beautiful. She was drawn to his success and he was drawn to her everything. It didn't take long before they began courting and talking about marriage and later life.

Kenda wanted a glamorous life, and she had heard about so many conveniences Earth had to offer. She had planned to go since she first heard about plumbing and air conditioning, but she didn't want to try to make it on her own. She needed someone strong and hardworking to support her. Toren was a perfect fit and he was smitten. It took a lot of convincing—and no one was sure what pushed him over the edge—but he decided to go. He reinstated the elder council, said a last goodbye, and was lost to them forever.

Teddy finished his story just as they reached the forest floor. Mara was glad to have so much of her history filled in, but she still had so many questions—questions it seemed only her dad would ever be able to answer. Her breath caught at the thought of never seeing him again. Never seeing her sisters. She absently twisted the silver cuff on her wrist, frowning. She couldn't dwell on those thoughts, for the forest floor was teeming with forest dwarves and bearkin—whispering about her trial, whispering about her training, some even trying to get her attention as Teddy waved and steered her along.

Soon they were alone in the forest, but not for long. It seemed as soon as Mara was blessed with silence, the world around her flared with light and sound. They had entered a clearing. Mara squinted into the light and looked around her. There were roped arenas on one side, roped runways to targets on another, a collection of wooden buildings in the middle, and various other stations as far as the eye could see. It looked like the far end was for horseback riding. There were forest dwarves of all ages at each station, the youngest maybe ten and the oldest fifty or sixty.

"This is our training ground," Teddy explained.

Mara had forgotten that Teddy was supposed to be the head warrior and the trainer of hunters and warriors. She turned to ask him why he had sat outside the Oracle's house all morning instead of doing his job, but he was already pointing at one of the wooden buildings. A tattooed figure bounded toward them, grinning ear-to-ear.

"Hello there, boss man!" Cora called, waving.

"Hard to train the young hunters if you're sitting in the stockroom!" Teddy called back.

They met Cora in the middle as the woman explained, "I did my job, thank you very much. You thrive on delegation, sir." Teddy shrugged and nodded. Cora continued, "I was trying to finish this before you guys came down here." She presented a small, plainly wrapped package and tossed it to Mara.

"What's this?"

"Open it and find out," Teddy told her, smiling.

Mara yanked the paper off, revealing a small wooden box. She glanced up at Cora before inspecting it. The box itself was beautiful with intricate leaf carvings. She tried to open it—it was locked. When she looked up again, Teddy held out a small key.

"It is up to the previous Ranger to decide the Ranger title of his successor—"

"Or hers," Cora put in.

"Yes, or hers," Teddy continued. "Your da was prepared for your arrival. He sent your title along. It's in that box."

Mara looked at the whorls of leaves on the box and wondered aloud, "What was my dad's title?"

"Toren was the Badger," Teddy told her. "He was given that title after completing his trial in the deep. Badgers are digging creatures, you see. After bringing back Aeun's token, there was no question."

Mara smiled, thinking of a beloved television character her father always seemed to have a deep connection to. The name was apt. "Shouldn't I wait to get my name until I've done something?" she asked.

"Ordinarily, yes, but your father said he knew what you would do as a campaigner and that the name would fit your role as a leader. He said ..." Teddy paused, then decided to commit. "He said that you were fiercely protective of everyone around you during a campaign. You do your best to help everyone and everything, even if they don't deserve it, and you're scary when you've been wronged. There were some other things in there, but I think you get the idea ..." Teddy trailed off when he saw the tears in Mara's eyes.

Curse it, she didn't usually cry at all! Now it's twice in one day! Mara quickly wiped her eyes and reached out for Teddy's key. When she opened the box, she saw it contained just a single leather bracer. It was chocolate brown and had its own intricate carving. Mara laughed out loud when she saw it was a dragonwolf.

One of the first times they had played D&D, Mara had invented this creature organically during a game. She combined the best qualities of both creatures and even argued fervently for their addition to the game, either as monsters or a playable race. She came up with them when she was barely eight years old and hadn't spoken about them at all in years. She couldn't believe that was what her father had picked for her, yet now that she saw the wild creature, she couldn't imagine it being anything else.

Once she had quieted her laughter, Cora spoke first. "It was quite a test for the tanner, trying to do that wolf-dragon. I'm not sure if it's what you wanted."

"Dragonwolf," Mara corrected her, "and yes, it's wonderful." The dragonwolf looked like a gryphon or a sphinx. Most of its body was that of a wolf—though the size of a small dragon—but it had dragon wings and a spiked dragon tail. Absent from this rendition, but present in all of Mara's drawings, were also curled horns and spikes all down its spine. Mara picked up the bracer, and Teddy took the box off her hands, murmuring that he would make sure it got to her room. She slid the bracer on her right arm and began tightening it. She thought she heard Cora nudge Teddy and whisper that she was even correctly wearing her first piece of armor. Mara was positively glowing. It fit perfectly. It had been made for her after all. She beamed as she looked up at the other two and asked them what was next.

Basic weaponry. That was next. Although Mara understood some about melee weapons, she'd only ever held a sword when she was trying to get her dad to buy one for her. She *had* thrown an axe before—at a fair. It didn't go well. Bows were a slightly different story. She had done a little work for her neighbor when she was in middle school and been rewarded with an old hunting bow. She'd practiced with it a few times but had to stop when her mother found out that she was using the side of the garden shed for target practice.

Cora took her through the weapons storage to pick out one of each of the practice weapons. The practice swords were heavier, blunted. When Cora told her to pick, she was confused at first because they all looked the same. After rifling through with no success, Mara found a practice sword with a slice on the handle and dings all up the blade. It had character. They'd given her a belt with a collection of leather loops, so she slid the sword into one of them.

Next was daggers, then small axes, a battle axe, and a mace. Mara picked out the saddest looking of those also. Here again, the bow was a different story. She wanted one that was in good condition, so she didn't pull back and have the weapon break into her face. Guessing how to test it and just hoping she had it right, Mara picked up one bow at a time, bending the wood back and stringing it. She tested the tautness of the string and the strength of the wood. The first bow made cracking sounds as soon as she started pulling it back, so she tried another. The second one didn't have any obvious defects or weaknesses, so she grabbed some arrows and turned back toward the dwarves.

What appeared to be barely stifled laughter was stifled no longer. Mara had so many weapons hitched to her hip she could barely waddle—plus she was holding a bow in one hand and a fistful of arrows in another. Through the laughter, Cora managed to force out an explanation.

"Y-you d-don't take them all at o-once!" she managed.

"You pick your weapons now, but you're only going to practice one at a time," Teddy explained, grinning ear-to-ear. He pointed to a door near the back of the room, snapping his fingers in Cora's face a few times to get her to get it together, before gesturing to Mara's weapons.

Teddy took the bow and arrows from Mara, Cora took the axes, and they led her back toward the other room. It was way larger than she'd expected it to be, and it was similar to a locker room. There were individual stations lining the walls and in the center of the room itself. Each station housed armor and weapons together.

"Whoa! Which one am I supposed to take?" Mara asked.

"Easy," Teddy replied. "You get the one closest to the door."

Mara turned and saw an empty space tucked behind the door. Cora and Teddy placed her other weapons there. "Alright, hand over the daggers. Won't be needing those right now either." He reached out a hand and accepted the daggers, making sure everything was in its place in the locker. After a few moments, Mara was left with nothing but the battered sword.

"Alright." Cora patted Mara on the back. "Are you ready to begin basic swordsmanship?"

Mara smiled, eyes wide, and followed them back out into the sunlight, hand on hilt.

CHAPTER FIVE

DRAGONWOLF

C ora and Teddy led Mara out into the clearing and toward the roped
arenas. As they headed out to a sword arena, the younger students in
nearby sparring matches turned to look, resulting in many landed blows
and shouts of pain.

Cora shouted back over her shoulder, "That's why you always need to
pay attention to your enemy!"

They headed to their own practice area. It was a circle the size of a
small room, ringed with red roping attached to a tree on one side. Teddy
plopped down under the tree and crossed his ankles, waiting. Cora paused
at the entrance, removing all her weapons and picking up a practice sword
from the edge of the arena, before taking Mara into the center.

"Now," Cora began, pressing her sword into the ground and resting her
hands on it, "show me what you know about swords."

Mara was alarmed. In just one short day, she'd already begun to idolize
Cora. She didn't want to make mistakes in front of her.

Teddy called over from the tree, "Everyone's been a beginner, Mara.
Even her. She won't judge you."

How did he know that was what worried her? Mara tapped the hilt of
her practice sword. "You carry the sword on your non-dominant side," she
began. Cora nodded. Mara awkwardly drew her sword. It got stuck in the
loop and it took her a few tries to actually get it out. Teddy grinned and
relaxed against the tree trunk.

"That will become easier with time," Cora told her. "What else do you
know about swords?"

"Uh … that's pretty much it," Mara replied. "I've seen sword fighting in movies and read about it in books, but I really don't know what's right or how to execute it. Pointy end goes into the monster."

"Too right!" Teddy shouted from the tree.

"Too right." Cora chuckled. "Though hopefully you won't have to face too many monsters just yet. Let's start with your stance."

Cora showed Mara how to steady herself, how to hold her sword defensively, and a few defensive positions. She gave her pointers for various exercises that would help keep her nimble and fighting fit. Mara was not used to exercise, so a little was so much when it came to that. After what seemed like hours, Mara heard a gong sound three times. All those practicing began to clean up their work and head to the armory. Mara tucked her sword back into her belt—after a few tries—and gave Cora a puzzled look.

"It's lunchtime, Mara," Cora explained. "When the gong sounds three times, everyone stops for lunch."

"What about when it sounds other times?"

"The gong sounds throughout the day for those training. Each ability group is on a rotation for weapons practice. Everyone begins the day with stretches and exercise. Once they are dismissed into their ability groups, they have until the first gong to practice their first weapon. At the first gong, they switch to their second weapon and at the second gong they switch to their third weapon. Next is lunch. There are two more rotations after lunch, then everyone does a cooldown stretch before being dismissed."

"So they're here for the whole day?"

"Twice a week, those in training are here for the whole day. Twice a week, they train only in the morning, alternating weapons, and twice a week, they just come in for exercise. They have one rest day."

Mara was exhausted. Cora had simply touched swords with hers to show her the right way to stand and to move. She hadn't fought at all, she'd barely exercised, and she'd only used one weapon. She couldn't help but wonder, *How on Earth—or on Ambergrove, I guess—will I be able to do this?*

"I can see that look of defeat on your face."

Mara turned to look at Teddy. His eyes were closed. "How—"

"Everyone to come through here has felt that." He opened his eyes and peered at her. "Everyone. It's hard, bitter work in the beginning—that's no lie. It is. But it does get easier over time, and the practice is necessary for everyone. Everyone in Aeunna comes out for at least the two days of morning exercise. Even Rhodi."

Mara could feel the skepticism on her face, but Cora added, "What he's trying to say, Mara, is that this is a good life. This will prepare you for your Ranger trial. It will help you to defend yourself wherever you may be, and it's necessary for survival here."

Survival. You need to be quick to survive. Mara nodded. "I'm sure I'll figure it out." She reassured herself more than them.

"Let's put all this stuff away and head to lunch." Cora gave Mara a reassuring smile.

Teddy jumped up at the mention of food and led Mara down toward the armory while Cora stabbed the practice sword into the ground by the arena and gathered her weapons. The crowd of students hardly seemed to notice their famed future leader amongst them. They deposited their weapons and raced off to a collection of tables. Mara did the same. As she neared the tables, the clamoring was deafening.

Benches around the tables were filled with sweaty students of all ages. Each table held bowls fruit and vegetables in the center, as well as a pitcher and a few cups. There were bearkin skittering around the tables, emptying their trays. Lunch was sandwiches, lovingly prepared by the bearkin. There was one table off to the side with only two inhabitants—Mapleleaf chatted with Cora, a tray of sandwiches in front of him.

Teddy led Mara over to the table, grabbed a couple sandwiches, and had one in his mouth before sitting down. Mara was a little more polite, greeting Mapleleaf and thanking him for the meal before sitting down. Cora poured her some water. Mara took an apple and some carrots from the middle bowl and two sandwiches from the tray and placed them on her own metal plate. The sandwiches appeared to both be ham and cheddar, on surprisingly soft bread with firm tomato slices and crisp lettuce.

"Mapleleaf, will you tell me a little bit about your people? Do you have time?" Mara asked.

"I have a little time, young miss," Mapleleaf rumbled. "What would you like to know?"

Mara took a bite of her sandwich—man, it was good—and thought for a minute. "Could you tell me where you came from and why you serve the forest dwarves—the nature of your relationship?" She took another bite, a bit too large.

"You're wanting to know if we're pets or people?" he asked.

She choked. And choked some more. Cora had been laughing, but after a minute Teddy began clapping her on the back, calling, "You good there, lass?" She swallowed, took a sip of water, cleared her throat, took another sip, then nodded.

Mapleleaf chuckled, a sort of growling cackle. "You're not the first to wonder. It's okay," he assured her. "Do you need a minute, or are you ready to eat and listen?" His lip curled.

Was he smiling? Do bears smile? "Sorry, yes," she replied. "Please tell me." As Mapleleaf began his story, Mara scarfed down her sandwiches and settled in to listen.

"Bearkin have been here since before forest dwarves. Before Aeunna. Our race is old, but weak. We are not like the bears you know. I guess you could say we're kind of like your panda bears." Mara chuckled into her sandwich. He continued, "All we wanted was to make good food, eat good food, and relax in nature."

"Same," Cora and Mara crooned in unison.

"Indeed." Mapleleaf's lip curled again—surely that was a smile. He continued, "Though while your kind have grown into fighters anyway, my kind did not. When Aeun made Aeunna, she made it for bearkin and forest dwarves alike. She brought us together. There are caves for us at the base of the Aeunna trees. Forest dwarves live above, and we live below. Since they are better equipped to be warriors, they protect us. Since we are better equipped to find food, and we love to make it, we make the food for them. We work and live together as equals."

"That sounds like a good system," Mara noted. She chomped on a carrot. "I'm glad. I was worried that ... uh ..."

"That we were servants? Or slaves?"

"Yeah," she replied sheepishly.

"Our world is nicer than all that. Around here anyway. There are darker areas of Ambergrove where people from Earth introduced slavery, but Aeunna has always been a beacon of light."

"That's great. I'm glad." Mara smiled at Mapleleaf before finishing her lunch.

Their lunch eaten, it was time to head back for weapons and go to the next training area. Students were starting to get up. Mapleleaf patted Mara on the shoulder. "You let us know whenever you want to learn more from us," he told her. "Right now, it's time for you to learn something else." He gestured to the commotion around them.

Cora and Teddy were getting up. They stacked everything from lunch into one big pile, thanked Mapleleaf, and headed back to the armory. This time, Cora had Mara get two small axes, a bow, and a quiver with blunted arrows. They were stocking up for the rest of the day. After collecting their weapons, they went to the practice areas on the other side of the clearing. There were dozens of runways to wooden targets, and the furthest runway was half under the shade of a large, old tree.

They headed to the runway closest to the tree. Just as before, Teddy settled himself under it and crossed his ankles. "Are these trees just here so you can nap under them?" Mara asked.

"Pretty much," he replied, folding his hands on his chest and grinning.

Mara shook her head, turning to face Cora. The Marked warrior kept her own weapons this time, and she began by asking Mara if she'd had any experience with axes. Mara revealed she hadn't much, but she'd still thrown at a target before. Cora told her to begin with throwing and showed her the stance.

"You only have two shots at a time. Make them count," Cora told her.

Mara threw the first. Miraculously, it hit the exact center—with the handle. She tried again. The second hit the lower right of the target with the head, but it didn't sink in. She retrieved her axes and tried again. After target practice, Cora called her back to explain the basics of hand combat with axes. The gong sounded.

Before they would be able to practice archery, they had to add another target. For the initial practice, the forest dwarves had just woven straw disks and hooked them over the wooden targets as needed. Teddy added this and sat back down under the tree while Cora asked Mara what she knew about bows.

"Why did you string the bow before you picked it?" Cora asked.

"Because I remembered that the tautness of the string is what makes it fire further. Stringing it and pulling it back some showed that the wood was still strong."

"Good. I'm impressed," Cora smiled at her and motioned for her to continue. "Now, how do you nock the arrow?"

Mara pulled an arrow out of the quiver she'd strapped to her back. Three feathers and a notch to one end and a slight taper to the other—no tip. She held the bow with her right hand and rested the arrow above her hand, setting the notch into the string with one feather facing out. Cora waited until she seemed finished before speaking.

"You have that backwards."

Mara looked down at her hands, frowning. "Which part is backwards?"

"All of it. You have this set up to shoot left-handed."

"Oh. Well ... I guess I shoot left-handed then."

"What makes you say that, Mara?"

Mara told Cora how she'd been given her first bow. "He had me try out some of them before picking, and the only way I could seem to shoot straight is to hold the bow with my right hand."

"Hmm ... you've shot before?"

Mara nodded.

"Well, let's see what you have first." Cora gestured to the target.

Mara stepped up to the edge of the runway. She remembered what her dad had told her about bows. The one she had used at home was a compound bow. Once you pull pack a certain amount, the weight releases, and you can hold it like that forever. Longbows are not that way. You feel the pressure the entire time, and your hand shakes more the longer you try to hold.

She exhaled deeply. She would aim quickly and shoot as rapidly as she could. She hoped she wouldn't embarrass herself. She exhaled one more time, pulled the string back to her mouth, and fired. It hit the target, just barely on the right edge. She fired again. Closer. Again. Closer. Her last three shots were all right around the bullseye.

"Well," Cora mused, "seems like you *are* a left-handed archer."

As Mara walked to retrieve her arrows, Teddy cheered. She spent the rest of archery time with Cora discussing stance, wind resistance, and aiming quickly. When the gong sounded, they were all satisfied with Mara's progress her first day training. After participating in the end of day stretching, they put Mara's weapons away and stood by the door as the others poured out in two directions.

"You did well today," Teddy told her as he clapped her on the back. "Really well."

"I think it was probably okay, but definitely not where I need to be," Mara replied with a smile. "That's okay, though, I think. I'll work on it, I promise."

"You'll have plenty of time for that," Cora assured her. "For now, I need to take you off with that worm of girls." Cora indicated one of the two groups leaving, and Mara noticed one group was all male and one was all female.

"I need to be off to check in with Freya and talk to Aengar," Teddy announced. "Cora will bring you to the evening meal."

As Teddy went off toward his home, Cora led Mara off with the females. According to Cora, they were going to the showerhouses to clean up. Once they made it into the woods, they arrived at a river by a waterfall, with wooden buildings on stilts spreading across the river. Then Cora and Mara followed the girls through the showerhouse and prepared themselves for the evening meal.

There were clothes laid out for them inside the showerhouse. Cora's regular robes were waiting there, but the clothes left for Mara were different—no soft pants this time. She held the dress up in disgust. It was beautiful, there was no doubt. It was a soft green with lighter and darker green accents. Covering the entire garment was delicate embroidery—vines and leaves, woodland creatures, and hunting symbols. It was so fancy, and it was certainly beautiful. She just didn't wear anything like that.

"Yeah, I know that look. You have to wear it though," Cora told her dryly.

"But it's a dress."

"Yeah, I know, but this is a special occasion. Apparently, even though they're announcing that you're leaving on a dangerous mission, you're still supposed to wear a ceremonial dress." Cora rolled her eyes and made a mocking gesture. "Tradition!" she exclaimed. She paused, then added, "You're supposed to wear your bracer, though, so … silver lining."

Mara eyed her dirty brown pants. She squinted, thinking. Then she smiled at Cora.

"Are you about to mess with tradition?" Cora asked.

"Ah, just a bit."

Cora and Mara walked up the little aisle toward the dais. There were scattered gasps and murmuring all the way, but Cora patted Mara's back and beamed. Mara had worn the dress, but she had twisted it to one side and hitched it up, wearing her dirty brown pants underneath. A small part of her felt guilty about scorning the traditions of a place she didn't even really know, but Cora was proud of her and she was proud of herself—and that seemed right. Honestly, if the Oracle was to be believed, she *was* about to embark on a perilous journey. It made absolutely no sense for her to be required to wear a dress.

She strode up to the dais, and mixed reactions awaited her. Teddy beamed, and when Freya saw him beaming, there was a fierce look on her face and Teddy's face changed, as if he'd just been kicked under the table. He'd definitely just been kicked under the table. Rhodi smiled pleasantly. Aengar just looked sour. Cora squeezed past Aengar to sit in her spot, but when Mara tried to do the same, Aengar caught her and had her stand next to him for his address.

"Aeunna, today our rangerling met with the Oracle and was given her trial. You have waited to learn what that trial would be."

Mara looked around. It really didn't seem like many of them cared what her trial would be. She probably should have tried harder to stick with tradition. She wondered if she would be able to inconspicuously let down her dress as Aengar continued explaining the trials.

"... and Toren was able to save many people, proving he was right to lead us—if only for a short time. Aeun helped him complete his task. Young Mara's task also involves Aeun. I have spoken to the Oracle and she has instructed me to reveal this task to you thus." Aengar placed Mara at the center of the dais, stood to her right, and held up her right hand, displaying her bracer, as he began to speak again.

"Toren has named her the Dragonwolf." There were scattered remarks, many in confusion. "Should she complete her task, this will be her name." Aengar scanned the room once more. "The Dragonwolf must complete an odyssey. She must earn allies from Aeunna, the Big Hill, and the Great Serpent." There was much murmuring at this, but Aengar just continued, "Once she has found companions, she will sail through the Dragon's Teeth to speak to Aeun on her island."

Aengar waited for some of the murmuring to die down, then continued, "If she makes it to Aeun thus, this will also prove her to be the rangerling prophesied to reunite Ambergrove. Aeun will tell her how to save us and we—" Cheers drowned out all that Aengar had been about to say. After a moment's pause, Aengar raised his hand for quiet as he'd done before.

"The rangerling will now give a speech," he announced. Aengar handed Mara the microphone stick.

She was alarmed. More alarmed than she had been the entire journey so far. She had no idea what to say to them or how to say it. An awkward cough informed her she had been staring wildly out at them for some time. She cleared her throat and gave it a try.

"I— Um ... I am Mara. You don't know me, but my dad was good. At least, I hope you saw him as good. I ... do." She was acutely aware of everyone looking at her. She glanced down at her pants, then shook off her fear and called out to them, "How many of you just hate that I wore pants today?" No response. *Okay.*

"I grew up watching movies about grand heroines who wore ridiculous clothes. They fought with their hair down. They fought in dresses. They fought in armor that was basically just underwear. No, I don't know much about this place. I don't know how to lead you. I don't know how to complete my trial, or even if I can, but my dad did." Mara paused. Her dad would be proud. She was sure of it.

She scanned the audience for a moment, then continued, "I know that I spurned your traditions in not wearing this ceremonial dress properly, but if I'm going to fight—if I'm going to try to do what's right—I don't want you to see me as some stranger in a dress. I want you to see a fighter. And fighters wear pants." She threw up her hand and slapped her thigh lightly. When she looked around, some were smiling, at least. "I don't know if I'm a leader you want or need, but I'm going to do my best to prove that I'm someone who can belong and who can help. I am my father's daughter," she finished, glancing down at the cuff on her wrist.

The forest erupted into cheers. Good—that had taken all her energy. She quickly passed the stick back to Aengar and went to her seat. Cora gave her a small pat as Mara sank into the seat beside her.

"There you have it," Aengar announced. "We shall see what the future holds. For now, let the evening meal begin!"

Mapleleaf and the bearkin brought out the meal, and the forest melted into celebration.

CHAPTER SIX

A NEW LIFE

Mara decided to sleep that night in her uncle's home again. With the day's events, she wasn't ready to be on her own. She woke up early the following morning, once again, and went to the kitchen. This time, she was awake before Teddy, but not before Freya. When Mara opened the kitchen door, Freya was waiting there with some more homemade muffins.

"Sit," the woman said with surprising coldness, motioning to the seat beside her.

Mara greeted her great aunt, thanked her, and accepted a muffin.

"Do you know what you're doing?" Freya asked.

Mara was surprised to hear such an ignorant question from such a wise woman. "Uh ... no. No, I have absolutely no idea what I'm doing," she said honestly.

"No need for sass," Freya told her dryly.

Mara sighed sharply. "I'm sorry, Aunt Freya, I am, but you know I don't know what I'm doing."

"I meant for your trials, Mara."

"Yeah, I don't know about those eith—"

"Mara!" Freya slammed a muffin on the counter, disintegrating her breakfast. "Listen to me!" She calmed herself before continuing in a controlled tone, her dark eyes icy, "Your trial requires you to get a wise companion from Aeunna to help you on your quest. A warrior. Didn't you stop to think who that might be?"

She hadn't, really. She had a few ideas when the Oracle had first told her, but she had just hoped that the person would magically fall into her lap—like they usually do when there's a quest in a magical land. Now that she wondered, there really was only one person she knew who would, without a doubt, be prepared to go with her. She stared wide-eyed at Freya.

"You can't take him, Mara." The woman was trembling and her voice was a whisper. "He's everything to me. I couldn't bear losing him. ... Someone always dies on a Ranger trial."

Mara was silent for a moment. Freya sounded so certain. Was this fact or superstition? Slowly, she replied, "I'm not experienced, but I could never let that happen to him."

"No ... *he* could never let that happen to *you*. Toren was his son—more than anyone's. He may be your uncle, but when he looks at you, he sees Toren. He sees you as a granddaughter. If it comes down to you or him, he'll make sure it's you. You have to take someone else."

"She doesn't choose these things, Freya." Teddy stood in the doorway, arms crossed. He continued, "You know fate has already decided who will go and who will not return."

Freya glared down at her ruined muffin, and Mara turned to look sadly at her uncle. "Uncle Teddy ... are you the person who's supposed to come with me?" she asked quietly.

"I believe so," he replied. Freya threw the bowl of muffins to the floor and stormed out of the kitchen. Mara tried to stop her, but Teddy shook his head and let his wife pass. "Leave her be."

Mara stared down at her muffin, tears filling her eyes. "I don't want you to die, Teddy," she whispered.

Teddy strode over to her and grabbed her by the shoulders, making her meet his gaze. "Look, if I die, it will be because I made a choice. Because fate made a choice. You cannot change it any more than you can cause it. If I am the best person to aid you in your quest, then I will be there for you and I will make sure you know everything you need to know to be successful."

"But ... what did she mean when she said someone always dies?" Mara asked, wiping a tear.

Teddy's brow furrowed. He looked down at the muffin mess for a moment before explaining, "It's fate. I don't know why Aeun wills it that way, but the Ranger trial is not complete until one of the companions has died."

"And you're willing to just go with me, knowing you'll die?" Mara squeaked.

"That's what Dakota did." Teddy wiped another tear from Mara's cheek and swept a russet strand behind her ear. "Your father told him before he agreed to come, because he was the only companion. It would either be Dakota or Toren. He went anyway. Your odds are better though, since you will have three companions instead of one." Teddy smiled at her reassuringly.

Mara smiled at him weakly. "I guess," she said. "There's nothing I can do about it either way."

"Now, now, that's not entirely true. You can make a difference with heart, brains, and skill. If you are going to be a great warrior, you are going to need to make it to the morning exercise and training. Today is a lighter day, though. It's just a morning train." He nudged her chin reassuringly.

Mara nodded and took a bite of her muffin, trying to shake the doom out of her mind and welcoming his changing the subject. "What does that mean we'll be doing?" she asked.

"You will do the exercises, then you will practice with the sword, then battle axe, then daggers. We still have communal lunches these days."

"Sounds like a plan," Mara said, trying her best to be positive.

She and Teddy grabbed some muffins to go, Mara got water for them both, and they headed out to the training grounds together.

The morning exercise was brutal. As with weapons training, there were different ability groups for exercise. Mara, being an out-of-shape teen from Earth, ended up with one of the lower ability groups. Specifically, Mara was exercising with the elderly group. Even positioned next to Rhodi, and only working to match the old woman's pace, Mara was exhausted. They began with stretches, ran in place, and did sit-ups, push-ups, squats, and various yoga poses. After this, they ran laps—the elderly group power walked—around the entire training clearing. The lower groups only had to make one lap, but it was still at least a mile around the clearing. They did a few cool down exercises before Mara split off to work on her first weapon of the day and the elders left the training grounds to go about their business.

Before leaving, Rhodi pulled Mara to the side, holding one hand in both of hers and patting it. "You'll get there, rangerling," she said with a warm smile. "If you measure yourself by the abilities of others, you'll never be happy. Do your best every day, okay?" Mara nodded. The old woman smiled softly and said, "Okay, then." With a last reassuring pat, Rhodi shuffled away back toward the village.

Mara smiled to herself and headed back to the armory to grab her things. When she came back out, it wasn't Cora waiting for her, but Teddy. This time, Cora was busy circulating among the other students, so Teddy taught Mara what he knew of the sword. She'd liked having Cora as a teacher, but Teddy's patience and quiet wisdom were so helpful. With Teddy's guidance, Mara worked through the same positions and exercises she had the day before, moving on to basic attacks when Teddy was satisfied.

When the gong sounded, Mara hefted the double-bladed battle axe. Teddy had her complete the sword exercises with the heavier axe before showing her how to hold it for various parries and basic attacks. Mostly, she just practiced swinging without losing her balance. She couldn't exactly roll a two and hit her own leg like she'd done with Danag on her birthday, but she could certainly make a mistake and hit her own leg—and not be able to just walk it off.

When the gong sounded again, they moved to daggers. Teddy showed her a bit of handling, swiping and parrying, and she spent the rest of the time throwing them at the target. Teddy told her to try it out and he would correct her, so she tried and tried. No matter what she did, she kept on hitting the target with the handle instead of the blade. Teddy just kept chuckling from the edge of the runway and telling her to try again. Once the final gong sounded, Teddy told her that he would show her the right way to throw the dagger before they headed to lunch.

"Watch me just this once," he instructed. Her uncle picked up the dagger by the handle, as Mara had done, and then he flipped the knife to hold the tip of the blade instead. He held her gaze as he threw the knife and buried it in the center.

Mara suddenly understood why Freya always gave him dirty looks. She stomped toward him with the remaining dagger and stared at him while she threw it at the target—just as he had done. It barely clipped the edge, but it stuck. She stomped over to gather the daggers and continued stomping all the way back to the armory.

When she headed up to lunch, she discovered Teddy was at the table already, with Mapleleaf and another bearkin. This one was slightly smaller and, at least to Mara, seemed younger. "Are you telling these fellows about your hilarious dagger joke?" she asked Teddy dryly.

"Nah, they wouldn't get it any more than you did." He chuckled, stroking his beard.

By the looks on their faces, they probably wouldn't. Mara sat at the table, glaring at Teddy as she did. Lunch today looked like some sort of roast beef sandwiches. As she gathered her plate, she looked at the other bearkin. This creature had reddish-brown fur and seemed to be very cheerful.

"Hello there," Mara called. "I know Mapleleaf, but I don't believe I've seen you before."

"My name is Ashroot." The voice rumbled like Mapleleaf's, but something was different, lighter. The creature continued, "I am Mapleleaf's daughter."

"Oh!" Mara exclaimed. How could she tell the difference between male and female bearkin?

Mapleleaf's rumble met their ears. "My daughter listened to what you said last night at the evening meal. She would like to aid you on your quest." His face was sour.

"Wow. Uh ... I thought you said bearkin don't fight?" Mara asked.

"We—" Mapleleaf began.

"We don't," Ashroot explained. "But you are going to be going on a long journey. I know many places. I know what's food and what's not. I can prepare meals for you throughout your journey. I would like to assist you."

"Thank you!" Mara exclaimed. "Your help really would be valuable ... but wouldn't you be scared? *I'm* scared. This is supposed to be very dangerous." She grabbed a grape from the center bowl and popped it into her mouth.

"Yes, but that is the kinship of forest dwarves and bearkin. I know that you and your companions will do your best to protect me," Ashroot reasoned.

Mara thought about how long it had taken for her to figure out how to throw a dagger just moments before. "But what if I can't protect you?"

Mapleleaf replied, a hint of anger in his voice, "You will. It is your duty as a forest dwarf. If you are to be the Ranger, it is your duty as Ranger to protect all your people. We are your people, and—"

"Da, it's okay," Ashroot cut in. She turned to Mara. "I want to see the world and all the different foods that are in it. I was hoping that if I came to talk to you today, you would consider spending time with me to learn bearkin ways." She paused. "I also hoped you might teach me how to defend myself. I don't want to be a great warrior, but if I at least know how to protect myself in the wilderness, that would help."

"I would love to learn about bearkin!" Mara smiled. "I'm not sure I'm the one to teach you to defend yourself though. Maybe Teddy . . .?"

Teddy looked at Mara, shook his head, and gestured to the two of them. "You need to bond with other beings in this world. Ashroot is a good girl," he said, patting the bearkin. "She will be a good friend to you. You will learn how to fight, and as someone new to fighting, you are better suited to teach Ashroot the basics. She only needs to know a little. What do you say, Mapleleaf?"

Mapleleaf glared at them, clearly disapproving but unable to object. Ashroot spoke up first, touching her father's arm. "Da, if I go on this journey, I will be able to speak to Aeun. There are so many recipes you've been wanting to perfect. I'm sure she can help you with the anamberry foods."

Mapleleaf squinted at his daughter. When he spoke, his voice was a low rumble. "Very well, daughter. Just promise me you will return to me in one piece."

"Oh, I will, Da! Thank you! Thank you all!" she cried.

There was a slight commotion as tables began to empty and clear. Lunch was over, yet Mara hadn't taken a bite of her sandwich. Ashroot opened her mouth to speak to her, but Mapleleaf spoke first.

"Daughter, remember our agreement."

Ashroot's face fell. She looked at her father as if to argue, then thought better of it. There was a touch of annoyance in her voice as she replied, "Yes, Da," and began to clear up the table.

"Ashroot has agreed to complete half of Mapleleaf's work during the months it takes for you to prepare," Teddy explained. "She is to one day take Mapleleaf's place in Aeunna, so she needs to learn his duties, just as you need to learn yours." Mara picked up her sandwich and nibbled on it as her plate was taken. Then something dawned on her.

"Months?" she cried. The bearkin rumbled their goodbyes and thanks to Mara before heading off with the other bearkin, and Mara stared, wide-eyed, at her uncle.

"Yes, lass," he said, rustling sandwich crumbs out of his beard. "It's going to take months. It's customary for the rangerling to train for six months before the trial."

Mara's brows furrowed.

"Did you think we'd train you one day and then chuck you out like a baby bird?" Teddy continued.

She shrugged, "I wasn't sure what to think."

Teddy sighed. "You will have six months. That's enough time for you to get used to life around you and to train well enough. You'll keep training along your journey, so you just need an even ground right now."

Mara was about to ask him about training on the journey, but he put up a hand before she could open her mouth.

"Don't worry now. First, you need to head to the showerhouse and get cleaned up. You smell like you've been throwing daggers all day." He ignored Mara's frustrated grunt, continuing, "When you're done, I will take you to your own home." He smiled slightly. "Not that you aren't welcome in ours, but I'm sure your aunt will calm down quicker without consistent reminders of your training for what she believes will be my imminent death."

Mara nodded and trotted off toward the showerhouse. She understood why her aunt would be upset. Yes, they were family, but they didn't really know each other. Teddy didn't have to participate in her dad's trial—but look what happened to her grandfather. She agreed that it was as good a time as any to venture out on her own and give the woman some space.

The showerhouse was large. She hadn't really taken the time to look at it the first time she was there. She was worried about the trials, facing Aeunna at supper, and what Cora might think. This time, she looked around her. Mara was amazed to discover how the forest dwarves had been able to make showers. The building was on stilts over the river, and the water was drawn up into the building from the river underneath.

There were tendrils of roots going down through holes in the floor of the building and dipping into the water. These tendrils connected to vines that ran up the wall, and the showerheads seemed to Mara to be relatives of the Venus flytrap. Water poured out of its mouth and back down into the river. She only needed to stand under this mysterious plant to clean herself.

Once she'd finished showering, she left that room and went into the locker area. There were wooden lockers with names lining the walls, and there were benches in the center for easy dressing. Mara strode to her locker and was happy to discover clean brown pants and a plain sage shirt this time instead of a dress. She dressed quickly and braided her hair. She wasn't as good at it as Teddy, but it would do.

Her uncle was waiting for her outside the showerhouse. "All better?" he asked.

"Definitely! No dress today," she replied, making him chuckle.

They headed off toward the village tree and began to climb. After a few moments climbing, Mara asked, "Where is my home supposed to be?"

"We're almost there."

They had barely started climbing the pegs when he paused and pointed at the trunk of the village tree. They were about three stories high, which didn't seem like much when Mara looked up at the surrounding Aeunna trees. She turned to Teddy and raised a brow.

"Ah." He patted his legs awkwardly,. "I guess I should have explained. The Ranger lives in the lower trunk of the village tree. This is so you are central to everyone in the village, including the bearkin living below."

"Oh ... Okay then. That makes sense."

"Are you ready to go in?"

Mara sighed and turned to the door, reaching out to slowly turn the handle. When she stepped in, Teddy waited outside.

Looking in the room, Mara realized how large the tree really was. The entrance seemed like it was meant to be a mudroom. There were rugs by the door, supplies, hangars, and a counter with a basin and pitcher. To the right was a sitting area—the couches and chairs looked surprisingly comfortable. There was a large window with a rocker next to it, and the rest of the wall seemed to be lined with books.

To the left was the kitchen. The walls were lined with counters and cabinets, and there was a basin in the center of the kitchen wall with a window above. Just like Teddy's kitchen, there was an island counter in the middle with stools around it. It seemed as though most of the rooms in the house were divided up in this one huge area, but there were also two curved hallways in the back half of the massive room leading to closed doors.

"Teddy?"

"Yes, lass?" Teddy poked his head in the room.

"What's down there?" She pointed toward the hallways.

"The left hall goes to extra rooms." He pointed unnecessarily to the left side. "Meeting rooms with outside access and storage areas."

"And the right?"

"Bedrooms."

"That's a *lot* of bedrooms!" she cried. She saw three doors before the hallway disappeared from view.

"It's made for a family, Mara. There's enough room here for many children."

Children. She hadn't thought about that. She figured her home would be just big enough for her to live in. She looked down that long hallway and gulped. She really was going to be here forever. They were planning those rooms for her children, and she would never go home again. Mara twisted the tips of her little pink bracelet and sighed deeply before turning back to Teddy. "Which room is mine?" she asked.

"Whichever one you want—it's your house."

Mara decided to ignore the left hallway for a while. Intimidated by the length of the right hallway, she walked straight to the closest room and opened the door. It was twice as large as the bedroom she'd had at home. There were dressers and wardrobes lining the walls, a bench, a mirror, and a large bed in the center with a large chest at the foot. This room also had two windows, one on either side of the bed. It was nice. *I could make this home,* she thought.

Teddy chuckled as he walked into the doorway. "First room, eh?" he asked.

Mara shrugged. "I figured there wasn't really a reason to walk further down the hallway if it's just me."

Teddy nodded and smirked before pointing at the doorframe right next to the hinge. Mara walked over to look and gasped.

"He had the same idea," he told her softly.

Mara reached out and traced the letters, T O R E N. Her dad was here. This was his home. This was his room when he was her age—when he was the leader of the forest dwarves. This would do.

Mara woke to knocking the following morning. She'd spent the rest of the day in her new home, looking through the books in the sitting area and pulling out a large to-read stack, working on *The Origin of Aeunna* until Cora came to get her for the evening meal. After the evening meal, she had fallen right into bed. The gathering had been relatively uneventful, save for Aengar announcing that one of the bearkin had been assigned to the rangerling. They weren't servants, but one bearkin always volunteered to assist the Ranger as his or her own personal chef and companion. This bearkin was responsible for all the Ranger's daily meals and preparations for any official meals to take place in the home. Apparently, when Ashroot had asked her father's permission to go follow Mara through her trial, she was also asking permission to fulfill this role.

Mara found Ashroot waiting patiently outside, grinning ear-to-ear. "Good morning, Ashroot!" Mara yawned. "Please come on in."

Ashroot thanked her and bounded into the kitchen with a covered tray. "Please enjoy your breakfast, miss," she called.

Mara closed the door, yawned again, and sat in one of the kitchen stools, replying, "Please call me Mara, Ashroot. I want us to be friends. Friends don't use official titles or any of that garbage."

Ashroot smiled again, baring pearly, pointed teeth. She nodded and revealed Mara's breakfast. Mara gasped. Bacon and sausage, an overloaded omelet, a banana, and fresh-squeezed orange juice. What an amazing breakfast! "Th-thank you so much, Ashroot!" she stammered.

"It's my pleasure, mi— Mara," Ashroot replied. "We rarely use the kitchens in the morning except for special requests, so the Ranger usually ends up with a nice, cooked meal. You'll need your strength today—it's a full day of training."

Mara had already inhaled half of her omelet. It was so tasty. At the thought of training, she groaned, "Ugh, exercise."

The girls made eye contact and giggled. Mara gave the seat beside her a few pats and started in on the bacon as Ashroot sat beside her.

"Will I be training with you today?" Ashroot asked.

Mara thought for a minute before replying, "Um, let me talk to Teddy this morning. I think what would be best is for them to teach me for the first part of the hour—until he's satisfied. Then if you want me to teach you basics of that weapon for the rest of the hour, I can. You are supposed to focus on the dagger, so I'll see if we can do that more. Maybe we'll plan for time outside of the planned training time for me to teach you that. I also think that you should be trained to use a bow. I think that would help you the most because you can protect yourself before danger gets to you that way. What do you think?"

She turned to see the bearkin positively glowing. "Yes, yes, yes! Yes, Mara! I love that plan! I am so grateful that you would set aside so much time for me!"

Mara smiled. "I just want to do what's best for my people ... and my friend."

CHAPTER SEVEN

FIRST TEST

Mara sat alone on the couch in her sitting room. She often spent her rest time thus, reading ancient tomes kept safe in the Ranger house—and she'd still only made it about halfway through the wisdom in the Ranger's library. Over the past few months, she had learned so much about Ambergrove. She had learned about herself and her family. She learned about different races. She learned to fight. She was getting pretty good—even Teddy admitted it. She had disarmed him one time during a training day, and he was sore about it all through the evening meal.

Outside of rest time, she spent most of her days with Ashroot, and they had become very good friends. Often, they sat cloistered in the kitchens discussing the bearkin, foraged together for food for Aeunna, or stayed late at the practice grounds sparring with one weapon or another. Ashroot had decided she wanted to learn every weapon, so they learned them all together, and Mara practiced with her afterward.

Freya had calmed down significantly since her initial outburst, so when Mara wasn't spending time with Ashroot, she was usually with Teddy or Freya—or learning how Aeunna was governed with the elder council. Many days, Cora joined her with her friend or her family to teach her in a more informal environment—and save her from Aengar's sternness. Mara enjoyed Cora's company and loved to listen as the warrior told tales about her adventures around the world as she'd discovered various cultures and battled strange monsters. Thanks to this, Mara imagined monsters during her training, and it had proven lucrative.

She had advanced to the top archery ability group, and even the trainers were amazed by her skill. Throwing daggers and axes came easily to her as well—once she'd realized she was supposed to hold the blade when she threw the dagger. She was still a little annoyed by Teddy's joke, but it was one of the endearing characteristics of her uncle. One of many. They'd become close over the past few months, and he'd taught her to use a sword. She enjoyed the time spent training with him and believed she was doing well enough to handle herself.

Close combat with daggers was more difficult for her. She didn't want to be close—especially not that close—to her enemy. It was hard for her to teach Ashroot effectively when she struggled so much with the weapon herself, and Mapleleaf was deeply upset by that. What both girls enjoyed the most was swinging the battle axe. Mostly, they just appreciated the fact that they could use the axe's own weight to drive it to its mark. Because Ashroot was so small, this feature was extra beneficial for her.

Mara sighed and placed her bookmark—a dried leaf—in her book. The book she was working on was an exceptionally exhausting history of the gods and goddesses of Ambergrove and their island homes. She gazed out the window. She really did have a great view from her home. *Home.* She wondered if, when she left on her Ranger trial, she would ever see it again. Funny how just a few short months could turn it into a home. Although she still missed her dad and Kara every day, and even sometimes missed Sara, it made a difference to have family there with her. Teddy and Freya were undoubtedly her family. Looking down at the clearing below, she noticed the lights strung down to the banquet tables had been lit. It was close to mealtime.

She placed her book on the end table and headed back to her bedroom. She had made it homier the past few months, rearranging some furniture and bringing in extra pillows from a few of the other bedrooms. She preferred dressers to wardrobes and had switched those as well. For the sake of convenience, she now had training clothes in one dresser and relaxation clothes in another. Special formal clothes like that ceremonial dress hung in a wardrobe in one of the extra rooms. She went to that room to get dressed.

Today was a special day. Teddy believed she was ready to begin her Ranger trial and the elder council planned to announce their decision during the evening meal. She had enjoyed her time in Aeunna so far, learning about the village, weaponry, and Ambergrove itself, but she wanted to get started on the actual quest. She knew it would be an ordeal, and she was ready to just get it over with so she could move on—and maybe even enjoy Aeunna without a weight hanging over her.

Mara pulled out a deep blue dress. Freya made it for her because she had believed Mara cinching the ceremonial dress up for the announcement ceremony was a disgrace. This was a way for her to wear a dress and still look like a warrior. Mara pulled on her undergarments—a sleeveless shirt and soft pants in light blue—and slipped on the dress.

It laced up the front, which was what required the shirt. It also had slits up both sides to the hip, which was what required pants. There were matching light blue cuffs at the elbows of the long sleeves which hung down to Mara's knees, and the deep blue of the dress was embroidered with Celtic knot accents and sea elements such as waves and sea monsters. It really was a masterpiece, and it was meant to smooth the waters, so to speak. Since Mara's Ranger trial was meant to involve a great deal of sailing, this dress was to show Mara that Freya had accepted this odyssey and was wishing her well.

Mara was still hopeless with braids, but there was a delicate-looking hairstyle she liked that was relatively easy to execute. She pulled her long, red hair to the side, twisted it into a rope, and tied it into a knot at her shoulder. Pulling on her boots, she gave herself a once-over and, satisfied, headed down to the evening meal.

Mara was annoyed that the announcement wouldn't be until after the meal, though she wasn't sure why she expected any different. She was, however, delighted to discover her favorite for the evening meal. They were having baked turkey with fresh corn and loaded baked potatoes. Dessert was vanilla and anamberry cupcakes. Mara raised her brows when Ashroot brought these, because they had never had cake before. Her friend only winked. Once they had all finished their cupcakes, it was Cora's turn to address the village. She gave Mara a pat on the back as she headed up to the center of the dais.

"Good evening, all!" Cora announced, "I'm sure you are all ready to head off for the evening, but the elder council has an announcement to make before you go."

There were scattered murmurs and nods in Mara's direction. She felt a nudge under the table and looked up to see everyone staring expectantly in her direction. Cora had called her up to stand next to her. She was glad she'd worn her fancy dress. Once she made it to the center, Cora continued.

"Our rangerling has been training hard these past few months. Some of you have had the displeasure of training with her." Mara noticed a few friends absently stroke bruises she had given them in the practice arenas and smiled. Cora continued, "The elder council has been deliberating with her trainers, and we have some to a decision. We have decided …"

Mara glared at Cora as she paused for effect.

"… Mara is ready to begin her trials!" Cora shouted.

There were scattered cheers. Many of the younger dwarves had trained with Mara and had grown to respect her over time, but there were still quite a few uncertain of an as-yet untried youth. It was now time for her to be tried. Cora waited for the noise to die down, squeezed Mara's shoulder gently, and continued, "Her forest trial has been decided! It will take place tomorrow!"

The forest was suddenly quiet. Mara felt like the only sound in the world was her heart pounding. *Tomorrow? How could it be tomorrow?* At the very earliest she figured they'd schedule it for a week or a fortnight or something.

"The first part of this trial is to prove herself worthy of the loyalty of a wise forest dwarf warrior. This trial is to prove she knows when to fight and to prove she can think like one of us. For this trial, our rangerling is to climb to the top of Grimclaw Hill and enter the cave of the Great Silver Bear."

Scattered gasps throughout the forest made Mara nervous. She began to fidget in place and pick at her nails. Cora continued, "She will be allowed to choose one weapon. She must confront the Great Silver Bear and bring back a token from the bear and a piece of his treasure. She will leave as soon as the morning exercise is finished and must be back by dusk."

That was it. It was decided. People had already begun to disperse. Mara was in a panic. How was she meant to defeat a bear with just one weapon? What weapon would be best? Why was everyone so concerned? She opened her mouth to ask Cora what it all meant, but the warrior stopped her with a hand.

"No, Mara," she told her, "It's customary with a trial to only ask one person for help. You must choose that person wisely. No questions now. Rest on it before you make your decision and ask your questions in the morning."

Mara sighed. "Alright. Thanks, Cora." When she headed back up the pegs to her home, she was in a daze. She would never remember how she had made it home, or what she had done before waking the next morning.

When Mara woke, it was still dark. She wanted to ask questions, or at least figure out who to ask, so she got up, gathered some of the glowing stones from her hearth fire into a lantern, and began to look through her books. She read books about bears. She read books about fighting animals. She reviewed some of the histories of forest dwarves that she had read before. By the time Ashroot came knocking with her breakfast, Mara had made her decision.

The breakfast Ashroot brought was Mara's favorite—a great way to start the day. There were three biscuits with warm sausage gravy, a hardy omelet, and two pieces of toast with honey. Mara brought some of her books, a roll of parchment, and a charcoal pencil over to the kitchen counter to eat her breakfast, beckoning for Ashroot to sit beside her.

"Ash?" she asked.

"Yes, Mara?"

"I've decided who I want to ask about the forest trial."

Ashroot was slow to reply. "A-and what did you decide?"

"Well," Mara gave her friend a long, hard look, "I wanted to ask you."

Ashroot exploded with excitement, hugging Mara and blubbering thanks and encouragement.

"Okay, okay, Ash!" Mara patted her to calm her. "I'm not sure what time we have, and I want to take notes."

"Right!" Ashroot settled in her seat and folded her paws in her lap, waiting.

Mara took a few bites of her breakfast before asking, "Being bearkin, do you know how to talk to other bears? Regular bears?"

"Yes!" Ashroot replied excitedly.

"How do I tell the Great Silver Bear that I mean it no harm? And tell him what I'm there for?"

Ashroot seemed to struggle to contain her excitement, as if there was a detail she desperately wanted to reveal and couldn't. She told Mara what sounds and gestures to make and Mara wrote them on the parchment with her charcoal. After a few more bites, she asked, "What do bears love to eat—uh, besides people?"

Ashroot rattled off a list of foods, various nuts and berries, fish and meats. Mara wrote these down also. She finished off her breakfast and asked her final question, "Ash, would you please gather some of these foods for me? I want to bring him this food as a gift when I get there. Also, could you tell me how to tell him that the food is a gift?"

Ashroot explained the sounds and gestures to Mara, who added these to her parchment. She then headed off in search of the requested items while Mara dressed for the day.

The morning exercise ended early. Mara couldn't help but believe that the whole community had been focused on her the entire time. Some of her friends had cut in to wish her good luck or give her unsolicited advice. Seoc, who was her equal with the bow, gave her some pointers about bow hunting, assuming she would choose to take that. Moire, barbarian with the battle axe, had brought her own axe out for the morning exercise to show Mara how *she* would fight in the forest. However, as Mara turned away, she saw Rhodi giving her a knowing smile. *If you measure yourself by the abilities of others, you'll never be happy.*

"I'll do my best, Rhodi," she told the elder, nodding, before the exercise group dispersed. She didn't clean up. She knew she would be getting dirty throughout the day, so she just headed toward the armory afterwards.

The elder council was waiting for her by the door, accompanied by Freya, Teddy, Mapleleaf, and Ashroot. Ashroot stepped up to her and wordlessly handed her a pack before moving back to stand next to her father. Aengar was the first to speak. "Young Mara, in a few moments you will begin your forest trial, the first of the three you must complete before you may complete your true Ranger trial. You may no longer receive any aid until your task is done. Do you understand?"

Mara nodded. Cora spoke next, "Have you chosen your weapon for this trial?" Mara nodded again. "And?"

"I have chosen to take a bow," Mara replied shakily.

Cora went into the armory and retrieved Mara's practice bow and a small quiver—with real, iron-tipped arrows. She handed these to Mara, who slung them across her back.

Rhodi spoke next, her voice a whisper, "Young Mara, you have until dusk tonight to complete your forest trial. Remember, you must return with both a token from the Great Silver Bear and a piece of his treasure."

Freya stepped forward and added, "Should you sustain injuries, you must tend to them yourself with these supplies." She handed Mara a small pouch that smelled like herbs. "Once your forest trial is complete and you have returned to Aeunna, I will see to your injuries myself."

Teddy was the last to come forward. He gave Mara an affectionate pat before he spoke. When he began, his voice was tightly controlled. "In order to be successful in this trial, you have to prove yourself a true warrior and a true forest dwarf. If you return by dusk and you have completed these tasks ... I will join you on your journey."

Mara met Freya's gaze. She could read the pain there, but also acceptance. Freya had made her peace with the idea. She had expected Teddy to be the chosen forest dwarf. No one else fit the Oracle's description the way he did. With tears in her eyes, Mara gave her uncle a tight hug. When she let go, he stepped back to stand by Freya, throwing an arm around his wife.

Mara looked at the group before her. A crowd had begun to form behind them, individuals who had finished cooling down or cleaning up and were curious. Mara addressed them all.

"I will do my best to complete this trial and return to you all by dusk. If, for some reason, I am not successful, please know that I have cherished my time here with you and have come to feel like I belong, like you are all my family, and I am grateful for the past few months I was able to spend here with you. Thank you."

Unable to bear the crowd any longer, Mara turned and headed off into the forest in the direction of the Grimclaw Hill.

Mara heaved and took a breath, letting an arrow fly. It sank into a tree next to a large wolf. The wolf let out a low growl and Mara shouted, "Go on, git!" from her refuge in a nearby tree. The wolf gave one last huff and lumbered off.

She hopped down out of the tree and retrieved her arrow. She was glad the wolf left without a fight. She didn't want to hurt it. She knew this was its forest and not hers, but she needed to keep moving if she was going to finish her trial on time.

After a few hours' trek through the forest, Mara made it to the crest of Grimclaw Hill. The cave opening was just visible through the trees. Mara crouched for a minute and listened. She heard a slight rustle coming from inside the cave. *Good.* She opened her pack and reviewed her parchment translation sheet, and then she headed near to the cave opening and deposited half of the food on a cloth on the ground. Retreating a few paces, she began reading off the sounds from the parchment as loudly as she could, hoping it was correct. She growled, *Great Silver Bear! My name is Mara. I am a forest dwarf and I mean you no harm. I have been sent to retrieve some things from you and have brought gifts!*

There was no movement. She repeated herself a little louder. After a moment, she heard a groan from inside. Slowly, out lumbered the most majestic grey bear she had ever seen. He looked ancient and tired, but still his fur was shiny, and his body was full. "I'm so sorry to bother you, Great Bear," Mara whispered. She repeated her little speech once more and presented the rest of the food she'd brought—a fresh deer thigh. She'd brought her bow to scare off other animals, and also to try to hunt something, as Seoc had suggested, though she suspected Seoc had planned on her hunting the bear. She hoped the wolf had found the rest of the deer after she'd left. She set the thigh down next to the rest of the food and retreated again, making what she hoped were the correct respectful gestures.

As the bear began to eat what she had offered, Mara sat and crossed her legs. She had left her bow at the edge of the trees so she would not appear threatening. She hoped that wasn't a mistake. "My friend, Ashroot, a bearkin, taught me what to say. I hope I did it right. I don't wish you any harm. You're a magnificent creature. I hope I can leave this place in peace when you are finished," she told the bear. She began pulling up blades of grass, waiting. She wished that she would be able to do the right thing. She wished she could prove that she was her father's daughter. She wanted to be a forest dwarf. After a moment, Mara realized the munching had stopped. She looked up and found the Great Silver Bear inches from her face, his eyes staring deep into her soul.

She tried to keep her breathing calm. What else could she do? She had left herself vulnerable to him. She was completely at his mercy. Slowly, she reached out her hand, palm up. She could feel the heat of his breath on her hand as he sniffed it. "Please," she whispered, "please let me complete my mission and go home. I promise I mean you no harm."

I know that you mean no harm, the bear told her, growling in its bear language.

"Wh-what?" she asked incredulously. "I-I can understand you? ... Am I understanding you?"

Yes, little one, you can understand me.

"H-how is that possible?" she stammered.

I know your mission. All who wish to prove themselves to the forest dwarves must attempt it. Only one other has been successful.

Mara squinted in confusion and wondered, *Was that why everyone had reacted the way they did? Wait.* She turned to the bear and ventured, "You said only one other had been successful. Does that mean I have been successful?"

The bear's lip curled in what Mara now recognized to be a bear smile. *Yes, little one. The only way you could understand me would be if you successfully proved that you were one of them. True forest dwarves can talk to animals.*

She would have to have someone explain this to her when she got home. "Does everyone need to bring back a token from you and a piece of your treasure?"

Yes. Though to take treasure, you must leave treasure. And my token will cause you great pain. His eyes seemed to soften. He nuzzled her hand. *Gather your belongings and come into my cave. There, you will select a treasure to give and to take.*

Mara nodded and retreated to the tree line, collecting her bags and her bow, and rolling up her parchment. She turned and followed the bear as he slowly lumbered back into his cave.

Green, glowing crystals lined the cave wall, so it was bright all the way back to the treasure. Looking around, Mara saw grand treasures and things she would not call treasures at all. There were golden statues and gems, down to precious weapons, down still further to discarded bones. She turned to the bear.

Select which treasure you will offer, he growled.

Mara opened her bag and emptied it, lining all her possessions on the ground before him. "If this is your treasure," she said slowly, "then you should be the one to decide what is treasure. Please choose what you would like to keep."

Good choice. The Great Silver Bear looked over her possessions, sniffing some and nudging others with claw or nose. When he sniffed the parchment, he stopped. He sniffed it again. *Bearkin,* he growled.

"Yes, my friend, Ashroot, helped me with that. She's a bearkin, so she told me how I could talk to you to show you that I meant no harm." Mara explained.

This. This is what I'll take. Please put it with the rest and select your own treasure.

Mara did as she was bid, then turned to the bear again. "Could you tell me who successfully completed this trial before me?"

The bear smiled again. *It was a young healer who had birthed the new forest dwarf leader. Not too long ago by your years.*

Freya. It had to have been Freya, Mara thought. "Could you tell me what she left for you?" she asked the bear.

The bear smiled again and moved to a further section of the cave. *She also treasured knowledge,* he growled. *Come.* He patted his paw on an object on the ground. Mara picked it up. It was a book of herbal medicine that had been published in Scotland. It was old and tattered, but still legible—definitely Freya's treasure.

"May I take this back to Aeunna?" Mara asked.

The bear nodded and she thanked him. *Now, you must be given a token from me to prove that you have seen me,* he said.

Mara nodded. "Yes, please," she told him, then paused, trembling. "... You said it would be painful?"

Yes, very much. But it is necessary. You will need that bag of healing supplies for this. Get them ready first, he warned.

Mara shuddered, imagining the worst as she laid out all the medical supplies. She took a deep breath, then stammered, "I-I am ready for your token, Great Silver Bear."

The bear raised a paw. *My token is a single swipe of my claws. I will not hurt you too dearly. I do know what I am doing, but it must leave a scar so the token is permanent. It is a scar you will bear forever, so I will let you choose the location. Choose wisely.* He waited.

Her legs turned to jelly, and she held the cave wall for support. So that's what he meant about it being painful. If this was going to be her token to prove that she belonged among the forest dwarves, she wanted it to be a place everyone would see. She shivered and sighed, trying to calm herself. She couldn't believe she was about to tell a bear where to attack her. After a moment, she looked up at him and drew her hand across her collarbone.

"C-could y-you do it here? J-just below my neck?" she managed.

Close your eyes, little one, he commanded. Mara's heart hammered. She closed her eyes and tried to focus on the beat. She felt slight pressure and then warmth trickling down her chest. Her eyes snapped open and she looked down. That was it. It was done and it hadn't hurt at all, though her chest was covered in blood. She was sure it would hurt later.

"Th-thank you," she managed. She wasn't sure how she knew, but the bear had cut delicately, so as to not seriously injure her. She didn't know how to properly dress the wound, so she assessed her supplies. There was a kind of bandage and an ointment she believed would be helpful. She coated the cuts with the ointment to try to seal in most of the blood, then she wrapped the bandage around her neck and under her armpit and stuffed it in the top of her shirt. That would have to do until she made it home. She packed up her medicine bag, then turned to the bear.

"Is that it?" she asked him.

He nodded. *Your task is finished. Go in peace back to the village, little one. Thank you for your offerings.*

"Thank you for your help," she replied, "and for your treasure and token. Goodbye, Great Bear."

Goodbye, young dwarf.

Mara gathered the rest of her things, stuffed the medicine book in her bag, and gave him one last wave. Then, she walked out his cave and headed back in the direction of Aeunna, triumphant.

CHAPTER EIGHT

TRUDGING

It was nearly dusk when Mara made it back to the village. The crickets had begun to chirp in the undergrowth and the villagers were beginning to assemble for the evening meal. Mara headed straight to the dais, ignoring all the people she passed. She simply sat in her chair and waited for the evening meal to begin, because she didn't have the energy to look for anyone.

The murmuring around her was deafening. It wasn't long before her aunt and uncle came rushing up to the dais, the elder council on their heels. The rest of the village had arrived in the commotion as well, clamoring to see their rangerling returned. Aengar looked at the clearing around him, grabbed the microphone stick, and stepped to the center of the dais.

"People! People!" he called, trying to settle the masses. "People, please!"

Gradually, the murmuring died down. Aengar continued, "Rhodi will stay here with you and conduct the evening meal. The rest of us," he gestured to Teddy, Freya, Cora, and himself, "will take the rangerling to have her wounds tended. We will return by the end of the meal and will convey the official outcome of her forest trial at that time. Thank you."

He handed the stick to Rhodi and then helped her to her seat as the others ushered Mara off to a stone building near the kitchens. Things had started to get fuzzy, and their words and panic just melded together. Teddy steered her into the building and helped her onto a bed, then everything went black.

When Mara woke, Freya was just finishing up wrapping her chest and Cora was mopping away the excess blood.

"Well, hello there, brave warrior!" Cora said gently. "Good of you to join us."

"Wh-what happened to me?" Mara mumbled.

"You," Freya snapped, "picked a terrible place for your token and you almost lost more blood than you could spare. Teddy was mad with fright, thank you. You already had an infection setting in, so I had to sterilize and disinfect what I could and stitch up your wounds. Now, we need to get some clean clothes on you so the men can come back in and you can tell your story." Freya disappeared in a huff. Why was she so angry? Hadn't she been the one to complete the same quest?

"She's just worried," Cora whispered, nodding into Mara's concerned eyes. "She doesn't want to let on, but she was more concerned about you than anyone, because she knew best what you faced. Don't take it to heart."

Mara smiled weakly as Freya returned with a soft, baggy, white dress. Mara didn't have the strength to argue. That dress looked like a nightgown, and she didn't have the energy for much else—especially not to balance to put on pants. Freya was right; she had lost a lot of blood. This was a battle she could afford to lose today. Cora helped her to her feet, and the two women helped her slip the dress over her head. She could feel it now—persistent searing pressure in her chest and unbelievable pain. She could feel a slight numbness in her limbs. This would linger. The women settled Mara into a chair and called the men into the room. Ashroot was with them, bearing a large food tray.

The bearkin reached Mara first, setting the tray on the bed and hugging her friend. "I'm so glad you made it home," she managed. "I'm so sorry I forgot to pack a meal for you."

Mara's stomach grumbled, and she realized she hadn't eaten since Ashroot's magnificent breakfast. "It's not your fault, Ash," she reassured her friend. "I was too nervous to eat, though I am pretty hungry now."

Ashroot jumped up and uncovered the tray. There was a plate for Freya and for Cora on the tray as well. Mara's plate was simple. There were only hardy foods meant for an unsettled stomach. Mara accepted them without a fuss and gulped down an entire glass of water.

Able to restrain himself no longer, Teddy rushed across the room to Mara and enveloped her in a hug. He was trying to be gentle, but it did still hurt all the same. "I thought I'd lost you," he whispered into her shoulder. She squeezed him back. Someone coughed and Teddy stepped back.

"I know this is a big moment for you all, but we need to hear your story so we can dismiss the village from their evening meal." Aengar's tone seemed cold, as usual, but they all obeyed. Mara nibbled at her food, Cora and Freya sat on the bed wolfing down theirs, and Teddy stood beside Mara with a hand on her shoulder as she told Aengar her story.

She explained how she had chosen Ashroot to ask about her trial, wanting to keep the peace with the bear instead of fight. She walked them through her meeting, discovering that she could talk to the bear after all, and her selection of a treasure. She told Ashroot that the bear had chosen the parchment as his treasure for the exchange because a bearkin had a hand in it, and her friend was giddy. When Aengar asked what treasure she had brought, she pointed to her bag and said there was a book inside.

"A-a book?" Freya jumped up and flung the bag open, retrieving her own book she had given to the bear all those years ago. Gently, she ran a hand along the cover.

"Well?" Aengar asked impatiently.

"Yes," Freya snapped. Remembering whom she addressed, she continued more softly, "Yes, Aengar. This is the book I left myself when I went up to meet the Great Silver Bear."

"Alright then. Now," he turned back to Mara, "where did he place your token and why?"

Somewhat put-off by his curtness, Mara stammered, "W-well, I wanted it to be a place people would usually see, since it would prove I belonged here. S-so I picked my collarbone." Mara gently laid a hand on her throbbing collar and winced.

"Very well. Tederen and I will announce your results to the village as soon as you are able to head back up to the dais," Aengar told her matter-of-factly.

"Now's as good a time as any," Mara said, shrugging. "Though I will definitely need help getting up there."

It was slow going. Teddy and Aengar murmured urgently to each other as they walked ahead, and Freya and Cora walked on either side of her, steadying her. Once they made it up to the dais, Teddy accepted the stick from Rhodi and moved to the center, the women still bracing Mara behind him. Aengar sat with Rhodi.

Looking out into the crowd, it was clear most hadn't noticed their arrival, so Teddy gave one sharp whistle to get their attention. As most of the people had trained under him at one point or another, it was effective. He took a deep breath and began, "We have set this task many times. Every time someone from Earth wants to be a true part of Aeunna. Most have failed. That was not the case today."

There were scattered whoops from the crowd. Teddy continued, "As many of you know, to be a forest dwarf, you must show compassion toward woodland creatures. Mara has done this, leaving her weapon in the woods and meeting with the Great Silver Bear as a friend. She was gifted our ability to speak to animals. She has also proven herself a true warrior. A true warrior knows when to fight and when to seek peace. Mara was respectful to the Great Silver Bear and was given a treasure—the same one your healer left with him many years ago—and was given his token."

Teddy turned and made a swiping motion across Mara's chest, where some blood had soaked into the white dress, then he turned back to the villagers. "The elder council has received proof of Mara's heart. Your Dragonwolf has passed this first trial!"

The forest erupted with cheers, applause, and stomping. After a moment, Teddy whistled once more for their attention. "As such, I will be accompanying the rangerling as she continues through her trials and attempts the final Ranger trial. I am accepting the responsibility to be her forest dwarf companion. Once she has healed enough to begin the journey, we will buy a ship from Port Albatross and will not return until she has spoken with Aeun, and the Ranger trial is completed."

Shouts of encouragement filled the forest. "Head home and rest," Teddy instructed. "Soon, the odyssey begins."

It only took a few days for the infection to leave her system, and Mara was weak for a few days longer. Freya still held Mara under observation for more than a fortnight. Once her wounds became scars and she could lift weapons and complete the morning exercise without pain—and even spar with Moire, who never held back—Teddy confronted his wife about stalling to prevent his leaving. At that evening's meal, she declared Mara fit to begin her journey.

Mara could hardly contain her nerves and excitement. As she tried to figure out what to pack, what to leave, and what to say, her two companions had the same problem. Teddy had prepared Cora to take his place as weapons trainer, and she'd been doing a lot of it already, but he still gave her a few last pointers and told the students to beware her wrath. He had been on journeys before, so he knew what he needed and packed quickly. He spent most of his time with Freya, reassuring her that he would return and stocking up on medical supplies and last-minute medical instruction.

Ashroot was gathering and making foods that would keep well on a journey and writing down recipes for foods they might be able to have along the way. Mapleleaf also gave her a token for Aeun and a written petition for anamberry recipes.

Mara began by packing a bag. She planned to wear some soft brown pants and a sage shirt, like she usually did, so she packed a few sets. She included the blue dress Freya had made as well, just in case part of winning favors included stupid banquets or formal clothes. She had planned to wear her bracer the whole time unless Teddy told her not to, and she refused to part with the cuff from her dad, so the only thing left was weapons. Cora was supposed to come by before they left to give her some that had been specially crafted for her.

As if someone was reading her mind, there was a knock at the door. Mara set her pack on the chair in her sitting area and opened the door to a smiling Cora and Teddy and, to her surprise, Ashroot and Freya.

"Good morning! ... uh, everyone." Mara beckoned them toward the kitchen table. Teddy and Cora deposited large bundles in the center, and they all gathered around it.

"There's more there than I expected!" Mara exclaimed as she joined them all.

"Well, there's a bit of a selection for you here, and Ashroot's weapons are here also. Plus, a surprise or two," Teddy explained.

Freya smacked him lightly on the arm. "It's no longer a surprise if you tell her about it!" his wife told him.

"Uh ... yes, that's true I guess," Teddy conceded as he began untying the bundles.

"What would you like to see first, Mara?" Cora asked.

Mara looked at the company around her and settled on Ashroot's giddy face. She patted her friend playfully between the ears. "Ash can go first."

The bearkin jumped up and down as Cora unwrapped her weapons. Before showing her any, Cora said, "Now, neither of you got all the weapons you've been using. You wouldn't be able to carry them all anyway. You have three, Ashroot."

Ashroot just nodded profusely. She probably hadn't heard a word Cora had said. She was just anxious to see what was hers. Cora obliged. First were twin daggers. These were sturdy and simple, though the pommels were adorned with growling bear heads. Next was a battle axe. Like the daggers, it was made well and simply except for bear accents. The axe sported a growling bear head on top, bear claws etched into the blades, and a leather-wrapped handle. Finally, at Mara's request, Ashroot was given a shortbow. This had Celtic knots and various bear symbols carved into it as well.

"I want you to stay far away from the fighting whenever you can, so I hope you never have to swing your axe. I want the bow to be your go-to, so we can keep you safe," Mara explained.

Ashroot smiled and nodded. She was afraid to fight. She didn't want to be a great warrior. She just wanted to make sure everyone was fed and to speak with Aeun. She turned back to Cora. Along with these weapons were hip sheaths for the daggers, a hip quiver for the arrows, and a rig to carry the axe and bow on her back. She would definitely be battle-ready. Seeing all these items, Ashroot began to cry and hug the others with more force than any of them realized she possessed.

Mara's battle axe and bow were similar to Ashroot's. However, instead of bear accents, Mara's were wolf and dragon accents. The most notable of these was the axe. It sported a growling wolf head and blades resembling dragon wings. Instead of daggers, she'd been given twin axes, made similarly to the battle axe. She did have one extra weapon Ashroot didn't have, because, according to Teddy, it was a staple for all warriors. Her sword was simple with a leather wrapped hilt and wolf pommel.

"Thank you so much," she managed. "Even though these are way to grand for a novice like me."

She glanced up and met Teddy's gaze. "Maybe not," he agreed, "but they are just right for a Ranger, and I'd rather you have good weapons you grow into than faulty weapons that may be unreliable in battle."

Mara glared at him, then smiled despite herself. He was right. This wasn't made for Mara, the teenager from a podunk town in a fly-over state. This was made for Mara, the Dragonwolf of Aeunna, who would do what it took to help her people. She hoped she would be able to grow into these weapons. She started to gather them back up to add them to her journey pile and was interrupted by throat-clearing and chuckling.

"What's so funny?" she asked, brows furrowed.

"You're forgetting the big surprise!" Cora exclaimed.

"Ri-i-i-ight!" She turned back to Cora and the final bundle.

"I have what I need because this isn't my first journey, but you girls are missing one important element." Teddy explained as he pulled the first item out of the bundle. It was a leather vest with a skirt, kind of like what an ancient Greek warrior would wear. Ashroot gasped and snatched it from his hands. "My own armor?" she cried.

"Why this design?" Mara asked him. The skirt seemed to her like useless armor most female warriors wore in stories or movies she'd seen, and that was disappointing.

"Ah, well." Teddy stammered.

"We were trying to figure out what armor would be best for a bearkin," Cora interjected. She turned to Ashroot and explained, "This seemed to be the best way to cover most of your body, since your body structure is different, and you don't usually wear clothes."

Mara felt like an idiot. Of course, that made the most sense. This wasn't one of her adventure movies. In real life, all warriors had functional armor and—despite how strange it all still was to her—this was real life. "So that means no skirt for me?" she asked.

"When have you ever seen *me* wearing a skirt?" Cora demanded, pulling Mara's armor out and handing it to her.

Her armor was very simple. It was one piece, a full leather tunic that was overlong to protect all the way down to her mid-thigh. She would be able to wear a basic shirt and pants underneath. Mara looked at the tunic and grinned. Her chest and torso would be completely protected, though the lacing only went up a little past her chest. *Good*, she thought. That meant that she would be protected, but the token from the Great Silver Bear would still be visible. There were slight shoulder pads, but otherwise this was made for mobility. She'd just have to be sure to protect her arms and lower legs.

They were ready. They had just about everything they needed. What would make the most sense would be for them to stay for the evening meal and one more night, but they could head off in the morning.

Mara was up before the sun. She went to her collection of journey items and dressed, also lacing on her armor and strapping her weapons to her hip or back. She loaded the remaining items into her pack, rolling her dad's old dagger up into her dress. She had delved into her D&D experience at the last minute, making sure to include a few staple adventuring items Jim had always insisted everyone carry. She'd never heard her father argue their usefulness, so she figured that was something that the game had gotten right.

She also skimmed through her little library to see if there was anything that might be helpful for the journey. She grabbed a small tome about gnomes she'd read a few months before and scanned for another. It was frustrating to see that, amongst all those books, there wasn't a single book about the sea elves.

The last thing she did was pick up her dragonwolf bracer. She wasn't sure what the protocol was, but she went ahead and laced it on anyway. She spent the rest of the time until sunrise trying to braid her hair. By the time she heard the knock at her door, she had managed a very sad, loose braid. As soon as the door was opened, however, her visitor nearly doubled over with laughter. Freya gave her husband a thump with her medicine bag and his laughing trailed to a halt.

"I-I'll fix that for you, Mara," Teddy managed, chuckling. They entered, with Mapleleaf, Ashroot, and the elder council behind them. Teddy thumped a chair and placed himself behind Mara to re-braid her hair as the council gave the group their final send-off.

Aengar and Rhodi began to explain the rules of the Ranger trial to Mara. Aengar warned, "Many things Teddy could tell you about trials are true—the good and the bad. Since the forest trial is over, you may ask him any questions you like, but keep in mind, you may not like what you hear."

"Freya's concerns were not unfounded." Rhodi added, placing a consoling hand on Freya's cheek. "Your companions will present themselves to you and will join you as they were meant to, but they will not all come home. You have to prepare yourself for that event and accept that there is *nothing* you can do about it."

Mara glanced up at Freya. Her aunt's face was white, and her lips were pursed. When Mara turned to look at Teddy, her uncle gently pulled her braid in the other direction so she couldn't. He was doing a modified fishtail braid, or so he said, so it would stay in for a few days on their journey without having to be redone, and it was taking a long time to finish. Mara gave Rhodi a slight nod in acceptance.

Aengar continued, "Once you leave Aeunna, neither you or any of your companions may return unless you have completed your trial or you are giving up. If you do return before your trial is completed, it will be considered forfeit and you will no longer be able to be the Ranger."

"Do you understand the gravity of this?" Rhodi whispered.

"Y-yes, I understand," Mara choked. So much rested on this. She was going to be in Ambergrove for the rest of her life. She had proven herself to be a forest dwarf. If she failed them, where would she go? Who would she be? She had to be successful, and she had to bring Teddy and Ashroot home with her. Teddy finished with her hair and gave her a little pat on the shoulder, so she stood and faced Aengar.

"With that in mind, Mara, we send you off on your trial," Aengar told her solemnly. He stretched out a hand for her to shake.

"You have your community behind you, young one, and we hope to see your safe return," Rhodi added. "When in doubt, trust your heart and trust your family."

Her father's words rang in her ears again. *You need to be quick to survive.* Rhodi clasped both of Mara's hands in hers, like she'd done before, and patted the top of Mara's hand.

"You show any monsters you meet what's what, and you come back with some Marks of your own, yeah?" Cora hugged Mara and winked.

Aengar shook Teddy's hand, Rhodi gave him a grandma hug, and they left without another word. Cora hung back. Mara glanced at Mapleleaf and Freya, wondering who would be next. This was family time. Mapleleaf wouldn't see his daughter nor Freya her husband until they finished this trial. It could be months or years. Watching her companions with their families, she remembered what this trial was supposed to achieve. She closed her eyes and made a wish, for what else should she call it when she wasn't sure what was real here? *Please,* she thought *Aeun, if you are real, please have the mercy to ensure that I can bring these two back safe.*

As if he had heard her thoughts, Mapleleaf stepped up to Mara, clasping her hands. His claws dug into her palm slightly as he growled, "Do not forget your promise. It is your duty to bring her back to me." Mara nodded, wincing, as Mapleleaf released her hand and turned back to his daughter. "I'll be waiting for you on the forest floor to say ... goodbye." With that, he turned and headed out.

Freya clutched her medicine bag with both hands as she stepped up to Mara. The stout woman came up just past her niece's shoulder, but Mara met her watery gaze. Freya handed her the bag, opened her mouth to speak, then wrapped Mara in a tight hug and began to sob. Mara's hands were smashed at her chest, holding the medicine bag. She turned desperately to Teddy and Cora, who both came over to join in the hug. Ashroot got some water for Freya to drink and the others hugged her and tried to calm and reassure her until the tears abated.

Freya sighed deeply. "You are my family," she managed. "All of you, even you have been recently, Ashroot, since you have been spending so much time with Mara. I-I don't— I can't—"

Teddy wrapped his wife in the warmest of hugs. "I know, love. I know it's hard, but it's also the right thing to do." He gently raised her chin with his hand, gazing into her eyes. "I promise you—I will do everything in my power to come home to you and bring them with me. I *promise*." He caressed his wife's cheek for a moment before turning to the others.

It was time to rip off the band-aid. The longer they drew it out, the worse it would be for them—particularly Freya. They all gathered their things and headed downstairs. Most of the village had started their morning exercise, so only the family was left to say one last goodbye before Mara, Teddy, and Ashroot headed out into the forest. Teddy didn't look back at his wife, but when Mara looked over, she saw the tears staining his face.

It was nearly midday when they stopped near a river to fill their water pouches. Ashroot spread out a simple yet hearty meal for them, and they discussed next steps while eating.

"How far is it to this village?" Mara asked.

"Ehm ... Well ... we won't get there today," Teddy mumbled, avoiding her gaze.

"Well how far is it then?" Ashroot pressed.

"It'll be the better part of two weeks," he said quickly.

"Two weeks?" Mara cried, inhaling her drink and breaking into a fit of coughing.

"Yeah," Teddy began, grinning. "What's better to prepare you for a long, grueling journey than a week or two of camping?"

Mara threw an anamberry at Teddy and laughed. Ashroot shouted, "Hey! Those are precious!" When she wrinkled her snout in disapproval they all laughed together.

Once they'd finished their lunch, they packed everything up and headed off again. The forest was dense. Light shone through the canopy above, peeking in little rays to the forest floor. As they walked, Mara marveled at all the new things around her. She'd gone out into the forest to forage with the bearkin, and when she'd gone to Grimclaw Hill, but otherwise, she hadn't really ventured out into the world. She'd kept tight to Aeunna and to the practice grounds.

Now, she noticed many trees, plants, and little skittering creatures she'd never seen before. She wondered later if she annoyed Teddy and Ashroot during those first few days in the forest. She wanted to know everything and see everything.

"What's that?" Mara whispered, pointing into the forest.

"Ah," Teddy whispered, pausing and looking out. There was a deer-like creature staring back at them, disturbed in its grazing. It was a deep brown with vines and leaves covering its body. "That's a woodland elk" he explained. "They're common in Ambergrove. Do you not have those on Earth?"

Mara shook her head vigorously, then touched a hand lightly on the scars on her chest. "Hello there," she said to the deer. "We're just passing though. We don't mean you any harm."

The deer's ears twitched. *Thank you, forest dwarf*, she replied. She made a short, light grunting sound, and two little fawns appeared and began grazing beside their mother.

"Come on, ladies," Teddy said, tapping Mara on the shoulder. "Time to move on and leave these gals alone."

Reluctantly, resisting every urge to surge forward and pet the fawns, Mara followed Teddy and Ashroot further in the forest.

By the time they'd made it to their stopping point for the day, Mara had seen brown squirrels, foxes, a badger, and some wild hares. She tried to talk to every animal she met. When she tried to speak to a wild hare, she learned there were limits to this ability. Teddy shot one of the hares, retrieved it, inspected his arrow before wiping it on his pants and returning it to the quiver, and then handed the hare to Ashroot. Mara stared at him in horror.

"We cannot speak to all animals, Mara. Some are too simple to converse with us, like the hares. Some are too wild, like boars. That is why we eat the ones we do. We don't eat friends, but now we have supper," Teddy explained cheerfully.

Frowning, Mara followed Teddy to a denser patch of trees, which seemed to work like natural walls. It would be a safe camping area for them. Teddy then gathered firewood while Ashroot dressed the hare and Mara watched.

That night, and many nights after, they slept on the earth under the stars. Mara stayed up late trying to see if she could come up with any constellations and made a mental note to see if she had a book about it back in Aeunna. It got rougher with each passing day, and they all grew crankier—so cranky and loud that they missed the approach of their first enemies.

During a tense silence in the middle of another spat about nothing, they heard a rustle nearby. Ashroot froze. Teddy gently tapped his sword and looked at Mara, unsure if she had heard it. She had. Her training was about to be put to the test.

Teddy picked up a stone and threw it in what he thought was the direction of the sound. There was a shriek and a grumble from the tall grass and the forest erupted in clanging and shrieking. There were little goblin-like creatures with gnarled teeth, pointed ears, and yellowed skin. They stormed the camp, drawing little curved daggers or swords from their tattered clothes.

There were six of them, spitting and shrieking. Teddy shouted, "It's a raiding party! Fight!" He didn't wait for them to get to him. He charged ahead and started slashing.

Ashroot looked at Mara for a second. She was afraid; that was plain. All that training hadn't prepared them for the moment of actually killing someone. Ashroot drew a dagger but still hung back, shaking. Teddy was growling and swinging. He brought his blade down hard and sunk it in a goblin's shoulder, all the way down to his belt. He yanked his sword back out and turned to the next nearest goblin. Mara could hang back no longer. Two goblins had broken past Teddy and were heading straight for her and Ashroot, and she'd promised to protect Ashroot.

Mara drew her sword and placed herself between the goblins and the bearkin. The nearest goblin swung his sword. In that moment, time seemed to slow. She brought up her sword to block his without even thinking about the motion. She thought the ring of the blades would echo in her ears forever. His stench overwhelmed her senses. His eyes glowed an orange-red and his cackle filled her with dread. She swung her blade this time, hard, and managed to catch him off guard, knocking his sword away. For a split second, she thought about bringing her sword down on him like she'd seen Teddy do to the other one, but she decided instead to kick him with all her might. He was less than half her size, so the force made him fly backwards into a tree and lie limp on the ground.

The other goblin was advancing on Ashroot, who was cowering and whimpering. Mara managed her best growling shout and swung her sword at the goblin. He blocked her and his lips curled into a terrible grin. This time, his blade was a blur. She seemed to barely have enough time to block before he was swinging again. She heard continuous whimpers, and it took her a moment to realize she was the one making the sound and not Ashroot. Afraid that he was going to get her, she was just blocking—and blocking in a panic. His blows stopped abruptly, and Mara saw the fire leave his eyes. Teddy's sword was sticking out through his chest.

Mara looked around and saw all the other goblins crumpled in bloody piles on the ground. It was over. She sheathed her sword and went to Ashroot, hugging her and trying to calm her down.

"Mara!" Teddy snapped. She was surprised to hear such harshness in his voice. She turned to see him standing next to the goblin she'd kicked into a tree. "Why didn't you kill him?" he shouted.

"I-I— w-well . . ." she stammered. She was afraid—that was why. She'd never killed anyone, and it was horrifying to her to see Teddy basically chop someone in half. Why was he so angry?

Teddy looked at her, no doubt reading her fear. To Mara's surprise, he stomped over to her, grabbed her by the arm, and drug her over to the unconscious goblin. "This is life or death, Mara! You know that! You knew before we left, and you have to remember that. If something is after us and you don't kill it, it will kill you. THIS—" He pointed his sword at the goblin. "This is a monster." He stabbed his sword through the goblin and into the ground.

Mara gasped and Ashroot began to softly sob.

Teddy wiped his blade disgustedly on his pants, sheathed his sword, then got in Mara's face, eyes blazing. When he spoke again, his voice was tightly controlled yet severe. "Tough love, Mara. This is not a dream. You can't afford to treat it like one. The next time we fight, you'd better be prepared to kill—or I'm taking you home."

Teddy strode through the forest, not realizing just how far the others lagged behind. Although Mara knew Teddy was trying to teach her the right things, and she'd had a couple days to get over being scolded, she was still feeling down. She'd had her first chance to prove herself on the road. She knew she'd made a mistake. She glared at Teddy and thought, *According to Dad, you used to say it's only a mistake if you don't learn something and boy did I learn.*

The trouble was, she was worried she wouldn't do well enough. She wouldn't be enough. She was worried she would disappoint him again. She was tired after so many days on the road, sleeping in the dirt, foraging for food, and getting attacked by a pack of goblins. She just wanted to be home, but she knew it would be a long time before she made it back. The few days to the next village would be nothing compared to their whole journey, and she would have to find a way to keep pushing on.

Teddy turned and saw the sullen faces behind him, with their feet shuffling weakly forward. "Hey now," he said, crossing his arms. "I know it's been a long road so far, but we'll make it to the village soon."

Mara nodded. Ashroot sighed and nodded, saying, "Yes, Teddy."

"Alright then! Let's keep trudging on!" Teddy encouraged, clapping and turning back around again.

Mara laughed, first one small "heh" and then a cackle. *To trudge,* she thought. *I suppose this is as good a definition as any.* Thinking of a hilarious moment in a movie she'd always loved, and hearing the character's voice and tone, she announced self-importantly, "Trudging!"

The others gave Mara a puzzled look, but she just grinned and began walking again with a new spring in her step.

CHAPTER NINE

HARRGALTI

Darach was a small village, but it was plentiful. Nestled next to a stream in a clearing surrounded by willows, it was its own little patch of peace. As Teddy led Mara and Ashroot into the village, a tall reddish man with long, green hair emerged from the nearest cottage.

"Ah, Teddy!" the villager called, stretching out his arm to clasp Teddy's.

"Callum!" Teddy called back, shaking the offered arm and shifting to one side to reveal Mara and Ashroot.

"This is the rangerling?" Callum asked as he stepped forward to shake with Mara too.

"I am," Mara told him timidly. "And you're a forest dwarf. Are you the leader of this village?"

Callum nodded. "I am the village guardian, but we do look to Aeunna for leadership just like every other forest dwarf village. The rangerling is always welcome here."

"Thank you very much, Callum," said Teddy. "We hoped we might rest, resupply, and catch a cart to the port in the morning."

"We can handle that," Callum replied. "I have some supplies for Bowen. We have his wagon from the last trip, so you could just return it while you're there. I'm sure Bowen will be glad to see you."

"That's where we're headed actually." Teddy clapped a hand on Callum's shoulder, and they headed off into the village to discuss plans for travel and accommodation, leaving Mara and Ashroot standing awkwardly at the edge of the village.

"What are you?" said a small yet powerfully judgmental voice.

Mara looked down to see a small, green girl with a lanky grey puppy. "I'm Mara," she said kindly. "I'm from Aeunna."

"No, you're not." The girl crossed her arms and the dog's hackles rose. "You're a human."

"Well, I was. I am. But I'm also supposed to be the Ranger," Mara babbled.

"Prove it," the girl said defiantly. "What does Pepper think about your friend there?" The girl pointed at her dog and then gestured rudely to Ashroot.

"Um ..." Mara began. Uncertainly, uncomfortable about the whole situation, she turned to the dog. "Hello, Pepper. What do you think about Ashroot here?"

New smell! New smell! Smells like bear but not bear, the dog barked. *Want to sniff. Want to friend.*

Ashroot laughed. Mara looked back to the girl and said, "She doesn't know what Ashroot is because she seems like a bear but different. She wants to sniff her and learn her smell and then become friends."

The girl scrutinized Mara for a moment, then nodded. "I'm Iona," she said. "Come with me."

The girl turned and walked into the village as Pepper took the opportunity to run up and sniff Ashroot. Ashroot scratched the puppy's ears while Pepper sniffed her and licked her, howling, *Pepper got a new friend!* Mara grinned and turned to follow the girl.

Iona led them to a cottage with a sign posted: *Brana's Boarding.* Brana was an elderly woman, a grandmother, who opened her empty nest to visitors when they came through. There were two rooms for visitors, and she would prepare their meals during their stay. Brana greeted Mara warmly, clasping one of her hands with both of hers, reminding Mara of Rhodi. She then showed Mara and Ashroot to their room—Teddy would have his own— and told them to rest while she prepared supper. She waved away Ashroot's protestations, telling the bearkin that guests in her home do not cook.

After a peaceful night in a soft bed, Mara woke feeling rejuvenated.

Brana cooked them a nice breakfast and thanked the "young man" for helping her clean the table, making Teddy grin and puff out his chest. Teddy had been out until bedtime making arrangements with Callum. Once their breakfast was finished, it would be time to go.

"You be good now, girls," Brana told them as they left her home.

"We'll do our best," Mara replied, smiling. "Thank you so much for your hospitality, comfortable beds, and wonderful cooking."

Mara said goodbye to Iona and Pepper—and gave Pepper a good belly scratch—shook Callum's hand again, and hopped up into the wagon. Their wagon was full of various supplies, some of which they'd use on the way, and some they were taking to an innkeeper in the next town.

"Good luck on your trial, young rangerling," Callum said as Teddy hopped onto the wagon and he waved them away.

Teddy clicked at the horses and said, "Let's get going, boys," and they headed away from Darach.

It would take them two days to travel the rest of the way to this port, but this traveling was much less taxing than before. They rode on the wagon for a large portion of the first day before stopping at a river to water the horses and stretch their legs. They crossed the nearby bridge and rode a few more hours before setting up camp.

Now that they had supplies in a wagon, they were able to pitch tents and lay on bedrolls instead of directly on the hard ground. The night was not as peaceful as Brana's boardinghouse, but it was way better than sleeping in the forest. They got up before the sun the next morning and headed off again.

When they stopped to water the horses the second day, Mara followed Teddy around, taking long, lunging steps as she did so she could stretch her legs. "So, tell me about this port," she said. "What are we going to do once we get there?"

Teddy tied the horses to the wagon by large ropes as he explained, "We'll get to Bowen's inn around suppertime. We should be able to get rooms at the inn and a nice meal, and we'll give him the supplies from Darach. We can rest and see about hiring a ship in the morning. We'll probably need to stay in the village for at least a few days until we can get a ship ready—maybe even a few weeks."

"And we'll get the rest of our supplies there? For the rest of the journey?"

"Yes—well, mostly. Port Albatross is a trading village. We can get just about anything there. I figured we'd wait to get the rest of our supplies until we could load them directly onto the ship, and we'll get as much as we can before we set sail."

"And … do you know what all we'll need to survive and make it back?" Mara asked quietly.

Teddy glanced at her sullen face and playfully flipped her braid. "Hey now. I've seen a thing or two. I'm your wise companion, remember? My great wisdom will see us across all of Ambergrove," he announced. One of the horses twitched its tail at a fly and whipped Teddy in the face.

"We're doomed," Ashroot muttered.

It was nearly dusk when they made it to the edge of the village. There was a network of buildings as far as the eye could see. Teddy knew where he was going, so he led the horses steadily past the distractions. They would have plenty of time for shops after they had some supper and rest. They passed dozens of little shops, homes, inns, taverns, and temples. Finally, they made it to a small inn called The Pleasant Mariner. Teddy hopped down and handed the reins to a stable boy before ushering Mara and Ashroot inside.

The dining room was bustling with people. There were raucous warriors downing ales, civilians and families eating dinners, and a group of children sitting by a hearth fire begging someone to tell them a story, all while young men and women raced around the tables, keeping everyone happy.

They were met at the entrance by a large, merry man with rosy cheeks. "Te-e-e-ed!" he shouted, arms wide. To Mara's surprise, he wrapped those arms around Teddy in a familial hug. "What brings you here to the coast this time?"

"My niece's Ranger trials have begun, Bowen." Teddy wriggled out of the big man's hold and gestured to Mara. "I can tell you the story in the morning, but for now we're in desperate need of meals and rooms."

The man beamed in their direction and then called two young men over. He sent one to prepare rooms for them and one to take them to an open table. After a few moments, the second man returned with water and food—sweet rolls with butter and a hearty stew.

As they began to eat, Mara noticed the children by the hearth fire had been successful in finding a storyteller. After some jeering and shoulder clapping from her table, a young woman with brunette braided hair and a crimson dress went to sit by the fire. She smiled at the children and asked them, in an enthusiastic voice one tends to reserve for children and pets, "Now, what kind of story would you like to hear?"

"Giants!"

"Sea elves!"

"Dragons!"

"Yeah, dragons!"

"Dragons it is," the woman announced.

She told a long, eloquent story about the Dragons' War. This story explained why the dragons had been split up into two parts of the world. Long ago, before many creatures had begun to exist, dragons roamed freely and lived peacefully. After the gods decided to create humanoids, some dragons became jealous and power-hungry. They believed that they should rule over the humanoids since they were older and fiercer. Because of the terror some dragons wrought over the rest of the world, dragons began to be hunted.

One day, dragons of all kinds gathered to decide the outcome of their kind—and they did not agree. They warred with each other and with the other creatures of the world for centuries. Finally, the gods had enough. They gathered and combined their powers to bind the dragons. All those they considered to be well-intentioned were sent to a northern land and were given curved horns. Those whose power-mongering could not be tamed were banished to a southeastern land and were given pointed horns. The dragons would be confined to those lands until they were able to coexist with Ambergrove's other creations.

"... and so, little ones, if ever you see a dragon in the sky, you will know by its horns if it is friend or foe. Though, you're likely to be consumed by dragon fire before you can see the pointed horns of an evil beast!" The woman finished her tale and splashed her remaining ale into the fire, so it came alive briefly—just enough to startle her listeners.

Mara clapped loudly, and the whole inn seemed to cheer. Teddy leaned back in his chair and clapped contentedly. As the woman headed back to her table, she was stopped by Bowen, the innkeeper.

"Please, good lady, what is your name?" he asked.

"Salali," she replied diffidently.

"I'll remember the name." He smiled at her, then addressed the room. "What better note to end the evening? If you are staying with us tonight, please allow one of my workers to guide you to your room. Otherwise, we thank you for your business and your company, and we ask that you return to your own homes at this time. Thank you."

Surprisingly, everyone seemed to obey his command without question. Customers rose and stacked their dishes neatly on the tables, giving Bowen a firm shake or a pat on the back as they left the inn or waving appreciatively in his direction as they got a worker to take them to their rooms.

Mara and Ashroot followed Teddy over to the innkeeper. "Thank you for your hospitality, Bowen. The food was tastier than I remembered it," Teddy told him. "If you'd like, I can be up before the sun tomorrow to tell you our tale."

Bowen let out a full belly laugh and clapped Teddy's shoulder. "I'd be delighted, friend!" he exclaimed. He turned to Mara and Ashroot, continuing, "And we will have breakfast available with the sunrise, ladies. You won't be disappointed." He winked at Ashroot, adding, "Though I would consider it the highest honor if a bearkin were to praise my food."

At that, Teddy nodded, and they all followed a young woman upstairs. They each had their own room, though all three rooms were right next to each other. When Mara asked for a key, the woman assured her there would be no danger in their inn, opening the door to a pleasant little room just large enough for a comfortable bed and a rocker by a small window.

Suddenly, Mara was weary. It had been a long day, and all she wanted was to sink into bed. She thanked the woman and shut the door, bracing the chair under the handle for good measure, no matter how safe the place was supposed to be. She wasn't sure how she managed to remove her armor before falling into bed, but as her eyes closed, she silently thanked Teddy for giving her armor that was easy to shuck off. That night, she dreamed of dragons.

Mara woke to the harsh sound of a seagull cawing outside her window. She blinked away the light, then she sighed, stood, and went to look out the window. How had she not realized last night how close they were to the coast? She'd never been to the ocean, so maybe she just didn't know what it looked like or sounded like. Beautifully carved ships with colorful sails lined the docks, and the waves crashed against a distant cliff face.

The seagull took flight, and hundreds of flockmates joined him from the roof. As they flew back toward the sea, Mara saw a whale splash near one of the ships. She opened her window and breathed deeply, taking in the cool air and the salt water. It was magical. She decided she wanted to see it up close, so she dressed, putting on her armor. She hesitated for a moment at her weapons, unsure what to bring along if she was taking a trip through the village, and she decided to bring just the small dagger her dad had given her. She tucked it in her boot, took her chair brace away from the door, and left her room.

The inn was quiet. When she got downstairs, she saw the dining room was empty but for one figure at a table in a corner. Mara walked closer to the figure and saw that it was the storyteller, Salali. She decided to go talk to the young woman before heading out on the town.

"May I sit with you?" Mara asked.

Salali looked up, startled. She had been immersed in a map. "Sure!" she replied, pulling out a chair.

Mara thanked her and sat. Salali went back to her map, and Mara watched her for a moment. Salali's map seemed to cover the north of Ambergrove. She was looking at the dragon lands. No wonder she'd known so much about them.

"That was an amazing story you told, Salali," Mara ventured.

"Thank you, um ..."

"Mara."

Salali smiled. "Thank you, Mara."

"How did you know about the dragons?"

Salali raised a brow, confused. "It's a pretty common story, Mara."

"Well you told it well. Really well. Everyone was drawn by your story," Mara replied.

Salali smiled. "I've always loved telling stories."

Mara paused for a moment. "Maybe, once you've finished whatever quest you're on, you should find an inn and tell stories there."

"There's an idea," a man called from the bottom of the stairs. He was a tall young man, stocky, with a thick, brown beard and twinkling brown eyes. He had been sitting next to Salali the night before. They seemed friendly.

"Garan, you know we have a job to do," Salali scorned, though she seemed to smile slightly.

"Maybe one day, when it's all over." Garan sighed, walking over to Salali. He put a hand on her shoulder and kissed the top of her head before looking over her shoulder at the map.

Mara decided she was probably intruding, so she thanked Salali for her time and rushed outside into the crisp morning air.

The streets were teeming with people of all kinds. Mara recognized the forest tones, beards, and height of forest dwarves. There were shorter men and women with more volcanic tones that had the same strong build. Maybe those were the mining dwarves? They looked like dwarves in the stories she'd read growing up, down to the sour glances. Bustling around them were people slightly taller, rounded more with padding than muscle. Some of them had beards, but all of them had big noses and rosy cheeks. Gnomes?

There were all kinds of people who must have been humans. The largest portion were definitely humans. The smallest portion were the angriest-looking people she had ever seen. They were tall and slender with pointed ears. Their skin and hair looked to be various blues and greens—colors of the sea. Their looks and mannerisms told Mara they believed they were better than everyone else. Those had to be the sea elves.

Mara walked through the streets to what appeared to be the market. The crisp morning air mixed with the stench of fish. This was a coastal town after all—no wonder it was bustling at dawn. All the other shops had opened with the fishmongers. There was a tanner working on a crimson doublet. His shop was filled with dyed leather clothing, armor, accessories and bags. Mara decided to look at his shop first. She was amazed at the intricate designs carved, stamped, or painted on the items.

Nearby was a burly blacksmith with a mining dwarf apprentice who appeared to be his mini-me. Their store was filled with magnificent weapons. Some of the weapons were simple and functional, some were elegantly molded, and some were jewel encrusted. They also had a few miscellaneous little things. On a short table, something caught her eye.

"Excuse me, sir?"

"Yes, young lady!" The blacksmith handed his work to his apprentice and came to stand beside her.

"What are these?" She pointed to the objects on the table. They reminded her of the domed jungle gym climber she used to play on in elementary school. Each little dome was made of iron and woven into various knots and patterns, some with stylized animals.

"Good eye!" The man glanced at her braid—a little mussed after a few days, but Teddy had done a good job. "Though I don't see why you'd need it with that pretty braid there." He pointed at it and raised a brow.

Mara grasped her braid self-consciously. "Oh this? Uncle Teddy did this. I'm useless with hair. These are for hair then?"

"Yes!" he replied, unperturbed. He picked one up—a simple knotted one—and picked up a simple pin next to it. "May I?"

Mara nodded. He explained the process as he put it in her hair. "First, you tie the hair up in a ponytail." He left her hair in the braid and just pulled it up into a low ponytail. "You wrap the ponytail around itself in a roll, then you slip this over it." He put the little cage over the bun. "All that's left is locking it in," he finished, slipping the pin into one of the holes in the knotwork, through the bun, and out another hole on the other side.

Mara turned to the blacksmith and felt her head. Her hair was completely pulled back and contained. She bounced up and down slightly and it held. It was also surprisingly light for a hunk of metal. She beamed up at him.

"Have difficulties with that hair, do you?" he asked with a grin.

"Always!" she replied. "I can never find a good way to get it up and out of the way without it falling down a few hours later, but I can't bring myself to cut it. This thing is perfect! It's just ..." Mara's face fell.

"What's wrong, young lady?" he asked, shocked.

"I— um ... I don't know how to buy things here ..." she managed.

Was there money or did people just trade goods or labor? She should have asked before she came to the market and saw all the cool stuff.

"Here?" The blacksmith saw the look on her face, and he softened, placing a hand on her shoulder. "Uncle Teddy, you said? You got forest dwarf in you, young lady?"

"Yeah ... My dad," she answered. "He—"

"He was the leader of them, yeah? Teddy is Tederen of Aeunna?"

Mara nodded, and the blacksmith gave her a pat on the head. "Well, lady, today is your lucky day. Ted helped me out before, and I owe him. Whenever you need anything, it's yours. You never have to worry about payment."

"Th-thank you!" Mara exclaimed. An old gnomish lady walked into a rack, knocking some swords over, so the blacksmith went to help her, telling Mara to head on out and explore the port.

As she was leaving the shop, she turned, "Wait! What's your name?"

"Gryffyth." When she made a face, he added, "It's Welsh. Ask your uncle about my mum sometime." He gave her a wink and waved her away without another word.

Mara ran into Teddy soon after as she was on her way to the water. She wanted to see a beach and maybe feel the wet sand—and see if she could spot a whale up close. Teddy was near the boats talking to a red-bearded sea elf.

"Mara! Here!" her uncle called, waving her over. The teal-skinned man held out a hand for Mara to shake as Teddy introduced him. "This is Lir, Mara. He's the reason dwarves and elves shouldn't marry."

"Hah!" Lir shook Mara's hand and gave Teddy a brotherly shove. "You're the reason young forest women are driven into the arms of better beings!"

"Uh ... what?" Mara looked back and forth between the two men.

"Rhodi's my great-great grammy," Lir told her. "Ma left as soon as she was old enough to sail. Grammy told her where to find the best sailors, and she met my da when he came into this port. They sailed the seas together.

Magical isn't it?" Lir chuckled. "This port is home for me. I make ships and send others out to sail the seas. Others like you."

"What kind of ship do you have for us, Lir?" Teddy asked.

Lir thought for a moment, and then gestured to Mara. "Ranger trial?"

"Ding ding." Mara sighed.

"Just you two?"

"We have a bearkin with us now and we're on our way to the Big Hill and then to the Great Serpent for two others," Teddy explained.

"Hmm, then what you need is a modified longship." Lir decided.

Teddy nodded knowingly, but Mara asked, "What do you mean?"

"A longship is a small ship, one-masted. It's good for small crews like yours and for maneuvering small places. It'll be fun for your sea elf to handle—once you get one."

"Thank you so much, Lir." Teddy clapped the man on the back.

"Now—she's a loaner, Ted. You make sure you bring her back to me once you're successful," Lir warned, tapping the dwarf's bald head.

"What if we can't?" Mara asked. "What if we fail?"

"Nah, don't think about that, girlie," Lir reasoned. "Think positive. If, for some reason, my ship does get damaged, I can settle up with Teddy later."

"Let's see it then," Teddy announced, rubbing his hands together.

Lir took them down a row of ships. They were large, magnificent. All the ships were ornately carved with brightly colored sails. Most of them had carved figureheads—mermaids, dragons, monsters of various kinds. Although many of them were oversized, they all reminded Mara of Viking ships. Halfway down the row of ships, Lir pointed.

Their ship was made from a reddish wood and the sail was a light royal blue. The figurehead was a simple stylized beast, but Mara could vaguely make out a recognizable creature.

"What is that?" she asked, nodding at the figurehead.

"A boar," Lir said. "See the tusks and the snout?" He pointed at the pieces he meant.

Once he'd said it was a boar, she couldn't see anything else. "It's perfect," she whispered.

Teddy grinned at her and Lir shouted, "Oh, wait until you see her from aboard!"

Lir led them up a plank and onto the ship. It was immaculate. There were benches lining the sides and steps leading below decks at the center. The wheel was at the stern, and it was decorated with knotwork. Teddy followed Mara as she strode up to the helm and traced the knotwork on the wheel. "Sea elves admired the first Vikings who came from Earth," he explained. "Their culture evolved and morphed into something fierce, so the sea elves modeled their ships and much of their culture after them."

"Like the names of ships. All ships have Old Norse names—even this one," Lir commented.

"Oooh, what is it?" Mara burst.

Lir chuckled and grinned at her. "Easy there, little one." He smirked. "She's called *Harrgalti*, but I sometimes call her Little Red."

"It's alright." Teddy shrugged.

Lir glared at Teddy. "*Harrgalti* means 'sea boar.' It has a boar on it, and it goes on the sea! What else would you call it?" he replied defensively.

"I love it!" Mara agreed, grabbing the wheel and pretending to sail.

They went below deck and toured the rest of the ship—a storage area, a galley, and six bunks. It would be perfect. They just needed the last of their supplies and they could be on their way to the Big Hill and Mara's second trial.

CHAPTER TEN

THE ODYSSEY BEGINS

They stayed in Port Albatross for a fortnight before they set sail. Mara walked through the shops with Teddy, and he explained to her how trade worked. They had money in Ambergrove, but not everyone used it. Many businesses were run on faith. Places like The Pleasant Mariner provided donations-based room and board. Some paid with fresh supplies for the kitchens or replacement supplies for the rooms, and some paid with money. Those who couldn't pay were given what they needed with a smile. Teddy had some money, but he needed it for other supplies, so the supplies they'd brought from Darach were also to cover their boarding.

Actual shops only traded for small precious items or money. Small copper coins were for most foods and small items, silver coins were for meats and small artisan items, and gold coins were for larger or complex items. Mara discovered Ashroot and Teddy both had money. Ashroot paid for the foods they would need, and Teddy paid for other supplies. Teddy also brought money for each of the girls to get one thing they wanted. Ashroot got a selection of sea spices and Mara got another bun cage, this one with a stylized dragon. Gryffyth took a few hours and made a wolf's head pin to go with it.

Mara didn't see much of Teddy or Ashroot in the two weeks they spent at the port. She divided her time between exploring Port Albatross and learning the basics of ship anatomy and terms with Lir. She couldn't do this on *Harrgalti* because Teddy was working on extra modifications and preparations for the trip and didn't want her underfoot.

Mara showed Lir the sailing book she'd brought, and the shipbuilder just laughed. "You can't learn what you need to about sailing from books! You have to do it yourself and see what you're working with," he explained. "Plus, with the kind of journey you'll be taking with your small crew, you don't need to know all this stuff anyway."

He explained the basics. Some she already knew, like the four sides of the ship. Instead of left, right, front, and back, it was port, starboard, bow, and stern. The wheel of the ship was the helm. Some things she remembered from movies after Lir mentioned them, such as the storage area of the ship was called the hold and the kitchen was called the galley. The riggings to hold up the sail were called the shrouds, and the ropes to anchor the ship were called mooring lines. Pirate movies and underrated cartoons had served her well.

Lir explained that the half wall on the deck was called the bulwark— he'd laughed when Mara just called it a wall. When Mara had asked about anchoring the ship, he explained how the anchor was used and how they would be able to anchor themselves at sea, in order to keep from veering off course if everyone needed to take a break. He'd also invented a feature to keep the ship sailing on course, and he had been sure to include this in all the ships he made. Really, it was just a pin that went through the wheel and post to prevent the wheel from turning. He also told her that *Harrgalti* was considered a weatherly ship. It was made for simplicity and for beginners. It would serve her well and be easy for her to use when she learned to sail herself.

Finally, once their preparation was complete, they sailed with the tide. Teddy took the helm at first, because he was the only one who knew how to sail. Ashroot was seasick before they had made it out of sight of the port, so she spent most of the first leg of the journey below deck, either trying to sleep or trying to prepare food for the others. Mara watched Teddy or tried to touch the creatures swimming in the water.

After a little while, Teddy showed her how to use each part of the ship, furling the sails when they stopped for meals so they wouldn't be blown off course. On the second day, Mara took the helm with Teddy's supervision. The waters were calm, so it was a nice stretch for her to learn. Teddy told her they would have at least a week of calm, open waters, so he had Mara do most of the sailing for those days.

On the tenth day, an island came into view, and they spent another day sailing around it before moving any nearer. When they'd gone around the tip of the island, Teddy took over once more. As they prepared to dock, a bustling village came into view. Mara had been right—the people she had seen in Port Albatross were gnomes. She was surprised to see *only* gnomes, and she asked Teddy why.

"Trust!"

"What?"

"They're some of the smallest people here. They don't spend their lives mining and smithing like dwarves, and they only really learn to fight for basic defense, so they're easily overpowered. It's hard for them to trust others, so they usually don't allow outsiders to live in their lands. We're about to have some fun." Teddy sighed as armed guards made their way up the docks to their ship, pointing spears at them as they approached.

"What is your purpose here?" one of them called. Most of the guards wore simple scaled mail armor. This guard's armor was fancier, with gold filigrees, so she suspected he was the leader.

Teddy stepped forward, palms up to show he meant no harm, and called, "I am Tederen of Aeunna. My family line is of the leaders of the forest dwarves. We are here so Mara can complete her Ranger trial, and we will be gone just as quickly. Please let us speak to Chief Sokti."

The men didn't move, spears still aimed at Teddy's face. One of the soldiers in the back, one of the many with earthy brown skin and coal black hair, turned and whispered something to the soldiers next to him. The commander snapped back at them before turning back to Teddy and glaring.

"Very well, Tederen." They all lowered their spears as he continued, "Anchor your ship. Leave your weapons below deck and follow me to the Big Hill."

All their buildings were underground, dug into hills. The largest of those hills was the village hall—and chieftain's home. It was massive and magnificent. The hall was rounded on the inside, with intricately carved pillars. A big man—wide as he was tall—stood in the center of a crowd of gnomes. The only way to distinguish him from the other gnomes was the small silver circlet he wore.

When they neared the crowd and Teddy caught the gaze of their chief, her uncle bowed his head and bent a knee in respect. When Mara saw this, she hurried to do the same. Ashroot hadn't seemed to notice, but then neither had the other gnomes.

"Tederen! Come now," the man boomed. "You are welcome in my halls!"

Teddy stood and clasped arms with the man. "Thank you very much, Chief Sokti. We do appreciate your hospitality and any help you may give us."

"Such formality!" the big man boomed, chuckling. "You'd think Tederen of Aeunna had never visited the Hills before!"

"I'm just trying to teach our new rangerling good manners." Teddy grinned.

"Ah!" The big man pushed past Teddy toward Mara. To his visible surprise, she clasped his arm as Teddy had done. The man sputtered some as Teddy burst into laughter.

"Wh-what's so funny?" Mara asked.

The chief cleared his throat, uncomfortable. "Hem, well ... miss ... Mara ..."

"You greeted him like a man, Mara," Teddy wheezed.

Mara jumped back, bowed again, and repeatedly apologized until the chief snapped at her to stop. "... Sorry ..." Mara whispered to the floor in response.

The chief glared at her. "What exactly is it you dwarves want from us this visit?" he ordered, crossing his arms. The hospitable moment was apparently over. It seemed that Teddy had been welcome, but because of her blunder, Mara wasn't. Still nervous, she mumbled at the floor and the gnome shouted, "Speak up!"

"I'm here for my Ranger trial," Mara whispered, glancing back at Teddy. This was about her trial—he couldn't help her. She continued a little more forcefully, "I'm supposed to prove myself to the gnomish people so I can get a gnome to come along with me to the sea elves and then through the Dragon's Teeth."

Chief Sokti raised his brows and glanced at Teddy. Teddy nodded. The gnome sighed. "I am the leader of the gnomish people. We will not make this task easy for you, though we will allow you to complete it. Due to your ... unorthodox manner, we will not allow you to remain in our lands any longer than necessary."

Mara nodded. "Yes, I understand. I am very sorry for the offense, sir."

The chief smiled slightly, then ordered, "Head back to your ship and stay there until noon. We will give you your task then and, with any luck, you will be able to complete it and leave by sundown."

"Mara of Aeunna!" a soldier announced from the docks.

They were eating their lunch below deck when the guards arrived. Ashroot hung behind to clean up while Mara and Teddy came up to the deck to meet the guards. When they were within view of the docks, they were surprised to see a cluster of soldiers standing with the chief next to the ship, with what appeared to be the entire rest of the village behind them.

Mara shivered, and Teddy put a reassuring hand on her shoulder. "Have you come to a decision?" he asked the chief.

The chief nodded. When the crowd began to clamor behind him, he thrust his arms up for silence and announced, "Mara of Aeunna, if you are to complete your trial, you must travel to the Caves of Chittering Darkness and rid our island of the scourge below. If you are successful and bring us proof of our liberation, one of my guards," he gestured to the soldiers around him, "will accompany you on your quest. You have until dusk to complete this task."

Mara nodded. Why was it always dusk? "May I speak to my uncle first?"

"You may."

"And will you tell me where to go?"

"My guards will take you to the cave's entrance. Speak to your uncle. You will leave in a few moments."

Mara nodded again and thanked the chief before Teddy pulled her over to the far side of the deck. When he spoke, his tone was serious. "Mara, this will not be like your first trial."

"What do you mean?"

"For your first trial, the goal was to return without killing. You survived the goblin attack without killing. To complete this trial, you *have to kill*. You *have to*, Mara. Sometimes the objective is to kill the monster. If you are going to be our leader, you are going to have to learn to kill the monster. Are we clear?"

Mara nodded, unable to speak.

"He didn't limit your weapons, but you need to be nimble. Take one melee weapon and one missile weapon. Travel light. You may need to bring an empty pack so you can return with proof."

Mara went below to gather what he'd suggested. If she was going in there, planning to kill monsters alone, she preferred the battle axe to the sword. She grabbed the axe, her bow, and a full quiver, then she dumped her pack out on her bunk. When she saw her dad's old dagger lying there on the bed, she decided to slide it into her boot and take it as well.

Ashroot met Mara at the foot of the stairs. She handed Mara a water pouch and a few hardy snack items to keep her going. Wordlessly, Ashroot gave her a hug, pulling her in for one tight squeeze before letting her go with a reassuring nod.

Teddy was waiting at the top of the stairs. He squeezed her so tightly, she almost couldn't breathe, and then he held her shoulders at arm's length and met her gaze. Were those tears in his eyes?

"Remember," he told her sternly. "If it comes down to them or you, make sure it's you."

Mara nodded, blinking back her own tears. "Uncle Teddy, thank you so much for—"

"Huh-uh!" Teddy exclaimed. "None of that. You say goodbye and you don't come back. You go, be on your guard, and come back."

Mara nodded. "I promise, Teddy."

Before she could cry, she turned and headed to the docks, passing through the crowd with the chief's guards without looking back.

No one spoke to Mara the entire way to the cave. Once they made it to the mouth of the cave, the guards retreated to a safe distance and pitched a tent. She stared at the opening.

"Miss?"

Mara jumped. She'd thought all of them had gone to the tent. She turned to the soldier behind her. It was the one who had been whispering when they'd first arrived on the island. His face, though hardened, still seemed kind. He barely came up to her shoulder.

"Y-yes?"

"You need to enter the cave now. We will sit until you return or until dusk, but we will not sit while you do nothing."

"Sorry. I'll get there. I'm going." Mara turned and headed into the cave, focusing on keeping one foot after the other.

"May Baerk watch over you!" the soldier called from the opening.

Mara didn't turn back but walked into the darkness. She realized she probably should have brought some sort of light, but when she walked further into the cave, she discovered there were glowing stones lighting the way, just as there had been when she met the Great Silver Bear.

She followed the tunnel in silence, wondering what would be chittering in those caves. After what seemed to be a lifetime, she came to a fork in the tunnels. She sat, crossing her legs, and listened. If she had been playing D&D, she would have gone right. Jim said that when creating dungeons, dungeon masters would pick right subconsciously and so it would be picked most often. This wasn't a game. When she ran into the monsters, they wouldn't take turns. There would be no healing potions. Life or death. Them or her. She exhaled deeply.

After a moment, Mara heard a faint rustle coming from deep within the left tunnel. *Not a game.* She took a few sips from her pouch and hefted her axe. She was ready—as ready as she'd ever be. She hadn't made it more than a few steps down the tunnel when she heard the chittering. A few steps more and the chittering seemed to become words.

Fresh meat! The little creatures have sent us fresh meat! Large and juicy! Stab! Stab it! Eat it! Close, so close!

Mara kept her pace, hoping the darkness would work in her favor. She shifted the weight of the battle axe in her hands. Whatever it was, it was

large. This would do the trick as long as she was ready. The chittering
continued.

Must get it before it comes to the nest! Quickly, quickly, above!

Mara heard scuttling nearing her and tried to inconspicuously glance
upward. It took all her effort not to scream. *Why'd it have to be a spider?* It was
massive, but at least it wasn't that much larger than a dog. It was smaller
than the Great Silver Bear had been, and she *had* been prepared to fight him
if necessary.

Mara clenched her jaw. It was easier knowing they were spiders. She
thought she could take their lives more readily than she would have if they
had been more person than monster, like the goblins. The spider was nearly
overhead when she decided it was time. She gripped her axe as tightly as she
could and swept upward with it. To her surprise, the spider's head and body
fell to the ground on opposite sides of her. It oozed a greenish black, and
she saw a hundred reflections of herself in its dead eyes. She couldn't help
it. This creature had spoken. It was alive, and she had killed it. There was
so much blood. She doubled over, and her lunch made a return appearance.

She wiped her mouth and was reaching for her pouch to wash down
some of the vomit when she heard a shriek. There were three other spiders
further down the tunnel, staring horrified at the other's lifeless form. They
charged her. Later, when she regaled this moment to Teddy and Ashroot,
she never knew now she'd been so calm. She waited until the spiders were
close to her, and it only took one swipe with the axe to kill all three. When
she heard louder shrieks, she felt more confident. She'd just killed four
spiders—she could do it.

As she made her way through the tunnels, she followed the sounds
of outrage and took down all the spiders she encountered. She counted
them, wanting to prove to Teddy that she had what it took to be a leader
by telling him how many she'd been able to kill. By the time she made it
to a large, rounded chamber, she'd counted twenty-seven spiders. All that
was left was the largest spider she could ever imagine, her eyes burning with
rage, shrieking about murder, vengeance, and eating Mara slowly. Mara was
terrified. That creature was massive and angry, and Mara was tired. She
didn't want to give the spider the chance to rush her like some of the others,
so she charged it, screaming.

The good thing about fighting a creature without weapons was that the only way it could avoid Mara's attacks was to dodge. Mara's first swipe of the axe neatly severed the last digit of one of the spider's legs. She brought her axe down hard overhead as Teddy had done when he split the goblin—and the spider dodged. The spider dodged the next few swipes before reaching out a hairy leg to grab her. The hairs on its legs were sharp. Mara had slices on her arms from some of the other spiders trying to grab her, cutting her in the process. This one caught her in the forehead, leaving a gash right where her scalp met her brow. Mara removed the leg. Its two front legs gone, the spider was off balance. She leaned forward slightly, teetering because her forelegs were no longer there to brace her, and Mara took the opportunity. Before the spider could catch her balance, Mara swung her axe down as hard as she could, splitting the spider's skull.

The creature collapsed. Mara panted with the effort and swiped some blood from her brow. She looked around. She figured that the largest spider would be the last, but she wanted to be sure. She listened for a few moments before she was satisfied there were no more spiders. Just as she was about to search the spider for some sort of token to prove she had actually killed all the spiders, she heard rustling and muffled cries.

She followed the sound, and it led her to a webbed bundle. Mara pulled her dagger out of her boot and carefully sliced the bundle open. There was a young gnomish man inside—alive. The young man shivered and cried when he saw her. No matter how she tried, Mara couldn't get him to speak to her. She left him standing by the entrance to the chamber as she investigated the room.

Mara started at the young man's cocoon and made her way around the room, slicing open every bundle. Most of the occupants had died—a few had been dead for some time. She found two women, three other men, and a child alive in cocoons. One of the women and the child hugged each other, crying and rejoicing. The other gnomes were in the same state as the first gnome had been. They were terrified and lost, and they weren't responding to Mara's prompts.

She had no idea what time it was, and she knew she'd need the soldiers to be there when she exited the cave, so she needed to find a way to expedite the process. She opened her bag and removed the food Ashroot had given her, passing it around to the survivors. She used the cloth wrapping to grab some of the strung webbing around her. Quickly, she walked through those present and wrapped some of this makeshift rope around each gnome's left wrist. Once they had all been tethered to her, Mara led the survivors back down the tunnel, past the spider corpses, and out into the fading sunlight.

As soon as the soldiers saw Mara exiting the cave with seven other people, they abandoned their tent and rushed over. For quite some time, the gnomes were hugging and crying. Mara sat on the ground outside the cave, mopping her sliced brow and cleaning her axe blades. She smiled as she watched families reunite, but she couldn't help but wonder how so many people had been lost, and why not one of those soldiers had gone to rescue them. A few of the soldiers, now the way was clear, went into the caves to gather the dead.

She saw the young man who'd nudged her into the cave greeting the young woman and child. She thought it must have been his wife and child, but he was just hugging the child and talking to the woman. Mara thought after so long someone would be more affectionate if they'd just found their wife and child. The man saw her looking at him and waved her over.

"Dwarf—uh, Mara," he corrected, "my name is Kip. This is my sister, Kina, and her son, Loli." He gave them a squeeze. "They've been gone for almost a month now, and we've been forbidden to enter the cave to save them. They're the only family I have. I can never repay you for what you've done. Thank you."

Mara smiled. "You're welcome. Really—I'm glad this trial involved helping people."

"Dwarf!" another soldier snapped. "It's time to go! The rest of you, follow!"

He was an angry-looking man, and he was the only one who hadn't been reuniting with a survivor or gathering the dead. He marched off toward the village and the others followed obediently, remaining close to their loved ones as they walked. Mara walked with them back to the village, listening to Kip and his sister talk. They discussed her captivity and what she had seen the spiders doing. If someone hadn't saved them soon, she and her son were the next spider meal.

Once they made it back to the village, they were bombarded by people trying to reunite with loved ones. Those whose loved ones hadn't made it were distraught—rightfully so—but they were at least glad to have some closure. Those whose loved ones had returned rejoiced, though the gnomish chief was not as responsive. The other villagers had met them as they returned, but they found Chief Sokti in the village hall. He was so surprised to see her, he nearly spilled all his food down his front.

"D-Dwarf! You survived!" he stammered. Survivors filed in behind Mara with their families. "A-and you seem to have saved the lost villagers ..." he continued. He seemed almost disappointed.

"Yes, sir. The cave was full of spiders. I-I killed them. .... All of them. Your people have no more to fear there."

"You have completed your task," the chief said reluctantly, sighing. "You may have one of my soldiers for your quest ... if one volunteers for the task," he sneered.

What? Mara thought, the color leaving her face. *What kind of person reneges on a deal like that, especially after so many people have been saved? Who would volunteer to go with a complete stranger? What—*

"I'll go."

They turned to look at the new speaker. Mara wondered later how she'd been surprised. Kip had volunteered to come with her. She smiled at him gratefully before she caught the gaze of the fuming chief.

"Fine! Be on your way by dusk then! Off with you!" He waved absently and went back to his meal, barely acknowledging his citizens who had just been rescued.

Kip bowed to his chief and turned to Mara, "Give me a little while to get my stuff and say goodbye to my sister, and I'll meet you at your ship."

"Thank you so much, Kip. Take all the time you need," Mara told him gratefully. When she turned, Teddy enveloped her in a tight hug, his eyes murky with emotion. She'd done it. The second part of the trial was over. Soon they'd be on their way to the sea elves and the next trial would begin.

CHAPTER ELEVEN

BREAKING THE ICE

Kip shuffled toward their ship right at sundown, his face a mix of sullenness and anticipation. His sister and her son walked out with him. Mara watched from the ship as the siblings shared a tearful goodbye, and Kip heaved his nephew up in the air and spun him before enveloping him in a hug. He handed the boy something small and tousled his hair before finally turning and boarding the ship.

They cast off as soon as his feet left the docks. Teddy shook his hand and thanked him for joining them on their journey. "Thank your Ranger here," Kip said solemnly. "I owe her a doubt I can never repay."

Teddy clapped a hand on Mara's shoulder, and she smiled at Kip. "Thank you, Kip, for standing up for us and for helping me prove myself," she said.

He nodded, and then asked, "And who is this?"

Ashroot stepped forward and bowed lightly. "Ashroot," she told him. "I'm Mara's—"

"Best friend." Mara interrupted. "She's my best friend. She's been my constant companion while I've been here in Ambergrove, and I couldn't do any of this without her." Mara hoped Ashroot wasn't upset by her interjection, but she wanted Kip—and Ash, come to that—to know that they were all equal partners here. Ashroot nodded to Mara and smiled at Kip in turn.

"Alright, young warriors," Teddy announced. "It's time for Kip to get settled and for us to make our plans for what's to come. Take a few moments and head back up here by the time the water gets choppy."

111

"Yes, sir!" Kip nodded respectfully to Teddy. He turned to Mara and Ashroot. "Lead the way."

Mara followed as Ashroot led him below deck to the bunks. He'd brought just one small bag, wearing his armor and sporting a large hammer instead of the guards' spear. As he hefted the weapon to place it by the closest bunk, Mara could tell it was a weapon that had seen much use. He deposited his bag on the bed and looked around. It was a small ship, but the belly was comfortable.

The ship's hold took up the third of the ship closest to the bow. There were crates and crates of supplies. Between the hold and the steps to the deck were six beds. Rather than bunk beds, they were all on the floor and spread out into two rows of three. It allowed all six sailors to have their own space and be comfortable. From stairs to stern was the galley. After Kip selected his bunk, Ashroot led him into the galley and gave him something to snack on.

"Mmm! I understand why the food made by your people is so prized!" Kip told Ashroot between bites.

The two began to bond very quickly. Ashroot started to explain that part of the reason she'd wanted to go on the voyage was because her father had wanted special recipes. Mara watched from the doorway for a moment before heading back up to the deck.

Teddy was at the helm, squinting into the distance. He didn't move when Mara approached.

"Why the face, Teddy?" she asked.

"We have a long road before we make it to the sea elves. There's only treachery ahead," he warned.

"What sort of treachery do we need to prepare for?"

"Near the end of the journey, we'll have to pass the Dragon's Teeth. You know that will be a difficult task." Mara nodded in response. Teddy continued, "Before that, we have to appease the sea elves. Most of them aren't as friendly as Lir. They make Chief Sokti seem warm and fuzzy."

"I knew they would be difficult, though I was surprised the chief was so cold after one mistake." Mara paused and stared out over the water a moment before adding. "What's so bad about this part?"

Teddy met her gaze, his eyes fiery. "Monsters."

"What kinds of monsters?" she asked slowly.

"Sea monsters. Ice monsters. The mountains are teeming with icy creatures, and the waters nearby are home to starving sea beasts." He saw the fear in Mara's eyes and added, "There are less monsters in the rest of the sea and other isles, mostly because the Ice Mountains drive off all warm creatures."

"So . . ."

"So, there's lots of monsters this way, little one." He sighed. "But we'll be prepared for them, and we'll make it through." He looked out into the distance and spun the wheel to one side to avoid a faraway obstacle.

Mara stepped up beside him and patted him on the shoulder. "We'll get there," she told him fiercely. "We will. And back."

"What are you talking about?" Ashroot had just reached the top of the steps with Kip close behind her. They both smiled deeply, as if they'd shared a delightful joke.

Teddy and Mara glanced at each other. "I was telling Mara about how beautiful the sea elves islands are," Teddy explained.

"Sure," Kip began, "and I'm a forest dwarf."

"I see, I see." Teddy grinned. "Take a seat, young warriors, and we'll talk about what lies ahead."

The Ice Mountains. Perhaps it wasn't the most imaginative name, but it sure was accurate. The area was plain, cold, rugged, and wild. Decent creatures didn't live in the frozen south. All sorts of monsters like the ones Mara had read about in the monster manuals roamed ahead. There were frost giants, ice goblins, snowy golems, and winter wolves on land, and in water, serpents, polar piranha, winter whales, and, somewhere, a beast that gave even Teddy pause.

"A what?"

"It's a . . . kraken. An ice kraken." Teddy told them.

Kip stood and strode to the bow, pacing. Ashroot shook her head worriedly and began to make herself small. Mara inched forward in her seat, calculating. "Okay, I know from games and movies that krakens are bad enough, but what's an *ice* kraken?"

"Well," Teddy sighed, "the first thing is icy tentacles. Their tentacles are more solid, with sharp ice shards on the back made to shred ships."

Mara shuddered, looking lovingly at *Harrgalti*. She swallowed. "And what else?"

"Its icy touch spreads and spreads. Anything it touches will be covered in a sheet of ice. And its final weapon is frost. When the kraken gets close enough for you to see its teeth, you're likely to die from its frosty breath. Like a dragon breathes fire, it breathes frost. Whatever that touches, you likely lose forever."

"Dragons?" Ashroot squeaked. "There's dragons here?"

"No, no, dear. Not here." Teddy assured her. "Of all the creatures who have called Ambergrove home, never has there been an ice dragon."

"So, what's the worst thing here?" Mara asked.

"The kraken is the worst by far," he replied.

"So, what do we do?" Kip turned back toward them and rested a hand on the mast.

Teddy sighed thoughtfully. "Well ... your usual weapons will be of less help here. You don't want anything to get close enough to stab with a sword—or beat with your hammer, Kip."

"So, again, what do we do?" Mara asked.

"We face them with distance and numbers."

Teddy stood alone at the helm. They'd been sailing for a few weeks, and the wind had just begun to chill the bones. He'd sent the others below for a meal before beginning preparations for what waited in the cold. He'd been through the frozen lands before, and he knew that the worst wouldn't come for another month, but they'd need to work in numbers to prepare for what else they'd face along the way. He sighed and placed the bolt in the wheel to keep it on course. He glared at it a moment, making sure it would hold, and then he turned to the bundles on the deck.

What he'd told them when they'd left the Big Hill was true enough.

Swords would be little use against the creatures they would face. If one of those icy fiends got close enough to cut with a sword, it would all be over anyway. He crossed to the bow and dragged the wrapped bundles out from the bulwark. Just then, Mara, Kip, and Ashroot came up to the deck.

"What's that you have there?" Kip asked, striding forward.

"Gather 'round." Teddy beckoned to them as they circled him. Untying the binds and flattening the casing for the first open, he revealed mounds of daggers. "I have specialist weapons for each of you. These," he picked up one of the daggers, "are for Ashroot."

"What?" she exclaimed, as he handed her the dagger.

"You've become proficient with throwing daggers, Ashroot." He told her kindly. "You aren't pushing this into a shark belly—you're chucking it there."

Teddy saw the apprehension in her eyes as she looked at the dagger. He hoped when the time came, she would have the courage to fight. He'd made sure the girls were taught to use missile weapons, laughing off the idea so they would enjoy the practice—so they would be prepared for this moment without worrying about it until it came.

"What's in the other bundles?" Mara asked, trying to hide the excitement in her voice.

Teddy slid each bundle out to the center of the deck. Ashroot stood, dagger in hand, while Mara and Kip went to see what Teddy had brought. "Mara," Teddy began, opening the smaller of the bundles, "these are for you." He revealed dozens of throwing axes.

"Oh, yes!" Mara exclaimed, grabbing one and testing the weight.

"I thought you'd like those." Teddy chuckled.

"What's in those other ones?" she asked.

"I know," Kip said.

Mara turned to him and began to ask him how when Teddy replied. "Yes, I thought you might."

"Both of them?" Kip asked.

"Both of them."

"Excellent."

"Both of what?" Mara asked.

Kip strode to one bundle as Teddy stepped to the other, pulling back the canvas to reveal—

"Javelins?" Mara exclaimed.

Kip picked one up and tested its balance before giving it one sharp thrust at an unseen enemy.

"Is that gonna work?" Teddy asked, crossing his arms.

Kip turned to Teddy and grinned before giving him one sharp nod.

At that moment, Ashroot came over, holding her dagger by the tip. "Um, Teddy?" she began softly.

"Yes, Ashroot?"

"This isn't very sharp," she told him.

"Ah, yes." Teddy stepped around the javelins and took the dagger. He stabbed at Mara a few times to demonstrate that it would take considerable force for the dull weapon to break skin. "I bought these in bulk, unsharpened, so we could get the most out of them. Our job for the next few hours is to sharpen these."

In a little cabinet by the entrance to the below deck, Teddy had stored two large bags full of sharpening supplies. He snatched the bags from the cabinet and brandished them with a grin, like newfound treasure. Receiving only blank stares from the others, Teddy dropped one bag by the dagger bundle and one by the axe bundle.

"Grab yourselves a stool," he ordered. "Two to a pile. We'll work together to sharpen them. Just make yourselves a 'sharpened' pile and we'll talk about it all when you're done. Alright?"

Mara grabbed a small stool and settled herself by her axes. Kip grabbed another stool and followed suit.

"You and me, then." Teddy motioned cheerfully to Ashroot, and they also grabbed stools before heading toward the daggers. They wouldn't take too much time on them. Teddy instructed the others to make sure there was a bit of an edge on each before moving to the next. They weren't meant to be everyday weapons—these were one-and-done weapons, which was why the men would use javelins instead of messing with sharpening spears. Demonstrating, Teddy picked up one of the daggers, ran just the tip over the whetstone a few times and started his sharpened pile. He looked around every so often, checking for lights on the horizon, listening for movement.

Ashroot copied Teddy's work, jumping at the sounds of the wind whipping ropes against the mast.

"Ours is a little different," Kip told Mara kindly.

"How so?"

"They just need to sharpen the tips, because that's what the dagger needs in order to do damage here. We need the full blade." Kip ran the full axe blade quickly and carefully along the whetstone once, twice, thrice. Again on the other side. Then he tested the blade on his right boot. It left a faint slice.

"See, Mara?" Kip handed her the axe. She ran a finger along the blade and nodded. Then she started their sharpened pile and picked up her own axe to start.

While they worked, Kip and Mara talked. Kip told Mara about the beautiful hills in his homeland, about his family. How his sister met a mining dwarf and had little Loli—a scandalous thing among gnomes—and how he always carved little creatures for his nephew when he told the boy stories. Kip pulled a lumpy piece of wood from his pocket and showed it to Mara.

"What is this?" she asked.

"Well, I drew some inspiration from you, actually. I'm going to give that one to him when I get back from my quest with the dragonwolf, so ..." He trailed off sheepishly.

"So, you're carving a dragonwolf. That's nice!" Mara smiled down at the non-creature, imagining what it would be, and then she passed it back to Kip and picked up another axe.

"What about you?" he asked her.

"What do you mean?"

"Well, did you grow up in Aeunna with your uncle or something? ... What?"

Mara laughed, first a small chuckle, then a chortle. "You didn't know I came from Earth?" she managed.

His look of bewilderment said no. Mara told him broadly about Earth. She told him about DUNGEONS & DRAGONS, cars, electricity, computers, and phones. She told him about how her parents hadn't gotten along and how her dad came from Aeunna. She told him more than she had planned, and not in a truly comprehensive way. It was only when Teddy butted in, barking for them to get back to work, that Mara realized Kip had been sitting still, open mouthed, the whole time she'd been telling her story.

They finished their task in relative silence for a while after. Then, almost in unison, they stood and stretched their freezing joints. Mara and Kip held their last few axes up for Teddy to see. "Where do you want these?" Kip asked.

"One of the finer features Lir and I added to Little Red!" Teddy exclaimed excitedly. "Look there." He pointed to various stations around the deck. "See those cups?"

They hadn't seen the cups before, but now that Teddy pointed them out to them, Mara wondered how she could have missed them. About every three feet all around the bulwark, the cabinets, the mast, bolted into the surface, were metal cups the size of half gallon milk jugs with the tops cut off. Teddy went to the nearest one and placed a handful of daggers inside.

"Stagger them," he told the others. "Daggers, axes, daggers, axes—so they're spread out and accessible."

"Finally," Teddy instructed, "pile the javelins between cups." Teddy demonstrated this as well, staggering this time. He rested a handful of javelins horizontally behind an axe cup and a dagger cup, skipped a space, and stacked a handful between the next two cups. They did as instructed and kept circling the deck filling cups until all the weapons had homes.

Mara stepped back to admire their work. With the weapons staggered like this, they would each be able to access at least a few weapons from any part of the deck. She strode to the nearest axe cup and drew one, testing it against an imaginary sea creature.

"Good, Mara!"

Mara turned to see Teddy nodding his approval. He then instructed them all to practice—practice drawing the weapons, practice aiming when the ground was less than steady. They took turns calling out enemies. Someone would run to one side and shout, "Here!" They would all draw weapons and turn in that direction, aim, pretend throw, and reset.

Finally, after a few hours, Teddy barked, "That's enough!" They returned their weapons to the cups as he continued, "Head below, get you some supper and some warm clothes. I've packed enough for each of you in the storeroom. Now that we're heading into the ice, we'll need to take the lookouts and wayfaring in shifts, two at a time, once we're all ready. Go on."

Ashroot began the supper as Kip and Mara hunted through the storeroom in the hold for their warmer clothes. Mara was amazed at just how much Teddy had prepared. Looking through the storeroom, she felt a sharp pang of guilt. She would not have made it so far without Teddy. Already, there had been so many things he had thought of that she hadn't. They'd just prepared weapons, there was a whole section of healing herbs, poultices, and wraps, there were duplicates of all the basic adventuring gear she'd naively thought they would need, and there were huge trunks of clothing for each of them, Kip included. Teddy must have gone into town in the Big Hill and purchased warm clothes for Kip. They pulled out all four trunks and placed them near each person's bunk before opening their own trunks.

Mara had three layers of warm clothing. First was a long shirt and pants most akin to long johns on Earth, made from a deep blue material. Next were a button-up shirt and pants made of light wool in basic brown. Finally, a there was a huge, red wolfskin coat and thick, green pants. She had layers for all forms of cold and all forms combined. Stuffed in the bottom of the trunk were a few pairs of balled-up socks and a pair of brown, fur-lined gloves. It was just starting to get cold, so she ducked back into the storeroom with her blue long johns, peeled off shirt and pants, and slipped the warm layer on underneath. The long pants were completely covered by her brown ones, but the blue shirt went all the way up to her neck, covering her token from the Great Silver Bear. *Oh well.*

Mara stepped back out of the storeroom to find that Kip had made the same decision, only he'd apparently tried to rush it while she'd been changing and was standing with black long johns on and his coal grey pants half pulled up. Kip gasped when Mara opened the storeroom door, and nearly fell over. Red in the face, he yanked his pants up the rest of the way and muttered under his breath.

"What did Teddy get for you?" she asked, trying to hide her amusement.

Kip stepped aside and gestured for her to see for herself. She peered into his trunk as he pulled off his ruddy brown shirt. Out of the corner of her eye, Mara noticed that every part of his terra cotta torso she could see was covered in scars. She cleared her throat and concentrated on the trunk. His first layer had been black. His second layer was a deep brown. The thickest layer was a brown coat and black pants.

"Your uncle really knows what he's doing, doesn't he?" Kip asked, adjusting the sleeves of his shirts so the bottom sleeves were pulled all the way to his wrist under his brown shirt.

"He really does!" Mara replied, shaking her head incredulously. Teddy seemed to have them both pegged—and he had certainly prepared more than they had.

"Supper's ready, friends!" Ashroot called from the galley.

Mara and Kip exchanged a look, then Mara announced, "You get started. I'll go get Teddy."

Mara turned and bounded up the stairs to the deck. Teddy stood at the helm, poring over a map and compass. "What are you working on?" she asked as she made her way over to Teddy. He didn't answer, so she looked at the map. Here, again, Uncle Teddy had thought of everything. The map covered just the waters surrounding the Ice Mountains and the land itself, but it was covered in various markings.

"Are those runes?" Mara asked.

"Hmm?" Teddy had been engrossed in his work. "Oh, erm, kind of."

"Is this another one of those things that made its way to Earth and got mixed with the truth?"

Teddy chuckled. "Yes, it is. Though they were a lot closer with this than other things, I've heard."

Mara peered at the map. "I remember some of these. That's a P. That's W. That's G. K …. Wait, are these—"

"Yes."

"But why here?"

"This map marks common sightings of each type of creature. Polar piranhas have mostly been sighted around here." Teddy gestured to the closest part on the map. "W in the water is the whales. On land it's winter wolves." These were a little further away. He pointed out all the other creatures sighted throughout. Then, about halfway past the land mass, ... K.

"This is where we'll meet the kraken?" Mara asked in a small voice.

Teddy nodded solemnly. "But we'll be alright—we're prepared. By the time we make it there, you'll be ready. And Lir built us a strong ship." He clapped her shoulder reassuringly, but she couldn't help noticing it didn't reach his eyes. She returned the gesture all the same.

"You dwarves coming down for supper?" Kip stood at the top of the stairs, arms outstretched to either side. "Ashroot's worried it'll get cold."

"We're coming." Teddy and Mara called in unison. Teddy rolled up the map and tucked it away in the cabinet at the top of the stairs as they passed.

They all went into the galley together. The back half of the room was a spacious kitchen, fully stocked. The way to the kitchen area was blocked by a long wooden table. Three chairs faced the doorway and three sat opposite. There were tall cabinets on either side of the table. Ashroot sat at the table, facing the doorway, and her handiwork covered the entire surface. There was a roasted bird in the center of the table, surrounded by bowls of steaming vegetables. There was bread and cheese on one end, and various fruits on the other. Four place settings had been made, with plates, utensils, and mugs of water.

"This is amazing, Ash!" Mara exclaimed. She danced around the table to sit next to her friend, grinning. Then something dawned on her. "Ash, where did you get a chicken to roast?"

Ashroot looked at Teddy, who laughed a deep, throaty laugh. Kip also chuckled as he settled himself at the table.

"What am I missing?" Mara asked, slightly annoyed.

Teddy laughed himself quiet, then sighed and sat next to Kip. "It's not a chicken, Mara."

"What is it then?"

"It's a gull."

"What?"

Teddy chuckled again. "It's a seagull. I shot it earlier this morning and gave it to Ashroot to prepare. She's done as fine a job, as usual, it seems. It looks tasty, Ashroot!"

Mara stared at the bird in front of her. She vaguely heard Ashroot make a crack about how it would have been better if they had come down earlier, before she carved it up and passed portions around the table. They filled their plates, thanked their cook, and dug in. None of the others batted an eye about eating seagull. Maybe it wasn't that strange—all Mara could tell by looking at it was that the meat seemed a little darker. She took an apprehensive bite before wolfing it down. It tasted just like duck. It was juicy and cooked to perfection, just like all the other meals Ashroot had made since Mara had met her.

As they ate their meal, they talked and laughed, discussing strange foods they'd had and funny stories about them. Once they'd all had their fill and had given their food time to settle, they decided who would take the first watch, ushering in the beginning of their frosty fights.

Mara stood looking out at the calm waters. She pulled her red coat tighter around her neck and rubbed her cheek against the soft fur. Kip paced on the opposite side, whittling away at his dragonwolf carving. Teddy had given them detailed instructions before they'd begun the first watch. He had inserted the pin to keep the wheel pointed true, but he instructed them to periodically check the course and adjust as needed. It was a straight shot for a few hours, so it should be pretty simple. Their main directive was to watch the waters. The slightest ripple could signal something sinister. Mara rubbed her hands together and breathed into them before turning and walking over to the bow. She should have worn her gloves.

"What are you thinking?" Kip asked, walking over, stopping next to Mara, and looking out in the same direction.

"I don't really know." Mara sighed. "I've only ever fought those spiders. I don't know if I'm ready for any of this." She glanced at the carving in Kip's hand. "I just want everyone to make it home." She finished.

Kip slid the carving into his pocket. "We won't. You know we won't. Not all of us."

"How did—"

"Your uncle told me before we left," he chuckled, "in case I wanted to change my mind."

"Of course he did." Mara hid her face in her hands.

Kip slid a little closer and nudged her side with his shoulder. "Hey now, it'll all work out as it's meant to. And this," he took the dragonwolf out of his pocket and handed it to her, "is getting back to Loli."

Mara traced the outline of one of the creature's wings, held it tight in her hand for a moment, and nodded. "Yes. It will." She handed the little dragonwolf back to Kip, who met her eyes with a reassuring smile.

Just then, there was a jolt, and the whole ship shook. Mara held on to the bulwark to keep from falling. "What *was* that?" she asked. Still holding on, she leaned over to peer into the water below. A piercing blue eye looked up at her from beneath. Frosty mist shot out of the sea.

"Where did that come from?" Kip shouted, stuffing the carving back in his coat.

"Blowhole," Mara whispered. "Blowhole! It's a winter whale!" No sooner had the shout left her lips then the whole ship shook again. The whale burst out of the water and hit the side of the ship, splintering some of the decorative pieces and splashing gallons of freezing water on the deck. "Go get Teddy!"

Kip nodded and rushed below deck to wake Teddy and Ashroot. Mara watched him go for a moment before grabbing an axe from the nearest cup. She glanced at a javelin, debating how an axe could possibly be as useful in this situation. As she looked, the whale burst out of the water a second time, so she turned and let her first axe fly.

The others made it up to the deck just in time to see the axe bury itself in the whale's side, just behind its left fin. "Back up NOW!" Teddy shouted.

Too late. Everything went black as Mara crumpled to the deck.

CHAPTER TWELVE

HERE THERE BE MONSTERS

When Mara woke later, she was tucked into her bunk. Her eyes fluttered open and took a few moments to focus. It was dark. She saw stars, and her head was aching.

"Ah, ah. Don't sit up."

Mara felt warm hands on her shoulders. She inhaled sharply and looked at the person with narrowed eyes.

"Oh, sorry. You got some frostbite there," Kip said sheepishly. He withdrew his hand. "You do still need to rest though."

"Mmm," she groaned. "What happened? Where's the whale? Is everyone okay?"

"Calm down, calm down." He laid a hand on her cheek this time to avoid her injury. "You hit it good, but the winter whale's defense mechanism is its frost. The axe shot back out and conked you on the head. The burst of frosty air got your neck and shoulder there." He gestured to her left shoulder where he'd touched before. "Luckily, you got it good and made it angry."

"Why is that lucky?" she scoffed.

"Well, it thrashed madly near the surface trying to get us with its frost, so Teddy and I were able to get it with our javelins. Just one good stab." Kip demonstrated a javelin jab. "He yanked me back right after. And ..."

"What? What happened?" Mara sat up quickly—too quickly—and fell back on the bed.

Kip's dark eyes met hers as he continued, "It exploded. This big burst of frost kicked the ship back and iced up the rudder. Ashroot and Teddy are chopping away at the ice to get us going again. Then Teddy is going to give us a thorough lesson about ice monsters so nothing like this happens again." He gestured to Mara's forehead and shoulder.

"Yeah, that'll be good." She grimaced and felt her shoulder. There was a bandage across her shoulder and the lower part of her neck on the left side. Feeling the padding, she noticed there was a little bit of give. She looked up at Kip and raised a brow.

He nodded. "Yes. Uh ... Teddy dug into your aunt's healing supplies and put some kind of red goo on the frostbite. He said that always helps."

"He would know," Mara replied. "Freya must have patched him up so many times ... he should be an expert."

They heard clomping on the steps, and Teddy appeared. "Well! She's alive!" He called with a grin.

Kip smiled sheepishly and withdrew his hand, standing and stepping away from her. "Yeah, I'm okay, Uncle Teddy," Mara replied. "I'm made of tough stuff."

"I guess so! Tough as the Oracle! Made from the strength of the Aeunna tree!" Teddy strode over to where Kip had been and sat on the edge of the bed, placing a hand on Mara's forehead and checking her bandages in turn. "How's this coming along?" he asked, gesturing the bandaged shoulder.

"Really well, it seems. I'll bounce back. When the next monster comes, I'll be ready."

"I have no doubt." Teddy patted her gently on the shoulder and stood. "I'm going to get Ashroot and see if we can't get some food in you."

Teddy nodded at Kip and headed wordlessly into the galley, leaving Mara and the gnome alone again. Kip stood awkwardly, hands at his sides, trying not to look at Mara. Mara, in turn, lie awkwardly looking at anything but Kip. Thankfully, it wasn't too long before Teddy returned, followed by an anxious Ashroot.

Ashroot rushed over to Mara's side with an assorted tray. Peanuts and anamberries, cubed cheese, some cubed meat, and a boiled egg. It reminded Mara of protein packs or snack packs she used to see in the store growing up. Ashroot really knew her stuff. She'd brought all the foods that were meant to sort Mara out and get her head together. She thanked her friend profusely and recounted her assessment of her injuries for the final time.

"Kip," Teddy called. "Why don't you and I head up to the deck and leave the ladies to it?" He gave Kip a pointed glance.

"Uh ... yes!" Kip followed Teddy up the steps and out of sight.

Ashroot sat on the bed next to Mara as the other two had done. Instead of poking at her injuries, however, Ashroot pushed her to eat. "Come on, Mara. You need to keep up your strength if you're going to be ready to fight next time. Eat some of this."

"Why don't you eat it with me?" Mara suggested, certain her friend was putting the others first and hadn't had much to eat herself.

"Okay, okay." Ashroot sighed.

She placed the tray on Mara's legs, and they both began to pick at the food. As usual, the meat was cooked to perfection, and the cheese was sharp and tasty. Mara had a little piece of each, savoring the emerald anamberry's taste. "It's so good, Ash. It's always so good when you make it."

"Thanks." Ashroot paused. "Though it seems like something else on this ship is more appetizing to you."

Mara's shock was clearly unconvincing. Ashroot gave her a playfully stern look. "You didn't see the way that boy was looking at you?" she asked.

Mara's face reddened. "He's still a stranger, Ash."

"Maybe, maybe—but he's a good person. And he likes you."

"He does?" Mara asked a little too quickly.

Ashroot laughed and tossed a peanut at her friend's nose. "Yes, he does! This is the first time he's left your side since you were hit. He kept swiping your hair back from your face and checking your bandages—"

"Okay, okay, I get it." Mara glared at her food.

"What's so bad about that?" Ashroot asked.

Mara ate a few more cheese cubes before responding slowly. "I just ... I don't know. I feel like he's just being nice to me because I saved his sister. I don't want that to cause his death. And ... well I don't want to get too close to him if he's just going to go back home when this is all over and he's done what he thought he had to do to repay me."

"So, you think he's just being nice to you to repay you for saving his sister?"

"I mean ... that makes the most sense, really."

"No—it doesn't." Ashroot took the tray away from Mara and put a paw under her friend's chin to make her look up. "Why do you think I came?"

Mara didn't reply.

"Answer honestly." Ashroot persisted.

"You wanted that recipe for your dad," Mara began. "And you said you wanted to come on an adventure for yourself . . ." She trailed off when Ashroot began shaking her head.

"I came with you because I believe in you. I wanted to help you because I knew I could. I may not be confident when it comes to fighting, but I can keep you all fed. I can support my friend."

Mara looked awkwardly at her hands. "Oh . . ."

"Kip would not have come on this journey—on a dangerous journey— unless he believed in you. He wouldn't leave the family you just saved if he didn't think he was going to make it back to them. He's a gnome. He wouldn't baby you or pretend to like you—that's not how his people are." The bearkin patted Mara's arm.

"Thanks, Ash."

"Maybe I'm reading some of it wrong," Ashroot conceded, "but even if he doesn't like you like I think, he does still like you. He's friendly and he seems to be bonding with you."

"Yeah."

"And you like him." Ashroot ventured.

Mara opened her mouth to respond just as they heard clomping on the stairs again. Ashroot slid the food tray back up on Mara's lap and resumed eating as Kip and Teddy came back downstairs. Mara and Kip sported the same red faces. The men came over, and Teddy informed them that the ship was set on course and would be set for some time. It was time for him to teach them how to avoid a repeat injury like Mara's. Kip went into the galley and brought in two chairs, one for him and one for Teddy. They all sat around Mara's bed, picking at her tray of food, while Teddy began to explain.

A few weeks later, Teddy and Ashroot roamed the deck, on watch while

Kip and Mara were supposed to rest. Kip had fallen into bed immediately, but Mara lie awake, staring up at the ceiling.

While Teddy had explained how they would survive the ice, Mara wished more than anything that she'd brought some type of journal. She thought about each creature in turn every night before she went to sleep, trying to memorize what Teddy had said. The monsters whose names began with winter exploded with wintry blast when injured. Just like the winter whale had burst frosty air at Mara, giving her frostbite and hitting her with her own axe, winter wolves would blast a wintry mix when injured.

Snowy monsters were actually created from the snow itself. The golem could appear out of nowhere, whisked up from harmless tundras. They were difficult to defeat because they were made of only snow. The only way to defeat the creature made completely of snow was to melt it, so—if they were unlucky enough to meet a golem—they would have to get the golem to the water so it would turn into a slushy puddle.

Frost monsters, like the giants, had armor of frost. Little ice crystals made their bodies a deathly blue. In order to injure them, they would have to pierce the armor. This is why the men had javelins—the javelin would drive through the frost and into its mark. Polar creatures, like the polar piranha, were the mildest of the ice monsters. They were white—to blend in with their surroundings—and they had powerful jaws with sharp teeth. The polar bears on Earth were likely named in this fashion.

The ice monsters were arguably the worst—and not just because one of them was the kraken. It was imperative to defeat them at a distance so they would be unable to use their frosty breath. Aside from this, the commonality with the ice monsters was their icy touch. The tentacles of the ice kraken would freeze whatever they touched. The water around the kraken turned to slush as it swam, and a swipe of the tentacle on the deck would leave an icy sheet where the tentacle had been—with a jagged edge out a foot or two wider than the tentacle itself. The ice goblins materialized icicle weapons. A cut from one of them would make Mara's current frostbite seem like nothing. In addition, their touch would leave an icy shell where their hand had been. On a person, this would be a frozen handprint. On the ground or other surfaces, the layer of ice would shoot out a foot or two like the tentacles of the kraken.

The touch was a force to be reckoned with. It could be deadly. Mara sighed and looked over at Kip's sleeping form. He lay on his right side across from Mara's bunk. In his left hand, he clutched the partially carved dragonwolf figure. His short, black hair was in laying every which way, with a little curl going slightly over his eye. His stony chin was obscured by a thick, black beard.

When he'd touched her face today, it was anything but icy—but was he interested in her? At sixteen, she was a bit behind in that department. Growing up, Sara had boyfriend after boyfriend, as early as fifth grade. Even Kara had a few boys interested in her the past couple years—but no one had ever shown interest in Mara. She had male friends—more male than female, really—but her friends had always been just friends. She was one of the guys. She was a weirdo more interested in dragons than dudes.

When she'd come to Ambergrove, it had been a miracle. She'd met family she'd never known. Family who loved her. She'd learned to fight, she'd spoken with the Oracle, and she'd proven herself. She was in the middle of a trial to determine if she was worthy to lead a community. She was on her way to see a goddess, to figure out if she was the one to help unite the world. She'd never really worried about romance. She'd never imagined that would be something to figure into her life.

She sighed again and looked at the carving. She liked Kip, and he seemed to like her. Without a doubt, she knew that carving had to make it back to Loli. Kip had to make it back there to give to him. She wasn't going to do anything to distract him from that goal.

"You'll see your uncle again, Loli." Mara whispered to the carving. "Both our uncles will make it home. Once we're all home … then I guess we'll see what this is." She rolled over and faced the walls, closing her eyes and hoping for sleep.

Ashroot's barefoot descent didn't leave the distinct clomping that the men's did, so Mara didn't hear her paws as she came below deck. Rushing over to Kip, she began to shake him awake, noticing a faint green glow in his carving fading as his eyes snapped open.

"W-what is it?" Kip asked Ashroot.

"Piranhas—a bunch of them."

Mara turned and sprung out of bed at these words. She and Kip rushed to add layers before heading up to the deck. Mara winced as she pulled layers across her injured shoulder, but she was ready. They all rushed upstairs to meet the moonlight.

The piranhas circled the ship. There were dozens of them, all nibbling at the hull. They were taking little chunks of *Harrgalti* with every bite.

"We'll need to work in teams!" Teddy commanded. "They're underwater, so our best option is to jab with the javelins." Teddy turned to Kip and instructed, "Don't throw. Stab as hard as you can and whip the piranha back on the deck."

"Yes, sir."

"Girls!"

"Yes?" Ashroot and Mara replied in unison.

"Grab two axes each. When we toss the piranhas onto the deck, chop at the eyes with one axe. Take the other into the body and sweep the carcass behind you to prepare for the next one. Understood?"

They both nodded.

"Do not turn your back on the piranha unless you are sure it's dead. It will ruin your legs and bleed you dry before you can blink." Teddy warned. "Okay. Kip—take that side with Ashroot. Mara—take this side with me."

As Teddy gestured Kip and Ashroot to the port side, he and Mara grabbed what they needed on the starboard side. Teddy nodded to Mara, who nodded back. He drove his javelin deep into the water. Mara could hear the grunt and splash on the other side of the ship as well. It had begun.

When Teddy flung a pearly white piranha in front of her, Mara barely had time to notice the wild eyes, large jaw, and jagged sharp teeth before it was her turn to act. She swept the right axe down toward an eye, but the piranha moved just as the axe came down. The blade glanced off the spiky upper jaw. It thrashed on the tip of the javelin.

"Get it, Mara!" Teddy shouted.

With a sharp breath, Mara brought the axe down again. This time, it hit its mark.

"Yes!" Teddy shouted again.

She chopped the left axe down and swept the piranha as far back as she could toward the center of the deck. She turned back to see Teddy had wasted no time stabbing down for the next piranha. He flung his javelin toward her again. Barely looking, she chopped at the eye and chopped at the body, discarding the piranha behind her near the other one. This process continued. Three piranhas, four, five, ten . . .

Mara heard a shout on behind her and turned in alarm. Kip had a piranha speared on the deck, and Ashroot was chopping at it with her axes, but her last piranha still flopped around. Its jaws snapped as it flopped nearer to her ankles. Locking eyes with Kip, Mara threw one of her axes across the deck. It buried itself through the piranha's jaw, pinning it to the deck. Kip nodded to Mara and she turned just as Teddy presented another piranha on her side.

"Good work," he called, reaching a hand behind him and tossing her another axe.

They continued for what seemed like hours, the men passing up and down the edge of the ship to hunt for more piranhas. Teddy hollered to Mara that their side was clear, so they moved to the port side and helped their companions. After a few more jabs, the piranhas all seemed to vanish. The companions peered at the water. Finally, all was still. Turning to the center of the ship, they found mounds of dead piranhas. With a sigh, Mara turned to Teddy.

Teddy grinned and grabbed two more javelins, handing them to the girls. "Spear as many as you can—like a kebab. When you can't get any more on your javelin, bring it to the side of the ship, stretch the tip over the edge, and pull your javelin back across the bulwark. If we peel them all off into the sea, other monsters will go for them and not us."

"Why can't we just grab them and throw them over?" Ashroot asked, stretching a paw toward the nearest piranha.

"STOP!" Teddy shouted. Ashroot froze. He strode over to her and pointed at the piranha carcass. There were hundreds of fine, clear spikes all over the body of the piranha. Truly every part of the fish would turn around and bite.

"Oh," Ashroot whispered, mutely stabbing the piranha with the javelin.

The cleanup proved to be just as much work as the fight. Many of the piranhas seemed to stubbornly stick to the javelins. Once the deck was finally clear, all four sighed in deep relief.

"Alright, everyone," Teddy began. "Let's all take a break before moving forward. Have something to eat. Sit and rest, and we'll reassess after lunch. Yes? Good job today."

Mara and Teddy stood in the galley, washing dishes. After they'd all worked so hard to fight the piranhas, Teddy said that Ashroot had done her part—making sandwiches for everyone after they finished cleaning up—and sent her for a nap. Kip headed back up to the deck to ensure they were still on the right course.

As the dishwashers left the galley, they saw Ashroot lying fast asleep in her bunk. Teddy tapped Mara's arm and pointed to the stairs leading to the deck. She nodded and climbed up to where Kip stood at the helm. Once they were far enough away from the stairs, Mara asked, "Shouldn't you be napping too, Uncle Teddy?"

"Yeah," Kip agreed, turning to them. "You've been up the longest of any of us."

Teddy put his hands up in surrender. "Okay, okay—I've just got one little instruction for you and I'll be heading down for my own little snooze."

"What's that?" Mara asked, walking over to the edge of the ship to check for piranhas.

"Come here," Teddy commanded, gesturing with his left hand and grabbing the map with his right.

Kip slid the bolt into the steering wheel so they would stay on course, and then he joined Teddy and Mara. Teddy looked around them and squinted at a sharp spire in the distance before kneeling on the deck and spreading out the map. Kip and Mara knelt on either side.

"That spire," Teddy gestured, "is here." He pointed at a peak on the map.

"Whoa," Mara and Kip whispered in unison.

"Yes. We've made it pretty far. We're most of the way past the Ice Mountains. There's just this little cove here and we're outside most of the danger. Trouble is ... this is where there have been the most sightings of the ice kraken." Teddy gestured to various markings on his map which indicated the kraken's presence.

"So," he continued, "I want you two to take watch now so I can rest. Don't give me more than a power nap—then we'll all need to be on deck and ready for the kraken."

"Understood," Kip told him.

"Yeah, we'll take care of it," Mara agreed.

"Good. Keep an eye on the map and keep scouting the horizon. If you notice anything, wake me up immediately. I'll leave you to it." Teddy nodded to each of them, handed Mara the map, and disappeared below deck.

Left alone, Kip and Mara fell silent. Mara stood with the map and strode to the bow. She peered up at the spire and looked back at the map as Teddy had done. Gazing around, she took in the icy coast on the starboard side. Far off in the distance, straight ahead, she could see a hint of green. She looked back at the map, and her face fell more and more with each tentacle marking she saw. Just the kraken and they'd have a straight shot to the sea elves.

Kip strode up behind her and laid his arm lightly over her shoulder before sliding his hand down to her side and squeezing her in a reassuring hug. She felt calmer for a moment. Reassured. Realizing where she was, she lightly shook him off and strode to the other side of the ship, babbling about needing to check all areas. She heard Kip's sigh as she walked away, and she suppressed a sigh herself.

Dutifully, they worked, not speaking. Kip patrolled the port side and Mara patrolled the starboard side, checking periodically through the water and their other surroundings. The sun had crossed halfway to the horizon before they'd noticed. Mara looked up and gasped. Based on the distance, it was probably nearing evening.

"We've waited too long," she told Kip. "I'm going to go down and wake Teddy."

Kip didn't answer. He stood still, staring out across the water.

"Kip, what is it?" she asked. When he still didn't answer, she walked over to him and looked out in the same direction. The water ahead seemed thick, almost slushy—No, it *was* slushy. About fifty feet away, Mara saw a tentacle whip across the water's surface, hitting an ice chunk. The contact blasted a bolt of ice around the floater and across the water.

Kip turned to Mara, his eyes full of what could only be fear. "Go now. Get Teddy and Ashroot. Quickly!"

She ran below without another word.

When Mara made it back to the deck, she saw Kip standing near the bow, javelin in hand. Teddy came up a few steps behind her, followed by Ashroot. Before his feet touched the deck, Teddy began barking orders.

"Mara, head over there and grab some axes. Be sure to strike true!" Mara ran over to the port side of the deck and grabbed two axes. Before she could more than open her mouth, Teddy shouted, "Sparingly! Make every toss count!"

"Ashroot!" Teddy turned and looked into the bearkin's frightened eyes. "Go to that side and get the daggers from those cups." He pointed to the starboard side. "You have to use them on your own. This side is your responsibility. You can do this. Protect yourself and us. Fight!"

At his call to arms, the ship rumbled with the force of a deep growl. Teddy ran to the back of the ship and grabbed a javelin. The ship lurched and shuddered. Mara peered into the water to see a blue grey tentacle slam into the side of the ship, leaving jagged, icy spikes in its wake. She pulled back just in time to miss the jagged spikes shooting up in front of her, and then she quickly chopped the ice away and stepped back.

"It's the kraken!" Teddy shouted, unnecessarily. "Get the tentacles as they come, but focus on the eyes—a few good stabs deep in the face and we can beat it!"

As Teddy commanded, two tentacles shot into the sky on either side of the ship and slammed down on the deck. They could see a glow creep up the creature's throat beneath the water. Just the two tentacles immediately turned half of the deck to a sheet of ice. Kip swore and jabbed at the deck with his javelin. His feet had been frozen to the surface.

As Kip was distracted by his feet, another tentacle came up at the bow, just over his head. Mara had turned her head when she heard Kip's shout, so she saw the tentacle rising above him. Kip did not. Mara threw an axe as hard as she could in Kip's direction. He looked up in time to see the axe blade slice through the tentacle, leaving the tip hanging on by a sliver of skin.

Mara turned back to her side of the ship, careful not to make the same mistake as Kip. When she turned, she saw another ship out in the open water. The ship itself was blue, nearly blending in with the waters below. She'd seen the seaglass-green sails and a dozen figures running around on the deck before she'd seen the ship itself.

"Teddy! Ship to port!" she shouted.

Teddy turned and saw the blue ship gliding past them across the water. "Sea elves!"

"Great! They'll help us!" Mara cheered.

There was a commotion on the sea elves' deck. Mara could hear shouting in the distance and see many of the figures disappear. Her face fell as the ship sailed further away from them, safely distancing the elves from the kraken.

"If it's attacking us, that guarantees them safe passage. They won't help other sailors because they believe everyone should be able to hold their own at sea," Teddy explained, jabbing a tentacle in front of him. The javelin went clean through the tentacle. When the beast roared and pulled the tentacle back, the javelin hit the edge of the ship and snapped, ripping the tentacle in two.

With a louder roar of anger, two tentacles shot up again, tangled in the rigging, and pulled the sail down to a frozen heap on the deck. Throwing caution to the wind, Mara ran over to the tentacles on the deck and chopped vigorously with her axes, hacking both tentacles clean through.

Having now lost the tips of four tentacles, the kraken roared again and disappeared for a few seconds before bursting full force at the stern. This time, they saw its piercing blue eyes and jagged gaping hole of a mouth as it pulled its body up onto the back half of the ship and twisted its remaining tentacles up the sides.

"To me!" Teddy shouted. Kip, Mara, and Ashroot ran up behind Teddy. "As one!" he ordered. "Now!"

Kip rushed forward, and he and Teddy thrust their javelins through the beast's mouth. With a sharp grunt, Teddy drove his still further—so it burst out the back of the monster's head. Ashroot threw both daggers, and they buried one right after the other deep into one of the icy blue eyes. With a shout, Mara threw her right axe at the same eye, opening a deep gash. She threw her other axe in the same motion, and it drove the first further into the beast's brain.

It screeched and flailed, falling back into the water. Grabbing two more axes, Mara leaned over the edge of the ship to see the piercing eyes dim and the body sink into the deep. Teddy peered into the water, Kip following close behind. They heard cheering in the distance from the elven ship. Kip hooted and hugged Mara. Teddy triumphantly beat a hand on the bulwark and shouted.

"W-we did it?" a timid voice asked behind them.

Teddy turned to Ashroot, rushed to her, picked her up, and twirled her around in the air a few times like a father would a small child, before setting her back gently on the deck. "Yes!" he told her. "Yes, Ash, we killed the kraken! *You* killed the kraken! Two perfectly thrown blades right to the eye!"

Teddy let her go and turned around to Kip. "And you! Perfect jab straight to the brain. Well done!" Kip and Teddy clasped arms in a respectful shake.

"And our dragonwolf! The killing blow! Well done! Well done, all!" Teddy cheered, giving his niece a peck on the forehead and playfully rubbing his beard in her face.

Mara grinned—Kip still had one arm around her. They had defeated the mighty ice kraken. *Them.* Who could believe it? Her face fell as she took in the wreckage around her. Their ship had been trashed. It wasn't moving—nor would it, with the frozen sections and the destroyed sail. They may have defeated the kraken, but like that sinking beast, they were all dead in the water.

CHAPTER THIRTEEN

SEA ELVES

Wrapped in all the layers Teddy had prepared for them, Mara and Kip sat on little rafts on either side of *Harrgalti*. Mara was taking a hammer and chisel to the hull of the ship. The icy spears shooting out all over would prevent the ship from sailing true. Teddy had tasked Mara with picking away at the ice on the starboard side while Kip took the port side. An angry grunt and a clatter told Mara that Kip had missed the chisel and hit his hand—again—and thrown the hammer back onto his raft.

Mara chuckled quietly and hammered again at a particularly stubborn chunk of ice. As she laughed at Kip's misstep, she brought the hammer down hard on her left thumb. She swore and chucked the tools back onto her raft.

"That's what you get!" Kip called from the other side with a sharp laugh.

"Yeah, yeah—but I did it once. How many bruises do you have, big man?" Mara hollered back.

"Hey! Kids!" Teddy called from the deck. "Try not to yell all day and draw monsters to us again, would you?"

"Yes, Teddy!" Kip replied.

"Sorry, Teddy!" Mara replied.

This was their second day ashore. On the first day, they'd had to drop everything and fight a pack of winter wolves because Kip and Mara had been laughing and running around on the deck while unhitching the rigging for the sails—whipping at each other with the ropes and flapping the sails. They'd heard the rasping, frosty howls before they'd seen the wolves. The good thing about that situation was that they had all still been on the ship

137

with weapons. A few well-tossed javelins by Teddy and Kip, just as the pack filtered into view, and the whole pack had been defeated. The wintry blasts were no threat at that distance—but Teddy had wasted no time scolding them and telling them how they'd gotten off easy.

Mara wrung her hands and stared ruefully at her thumb. Although she was wearing lined gloves, she was sure her thumb was already blackening underneath. She picked up her hammer again and continued chiseling away at the ice. Teddy was on the deck with a hammer, nails, a handsaw, and a few other tools. He was repairing the actual structure of the deck. They wouldn't know about the hull until the ice had all been picked away, but Teddy already had his work cut out for him.

Ashroot was Teddy's occasional helper as he nailed boards back into place, replaced others, shaved down splintered sections, and restrung some of the rigging. When Teddy didn't need Ashroot's help, she was sewing. The sail had been thoroughly ripped to shreds by the kraken. After they'd determined that only Ashroot knew how to sew effectively, Teddy had pulled a collection of different colored canvas sheets out of the storeroom and tasked her with repairing the sail before they continued on their journey.

It was grueling work, and it took over a week before they had repaired the ship at least well enough to sail to the sea elves. There were a few minor issues with the hull, but there wasn't anything they could do to repair that stranded in the frozen south. They'd seen a couple snow golems in the middle distance and a frost giant in the far distance. They'd been safe from those, luckily, though they did have to fight some ice goblins in the middle of the night on the third night, and a polar bear on the sixth day.

Ashroot was conflicted about fighting a bear, but the polar bear had been volatile. Mara, Teddy, and Ashroot had all tried to talk to him, but he had been insulted by Ashroot working with humans and was angered that they had spoken as an equals. Out of respect for Ashroot, rather than keep the meat and pelt, which would sustain them for a large part of the journey and provide warmth or valuable trade, Teddy had dragged the polar bear off into the distant woods, with Kip's help, before getting back to work. Once Mara and Kip had cleaned up the hull, they'd helped Teddy on deck so Ashroot could focus on the sail. Once Teddy had determined they had done all they could, all four of them worked to raise the sail.

Although Ashroot had worked tirelessly for a full week to complete the sail, she did not want them to sail to the sea elves with a patchy mess to show their way. Her sail was beautiful—especially for the time she'd had to work. She had spliced the new material together into chevron patterns. She'd cut the blocks into strips so she could get the shapes she'd wanted, using cream, brown, and green, but she hadn't had enough material to complete a new sail—nor did she want to throw out the old one.

At the center of the sail, Ashroot had used the blue material shredded by the kraken to pay homage to its destruction. The sail had a simple kraken silhouette sewn in the original material over the new chevrons, and the tentacles were creatively placed so they could use the most material effectively. They had been able to defeat the kraken. When the elves had run, when others had lost their lives in the attempt, this small group, who had no business facing a beast of that caliber, had slayed the kraken.

"Great job, Ashroot," Teddy crooned.

"It's perfect!" Mara squealed, looking up at the softly rippling beast.

Kip squinted up at it for a second before bursting into laughter. The others turned to him, Ashroot affronted. "Imagine," he choked. "J-just imagine the look on the sea elves' faces when we sail to their island with this up!"

Ashroot and Mara grinned at each other as Teddy offered, "The crew that saw us slay it will have trouble missing our triumphant banner!"

Mara had always thought group hugs were something stupid that only happened in feel-good movies, but just then, all she wanted to do was hug that group. Teddy read the look on her face, reaching an arm out. Mara grinned and hugged her uncle before opening her arm to Kip. Kip wasted no time closing the circle, hugging Mara and Ashroot.

Teddy looked around the circle at each of them before nodding to Mara. "Anything you feel like saying, lass?" he asked his niece.

"Um …" Mara thought for a moment, her face going beet red. "Just … we've made it so far already. We've done things no one else has ever been able to do. There's a fight ahead of us—with the elves and with the Dragon's Teeth—but this is the crew I want by my side. Any bearkin that can face a kraken can face any other terror any day." Mara grinned at Ashroot across the circle.

"Thanks, Mara," Ashroot whispered.

Mara turned to her uncle. "We wouldn't have made it without you. You prepared us by teaching us about the things we would face here, preparing the equipment we would need, and leading in a way I hope I can one day. You got us here. You led us to fix the ship. You'll lead us through and get us home."

Teddy smiled at her. "Well, it is your job to lead us through and get us home, but I will always guide you in any way I can and try to bestow the wisdom that only comes with age and experience."

Mara laughed and shared a loving look with her uncle. She glanced at the cuff on her wrist, which rested on Kip's shoulder. She could never have imagined having a bond like this with anyone other than her merry father. Uncle Teddy had been a blessing. With a deep sigh, Mara turned to Kip. "Where to start?" Her face reddened still further. "These two have known me for months. Ash is my best friend. Teddy is my family. You came along knowing little about me. You believed in me—and in us—before the journey began. You're risking so much for a cause that isn't yours. It means so much to have your help. Thank you." The more she talked, the more she avoided Kip's eyes, lowering them finally to the deck. She felt Kip squeeze her side tightly, but neither of them said another word. It was Teddy who broke the silence.

"Alright, adventurers, shall we set sail for the sea elves?" he asked.

Mara looked up and they all nodded to each other, squeezed the hug tighter briefly, and prepared to set sail once more.

They sailed for over a month without incident. The stretch from the Ice Mountains to the sea elves was a long one, but it was also relatively safe. Once they entered the area between the mainland and another, Mara was concerned about what dangers lurked in the distance. Teddy's map had it labeled as Fengel, but there was no sort of indication as to who—or what— lived there. She could hear roaring and see bursts of flame. However, the land came around in a jagged dome, so she couldn't see much more than figures. Ashroot was below in the galley, preparing their lunch. This was good, because Mara knew if the roaring unnerved her, it would terrify the bearkin.

Kip was below deck, napping in his bunk because he'd had final watch the night before. Teddy stood at the helm. Mara made her way over to him, glancing uneasily in the direction of the roaring.

"Teddy?" Mara began.

"Yes, those are dragons," he replied, not turning.

Mara spun around in front of him. holding the wheel between them. "Um ... excuse me?" she asked, eyes wild.

Teddy chuckled and hung his arms across the wheel, sighing and looking into Mara's eyes.

"Oh, dragons, whatever," Mara mocked, flailing her arms and making a face at Teddy.

"In this case—yes!" her uncle mused. Seeing the exasperated look on Mara's face, he continued, "Okay, okay. That over there is where all the bad dragons live."

Mara's eyes widened and darted in the direction of the dragon fire. "Wh—"

"It's okay!" Teddy said quickly. "They're trapped there—so they cannot harm anyone. Remember that story we heard while we stayed at Port Albatross?"

"Yeah ..." Mara remembered it had something to do with dragons and that it was really well told, but that was it.

"The good dragons live in the north, near the Dragon's Teeth. They fought the other dragons ages ago and, with the help of the gods, banished them to this land." He gestured to the domed mass spanning the horizon, continuing, "The gods and goddesses worked together to trap the dragons and contain them in this land. They cannot leave here as long as they bear ill will toward beings outside. Salali didn't completely finish that story. The good dragons are free, though they remain near their land by choice. These dragons are bound by magic. That's why we call it Fengel—that means prison. Until the magic is lifted, no one will ever see a pointy-horned dragon up close. They can do no harm here."

"Oh. Well ... that's good then," Mara muttered, relinquishing her arms, but leaving her eye on the dome. Teddy laughed again and reassured her.

Mara wondered if part of bringing everyone back together meant the dragons too. She hoped not—that would be a little much. She retreated into her own thoughts until lunchtime, when Teddy rolled his map out again to show them where they were headed. The lands of the sea elves included four different islands. There were three rounded blobs on the southern side of the cluster with a large island shaped like a sea monster curled around them.

"The sea elves tell that the islands are sacred for that reason," Teddy explained. "They believe they are the protectors of a giant sea creature. This grants them the rule over the seas and gives them their expertise with the water. They believe they are worthy of the island and the sea when no one else is."

Mara nodded. "That makes sense."

"So, what's going to be the first challenge here?" Kip asked.

Teddy sighed. "First will be nearing the island. This is where the queen rests," he pointed to the mouth of the sea monster shape and continued, "so we will need to come across the back here and gain permission to dock near the top of the spine."

Teddy drug a finger across the map to indicate a path between the mainland and the sea elves' lands, up to the base of what would be the sea monster's skull. "At any point, we could be surrounded by elven ships. Unless we effectively prove our worth, they will not let us set foot on any of their lands. Only the worthy may pass."

"What if we're not worthy?" Ashroot whispered.

Teddy paused for a moment, then replied, "They will turn us away or they will kill us—depending on just how unworthy we are. The thing to keep in mind is that they most greatly value courage. Keep your chin up and don't let them see your fear."

Mara squeezed Ashroot's shoulder, and they shared a reassuring grin before turning to Teddy for the rest of his explanation. Before long, the whole crew was up on the deck, watching and waiting. It had warmed significantly as they neared the islands, so they shucked off their warm layers and stowed them back away in the storeroom. Teddy had instructed them all to wear their armor, so they would appear more like worthy warriors—and so they would be prepared to fight if they needed to.

Weapons were stowed below deck. All the weapons they had stationed around the deck had been left, as those were meant for fighting monsters. The weapons they'd brought on the journey would make them seem disrespectfully threatening to the elves, so they would have to make do with javelins and throwing weapons to defend themselves if the elves attacked.

A few weeks later, they'd made their way halfway up the islands when two elven ships appeared out of nowhere. The blue hulls and sea-colored sails popped into view within seconds, and Mara realized what had made the sea elves so revered as sailors. They were good—but it surely helped that their ships blended in with the sea. Everyone on *Harrgalti* gathered at the helm as Teddy had instructed.

The elven ships closed in on either side of *Harrgalti*. The crews lined the edges of their ships closest to the intruders. With a lurch, Mara noticed they all carried sharp spears like harpoons. Like the ships, the elves themselves were all the colors of the sea. That seemed to be common of all the races here. Teddy had green skin like the trees, Kip had brown skin like the earth, and the elves had varying shades of greens and blues—seafoam green, ocean blue, seaweed green, ocean mist blue. Their hair complimented their skin, also in varying sea greens and blues—but what stood out the most to Mara was how fierce they looked.

"State your business!" a huge, muscular, male sea elf commanded.

Mara stepped forward. Teddy had coached her for this moment. She was the one who needed to be here. She was the one who needed to convince them. Hands clenched tightly behind her back and head held high, she began, "My name is Mara. I am completing my Ranger trial. On the course of my journey, I am to prove my worth to the masters of the seas so I may have a volunteer to help me through the Dragon's Teeth. I've been told that's something only your esteemed kind is capable of."

The elf glared at her, surveying the ship. He scoffed. "Clearly, you are in need of assistance. The state of your ship is disgraceful." The sea elves on both ships began rhythmically pounding the butts of their harpoons on the deck.

Mara saw Ashroot flinch out of the corner of her eye. With a deep breath, she continued, "We've just sailed past the Ice Mountains. We faced the mighty ice kraken and defeated it. We—" Mara was cut off by angry shouts. She tried to speak over them but was drowned out. The big elf sharply raised a fist, commanding silence—it was as if a switch had turned off.

"Your story will be investigated. You may pass and dock on the Queen's Crown. The queen will see you for judgement when you arrive." The big elf pounded his spear three times on the deck and turned away. The other elves pounded their spears three times in response, and then they sailed off without a word.

The port was much different than Port Albatross. The Queen's Crown was the head of the sea monster shape—where a crown would have been. The docks were made of stone and covered in algae. All the buildings were made of stone, covered in algae, with seaweed thatch. All except for one building in the distance, near what Mara suspected was the sea monster's mouth. There, Mara could see a castle made of what she could only describe as sea-worn glass. It was a beautiful green, with towers and parapets like a classic castle. High over the center spire, there was a coral colored flag, but Mara couldn't make out the shape that was on it.

Leaving their weapons on the ship, and taking only the essentials, Mara and her companions stepped off onto the dock. They were surrounded by gruff sea elves with spears and were marched silently up toward the seaglass castle. As they walked, Mara took in all that was around her. The sea elves were clearly a marine-centered society. All buildings and decorations were made of objects from the sea.

Looking around at the soldiers, Mara could also see sea elements in their garments. The people themselves were naturally colors of the sea. Beyond that, they wore spiked knee-high boots that appeared to be made of fish scales. Rather than pants, they wore strange, tight shorts. The material glistened—reminding Mara of something surfers or scuba divers would wear. Around their torsos, they wore tunics of brightly colored chainmail. From watching a blacksmith at a festival, Mara realized the effect of blues and purples in the metal was achieved by scorching in the forge. There appeared to be something like swim shirts underneath. Looped into the shoulder of the chainmail were large shells that were used like shoulder pads. Most of the elves had long hair, partially knotted or braided to pull it back out of their faces. Some of them had pulled the small knots or braids into a large, high ponytail. Some had just left them loose.

Blinking at the light glinting off the surface, Mara squinted up at the castle. She hadn't realized how far they'd walked. It seemed as though they had just begun, but they were already at the entrance to the queen's castle. Mara could see now that the figure on the coral flag was a sea monster. Fitting. They passed under a high arch and followed a flight of stairs into the castle. Down a few twisting hallways, they stopped in front of two burly guards in front of a coral colored door. When they arrived, the guards pounded their spears on the ground three times and opened the door.

They stepped into a large hall—a classic throne room. Sitting on a magnificent sea throne was a beautiful blue elf with coral pink hair matching the other coral Mara had seen. Her hair was braided and curled, looping around a yellow coral crown. There were guards on either side of the throne. Behind the throne, a woman stood on the left. She had seafoam green skin and short, spiked, deep blue hair. One hand was on her sword's hilt. To the right of the throne was a young man with blue skin and bright green hair.

The soldiers led the group up to the foot of the throne and dispersed to line the hall. Teddy stepped forward and kneeled respectfully. Following his example, Mara, Kip, and Ashroot stepped forward in a line next to Teddy and lowered to one knee. The queen grinned. Ashroot shuddered quietly, seeing the queen's teeth were sharp and pointed like a shark's. Thankfully, the queen didn't notice.

"Dwarf," she boomed, looking at Teddy. "Who is your leader?"

Teddy gestured to Mara. "This is Mara, who is completing her trial to be the Ranger of Aeunna."

The queen raised a hand. "That's enough—I don't need your family history." She turned to Mara. "Why do you raise the kraken as your ship's banner?"

"We defeated the ice kraken in the south on our way to your islands." Some of the guards growled as Mara spoke.

The queen raised a hand again, and all was silent. She glared at Mara. "A claim like that could lose you your head in my kingdom, did you know?"

Mara withered a little, but answered clearly, "Respectfully, ma'am, it's only a claim if it isn't true."

The queen's eyes flashed. Teddy sighed softly.

"Hmm ..." The queen assessed each of them in turn. "It so happens, you are the only crew who may not lose their heads for such a *claim.*" She locked eyes with Mara for a moment before gesturing to the man behind her. "It so happens, my son witnessed your battle with the ice kraken—and made quite a fool of himself at the sight." She turned and raised an eyebrow, glaring at her son in disappointment.

Mara looked at the man and realized she'd seen him—or someone who looked like him. Right when she'd seen the sea elves' ship, there had been a commotion on the deck, and a man had been dragged off. What had he done?

"Since your story bears some truth," the queen continued, "I will reserve judgement until this evening. My shipsmith will assess the damage to your ship and the guards will take you to our visitor's inn. You will be allowed to take the day to roam around this island—with a guard of course. Once we have completed our evening meal, your guards will bring you back to this hall and you will receive my judgement." The queen waved a hand. They had been dismissed.

Rising, the group quietly followed the guards out of the castle and toward the inn. Ashroot breathed a sigh of relief, but Mara's brow furrowed. They'd survived docking, they'd survived the first audience with the queen, but this judgement surely wouldn't be good. The matching look on Teddy's face told Mara there was much still to worry about.

As they approached the only inn, likely in the entire sea elf kingdom, Mara cracked a smile. This was no Pleasant Mariner. This inn was called The Skewered Shark—fittingly with a gutted, harpooned shark on the sign. The interior was less welcoming. It was clear this inn was meant to keep even those deemed worthy enough to be on the sea elves' island uneasy and alert. The decorations were mainly blood red. There were various carcasses hanging on the walls—squid, piranha, some kind of many-toothed eel, and yes, a giant shark. Additionally, there were shrunken heads hanging in the doorways and a few heads in jars.

The barkeep was a muscular, blue woman with blue hair so dark it was nearly black, with a yellow stripe up the side like a poisonous sea creature. She wore a necklace of shark teeth and bore scars on all her body they could see—to the point she had an eye patch covering part of a deep scar across her right eye. She'd been cleaning a meat cleaver, Mara suspected as an intimidation tactic rather than because the blade needed cleaning. As they drew closer, the woman stomped out from behind the counter and looked them over.

"I've seen worse come through here … but they didn't leave." She chopped with the cleaver and drove it into the top of the counter. "We'll see about you. The rooms upstairs are all empty—we don't get many visitors. Pick whichever you like, take care of it, and leave it as you found it. Supper will be ready at sundown. Understood?"

There were various murmurs of agreement. The woman nodded curtly at them, yanked the cleaver back out of the counter, and disappeared into the kitchen behind it. They made their way upstairs to find the decorations in the rooms much like those downstairs. There was a reddish hue to each room, jagged bones for decoration, and some many-toothed carcass hanging on the wall.

"Cozy," Mara muttered, closing the door quickly and heading back downstairs.

The others followed soon after. Mara had wondered what was supposed to happen with the guards. Would they have to ask someone to accompany them each time they wanted to leave? Could they only leave when there were guards present? Would the guards take them out for walks like pets? This was all answered when Mara reached the foot of the stairs. Four guards sat around a table, waiting. As soon as Mara appeared, they all stood at attention and grabbed their spears.

"Um … hello," Mara began nervously. "Were you going to take us around the town?"

"That is correct." The largest of them grunted. "Once your companions arrive, we will depart."

Mara turned away back toward the stairs, exhaling exasperatedly and widening her eyes in frustration. Kip came down the stairs right at that moment and, seeing her face, laughed one short "ha." Teddy came down right after, followed by Ashroot. They didn't have time to discuss why Mara had been making a face or what exactly they were going to do or see, because as soon as the last person hit the bottom of the stairs, the guards approached.

"Come with us. We will take you around the docks." One of the soldiers opened the door and beckoned as he spoke.

With a sideways glance at Teddy, Mara followed the guard out the door. It seemed one guard was there for each of them. They couldn't go through the door as a group. A guard went through, Mara followed, a guard went through, Kip followed, guard, Ashroot, guard, Teddy—and a guard who'd been standing outside brought up the rear. They wouldn't be able to talk to each other on their little tour, and it seemed more and more that the opportunity to look around with an escort was really meant to be to keep them apart so they couldn't conspire together. They were being monitored.

Determined to learn all she could—and to at least keep up some small talk for what would otherwise be a miserable afternoon—Mara ventured a question. "I thought the queen would introduce herself or someone would announce her when we arrived, but no one mentioned it. Does she have a name or another title or anything?"

"Ula," said the guard in front of her.

Whether that was a name, a title, an insult, or all of the above, she didn't know. The guard didn't offer any further explanation. They walked in silence for a while, just looking around. There were fish stalls, there were three blacksmiths, two armorers, and a miscellany.

"Could we go in here?" Mara asked as they came up to the miscellany.

"This one?" the soldier asked, pointing at the shop. "Yes, this one you may enter."

So we aren't allowed near the armor or weapons? Okay. The guard led Mara into the shop and the line followed. The shop was magical. There were little trinkets made from shells, seaglass, teeth, and dried plants. There were cuffs and books made from shark skin. Mara picked up one of the shark skin books and opened it. It was a history of the sea elves, written by Marlin the Marauder. Intrigued, Mara took the book up to the shopkeep.

It was the kindest-looking elf Mara had seen to that point—a shorter, stooped man, whose olive-colored skin was leathery and whose hair had gone white with age. He stretched out a wrinkled hand and smiled at her toothily. "Could you tell me how much this is?" Mara asked.

She handed the book to the shopkeep, who smiled good-naturedly and murmured, "Good choice!"

The guard appeared behind her and asked the shopkeep what Mara had given him. Looking at the book, he shook his head at Mara. His face deepened and he seemed angry. "This is not for you, human. You are not going to come here and steal our secrets. This tour is over," he barked at her, handing the book back to the shopkeep and gesturing toward the door.

Mara turned and thanked the old man for his help before following the guard back out to the street. They all followed the guards back to the inn like baby ducklings.

Supper in the Skewered Shark was surprisingly good. Stereotypically, there were eyeballs in the stew, but the stew itself was tasty. Mara just plopped her eyeball into Teddy's bowl. With their guards hovering even over their meal, not eating anything themselves, the group didn't have much opportunity for conversation. They quietly ate their stew, exchanging various glances.

Halfway through their meal, another guard entered the inn. He murmured something to the guard standing by the door and left without another word. The guard nodded to the others, who stood.

"Time to go?" Mara asked, with a slight edge in her voice.

"The queen is ready to cast judgement," the nearest guard said. "Leave your food here and make your way up to the castle."

CHAPTER FOURTEEN

THE FINAL ADVISER

They entered the throne room to find the same sight as before. The queen sat regally on her throne, the female elf stood stoically to the left, and the queen's son stood to the right, but this time, he had his hands clenched and looked distressed. This time, Mara stepped forward and knelt in front of the queen. Teddy beckoned for the others to hang back, so they knelt in a line behind Mara.

"Human," began the queen, in a booming voice. "We have inspected your ship and reviewed your story."

Mara's brows furrowed. She hadn't realized that part of assessing the damage to the ship was for the guards to root through it. They had been dragged around town, unable to really look at anything or talk to each other, because this queen had wanted to dig into their lives. She exhaled slowly and forced her face to soften.

"You have been through the Ice Mountains and the damage to your ship is consistent with the ice kraken's might. My son—and the crew of the ship he was on—confirmed they saw you fighting the kraken and that they saw it slain." The queen paused for a moment as Mara nodded, then continued, "You wanted to come here to get someone to help you on your trial. You cannot complete your task without the aid of the sea kingdom, but we will require you to further prove yourself before giving you the aid you so desperately need."

It wasn't Mara to get frustrated at these words. Kip swore softly behind her, Ashroot growled, and Teddy bumped them both for quiet. No one had been so conceited about the need for their help—even Chief Sokti, though cold and gruff, hadn't been rude. The queen was right though. She couldn't complete her trial without the help of the sea elves.

The queen glared at Mara's companions for a moment before continuing. "In order to earn our expertise, you have to prove that you possess the courage we prize. Tomorrow, you must prove yourself to us beyond all doubt. . . . In the morning, you will be summoned for the Serpent's Gauntlet."

The queen's son sighed sharply and crossed his arms.

"Enough, Finn!" the queen shouted, clutching the arms of her throne and glaring at the floor. "Candiru! Get him out of here."

"Yes, Queen Ula," the scary woman to the left of the queen replied, stepping forward and leading Finn out of the hall.

The queen sighed and drummed her fingers on the arms of her throne for a moment before continuing, "The Serpent's Gauntlet will test you according to the standards of my people. You will complete a series of physical tests to determine your skill, your resilience, and your courage. If you complete the gauntlet, your final test will be to defeat my champion."

Mara looked around at the guards that surrounded her, wondering which one of them was the champion. There was a harsh, cold laugh in front of her. "No!" the queen exclaimed. "None of these soldiers is my worthy champion—only Candiru has that honor. If you are able to complete my gauntlet tomorrow and defeat Candiru in battle, you will have earned the right to remain on our island and I will allow someone to accompany you to complete your trial."

Mara nodded. "Thank you for the opportunity." She couldn't think of anything else to say. She was wracking her brain trying to figure out what she was going to do, thinking about what the gauntlet would entail, and wishing she was somewhere else so she could just talk to Teddy.

"You know the way back to the inn. My guards will remain here. You will be allowed to roam this island as you desire, but your ship must remain docked until you have faced the gauntlet." The queen waved a hand to dismiss them as before.

Mara stood and turned. Her companions stood staring at her for a moment before Teddy wrapped an arm around her and they all headed out into the night.

The castle gates closed behind them with a loud clang. Mara stood still for a moment, fists clenched, staring at the ground. Looking down at the lights on the ships in the distance, and a few of the lights in the shops still open, Mara suddenly shook her head and broke into a run. She faintly heard Teddy behind her saying, "No, lad. Let her go." She ran down past the stalls, past a slew of alarmed sea elves, until she saw the miscellany.

Mara halted in the doorway, panting and trying to slow her breathing before stepping into the shop. The kind, old shopkeep stood behind the counter and smiled at her as she came in. "Ah, back again so soon?" he asked.

"Um, yes, I was wondering if I could buy that book from you that I was looking at earlier today."

The old man's face fell. "Sorry miss, but that's no longer available."

"N— Wh— Because the guard said no? I'm allowed out and stuff now, so if that's why ..."

"It isn't. I'm sorry, but someone came and got that book soon after you left the shop." He paused for a moment, seeing the dejected look on Mara's face. "Uh ... but it is special that you were able to prove yourself enough to our queen to stay the night here, so ... I have this for you."

The old man disappeared into a back room and came back with a chainmail shirt. He held it out to her. It was pretty rusted, but underneath Mara could see the bluish coloring of the sea elf mail. It would be a little big on her, but that was just fine when it came to chainmail.

"W-what?" She held out a hand to touch the metal.

"Take it," he told her, laughing at the disbelieving look on her face.

"I don't have enough to pay or trade for this," she told him, pulling her hand back.

"That's okay—because I can't sell this anyway."

"Wait, what?"

"Yes, I am a miscellany. I'm not permitted to sell armor. This is my old mail from my younger days. As I'm a little older now, you can see it hasn't gotten much use. If you're going to be standing up to the queen, you'll need some mail. This will help you." He smiled at her kindly and jingled the shirt.

Mara sheepishly accepted the mail. "Thank you. Thank you so much. I don't even ..."

"Don't worry about it, young lady. Complete your quest—and don't get any holes poked in you. Now why don't you head back to the inn? You might find a visitor waiting for you there." The old man winked at her and turned around, heading back into the back room again.

Mara clutched the chainmail in both hands and rushed back out of the shop, barreling right into Teddy.

"Oof. Hey there. Where's the fire?" Teddy asked, a little winded.

"I ... I needed my person to ask questions. I wasn't sure who I could ask here without them yelling at me, so I wanted to get that book I saw in the shop earlier today."

"That's not a book." Teddy grinned, pointing down at the chainmail.

"No, uh, the shopkeep gave it to me."

"Well then ..." Teddy clapped her on the shoulder and turned with her to head back to the inn. "You didn't leave with nothing at least."

"No, I didn't." Mara clutched the mail shirt and allowed Teddy to steer her toward the inn, where their other companions stood waiting.

They headed up to Mara's room, wanting privacy before they began discussing the day's events. Ashroot lead them up the stairs and opened the door, letting out a frightened squeak as she looked inside. Sitting on the floor, with the history book from the miscellany in his lap, was Finn.

"Hello there." He grinned, greeting them. Mara was glad to see he didn't inherit his mother's shark teeth.

"Can we help you with something?" Kip asked, an edge to his tone.

Finn's smile faded. "Uh, yes, um ..." He scrambled up, holding the book. After an awkward moment, staring at the wall of outsiders who were not looking welcoming, he offered the book to Mara.

"Wait, you're the one who bought that from the miscellany?" Mara asked. She didn't move to accept the gift.

"Yes, I ... I was following the guards when they were taking you around the shops. I wanted to make sure you weren't mistreated—"

"Hah!" Kip scoffed, flailing his arms in exasperation.

Finn glanced a Kip and fumbled for a moment. "I ... uh ... I saw that you were interested in this, and the guards wouldn't let you get it, so I got it for you. I thought it could help you out while you're here. I thought *I* could ... help you out ..." Finn looked down at his hands.

Kip and Ashroot both scoffed this time. Kip crossed his arms and glared at Finn. Ashroot growled. Mara turned and assessed them both. "Kip, Ash, could you leave us for a minute?" she asked.

Kip raised his eyebrows but shrugged and left without a word. Ashroot followed and shut the door behind her. Teddy backed up to the corner of the room and crossed his arms, watching. Mara paced back and forth for a moment, not looking at either of them. She sighed deeply before looking at Finn—who seemed terrified.

"Why do you want to help me?" she asked.

"Because I saw you fight. I saw you and your crew face the kraken and win. My crew— Well, they held a mutiny because I wanted to come help you then."

"You were the one who was dragged away," Mara gasped.

"Yes. They would have thrown me overboard if I wasn't the son of the queen."

"Right." Mara paced around some more, thinking. Finally, she asked, "How do you want to help me?"

Finn stared at her for a minute before saying, "I know what you need to do to complete the gauntlet, so I can coach you and train you a little bit tonight so you're better prepared in the morning."

Mara turned to Teddy, who shrugged and nodded. "It's your choice."

She nodded, turned back to Finn, sighed, and rubbed her face for a moment before speaking. "While completing my Ranger trials, I'm allowed to get advice from one person for each. I asked Ashroot for help with the first trial. Teddy helped me with the second trial." Mara gestured to her uncle before continuing. "Will you help me with the third trial, so I understand what I need to do to be successful with the gauntlet and to be able to move forward on this journey?"

Finn straightened and grinned. "I will."

"Awesome," Mara replied, causing Finn to look very confused. She laughed. "Where do we start?"

"Here." He handed her the book. "Turn to the marked page."

Mara opened the history of the sea elves and read *The Serpent's Gauntlet* at the top of the page. Beneath and across a few pages after that were various diagrams of sea elves traversing dangerous obstacles and contraptions. There were little headers to explain each step and broadly what that step would entail. No wonder the guards didn't want Mara to have the book.

"Thank you, Finn!" Mara called, smiling up at the elf. She looked back down at the book, skimming through the first section. "And thank you, Marlin the Marauder."

Mara thanked Finn and waved goodbye before closing the door to her room behind him. Teddy had fallen asleep in the chair a few hours earlier, but Mara decided to just leave him there to rest as she fell into bed. Finn had stayed with her through most of the night. She would only have a few hours of rest before she would be summoned for the gauntlet.

Finn had allowed her to look through a few different sections in the book, which explained various steps in the gauntlet. He then went through the obstacles step-by-step. He didn't explain everything to her outright. There were puzzles to solve—and being handed the answers right before was no way for her to prove herself—so he'd given her hints to help her figure them out on her own. Her mind was racing, planning the day to come, running through all the possibilities in her mind. After some time tossing and turning, Mara thought she heard a voice commanding her to sleep. She finally drifted off.

She was awoken just before daybreak by Teddy.

"It's time," he told her quietly.

Mara rolled out of bed and stood, feeling all the smallest aches in her body. She was as ready as she could be, but she didn't feel ready at all. With a heavy sigh, Mara pulled her boots on and slipped her chainmail down over her shirt. She slid a hand underneath the chainmail sleeve and pulled the sleeve of her green shirt back down to the elbow. It was lucky the chainmail was three quarter sleeved as well.

Once she'd straightened her sleeves, she made sure the chainmail was adjusted correctly before putting her dragonwolf bracer on her right wrist and tightening it. After lacing her bracer, she paused. She traced the Aeunna tree on her cuff and twisted the tails of the little pink bracelet. *I'll do this, Dad. I'll do this, Kara*, she thought.

She turned to see Teddy standing behind the lone chair in the room. "Come here and sit," he said, patting the back of the chair.

Mara obeyed, sinking heavily into the chair. As Teddy began to pull her hair back, Mara asked, "Is this necessary?"

"Of course it is," he told her. "You need to have your hair out of the way, but if you slip it into one of your little bun things, you'll have trouble keeping it up through some of those challenges. I'll take care of it." He patted Mara on the shoulder.

Thankfully, her frostbite had completely healed. She was as fit and healthy as she could be. Teddy began braiding her hair as she fiddled with the lacing of her bracer. She traced the dragonwolf engraving and thought about how far she'd come and how far she still had left to go.

She hadn't really thought about how long it had been. She'd been in Ambergrove for nearly a year already. Time had passed so quickly while she was learning about Aeunna and while she was on her journey. She was nearing her seventeenth birthday. If she made it through the gauntlet, she'd be spending her birthday at sea, on the final steps toward the Dragon's Teeth. All she could really wish for her birthday would be to make it through unscathed—for them all to make it through unscathed. Time would tell.

She'd earned the respect of the forest dwarves. She'd made it to the gnome hills and gained a friend and companion. She'd conquered monsters no one imagined could be conquered, let alone by a teenage girl who'd been a couch potato just a few short months previously. She'd earned the chance to stay on the sea elves' islands. With some effort, today she would earn her final companion and they would be on their way across sea. *So close.*

"Yes, you are," Teddy replied. She turned slightly before he pulled her braid to get her to straighten her head again. "Yes, you did say that out loud." He chuckled. "Just keep a clear head on your shoulders and listen to Finn's advice. You'll do alright."

"I'm doing my best."

"I know you are."

"Listen, Teddy," Mara began, trying to turn again and being pulled back by the braid. She sighed.

"I'm nearly done." He'd braided her hair tightly into three braids. After tying the third, he pulled the three braids together and tightly twisted them into one large braid—but he wasn't finished there. He pulled a small stiletto out of his boot, twisted the braid into a knot, and slipped the blade through. "Now." Teddy came around the chair and stood in front of her. "You'll have a little weapon to use if you need it."

"Thank you, Teddy. Before I do this, I just want you to know—"

"Nope. None of that."

"None of what?"

Teddy stepped in closer, his eyes flashing. "No saying goodbye. I told you last time—if you say goodbye, that means you're giving up. You will not give up. You will complete this task like all the others, and we'll keep going on our way. Is that clear?"

"Yes, Teddy," Mara replied with a small smile.

"Good." Her uncle turned away and headed toward the door.

"Uncle Teddy?" Mara stood and walked over to him, not meeting his eyes.

"Yes, lass?"

"I'm glad I met you. I-I love you, Uncle Teddy."

Teddy was silent for a moment, then sputtered something that sounded a lot like "I love you, too."

Mara smiled up at her uncle, meeting his eyes and seeing they were watery. She cleared her throat awkwardly and announced, "Alright, time to go."

Kip and Ashroot met them downstairs. Ashroot made Mara have breakfast and Kip pulled her to the side to give her something before the guards arrived—but he was a little too late. He'd only had time to say, "Here," and stuff something in her hand before he, Ashroot, and Teddy were all led away down one side of the street and the guards took Mara the other way. She looked down at the object in her hand and smiled. It was a little necklace. Kip had carved a wooden token for her and strung it on a leather cord. She didn't recognize the symbols, but she thought she recognized the gesture. She smiled warmly and slipped the trinket onto her neck as the guards led her to the gauntlet.

CHAPTER FIFTEEN

THE GAUNTLET

Two guards on either side, Mara walked through a dark tunnel. She imagined a football movie, but she wouldn't be walking triumphantly out to cheering fans. She would be walking out alone to fight for her life and for the future of Ambergrove. She tried to slow her breathing, deeply inhaling and exhaling, clutching the token at her neck. Reaching the end of the tunnel, she stepped out into the light.

The first thing Mara saw was a wall with double doors. Two of her guards marched forward to line each side of the doorway, waiting. Over the wall were huge sets of grandstands. It seemed as though all the sea elves in the nation had come to witness her attempt at the gauntlet. Far off in the distance, in the highest stands, Mara could see distinguishable features.

There was a dot of coral pink—which could only be the queen. Underneath her were two brown splotches and a big green one—Ashroot, Kip, and Teddy. She breathed deeply, looking determinedly at the doors. Off in the distance, a bell was rung. The two guards in front of her pounded their spears three times. A guard next to her stepped forward.

"Once you enter those doors, you will be sealed into the gauntlet. You will not leave unless you make it through all ten stages. Your time does not matter, only your completion. The gauntlet can sometimes last all morning or all day. Step up to the doors. Once the bell sounds again, your trial will begin."

Nodding to the guard, Mara stepped forward. She glanced down at her bracer, patted the dragonwolf, and clutched Kip's trinket while she waited. Somewhere in the distance, the bell sounded again, and the guards slowly opened the doors. Mara stepped through them, listening as a lock clanked in place behind her.

She stood on a small platform facing a strange canopy. There were six poles standing over a large pool. Spanning the tops of the six poles was a large net that appeared to be the rigging from a ship. Finn had told her that, for this first area, she had to cross the pool without getting in the water. It was a significant distance to try to cross—probably around fifty feet.

With a deep breath, Mara stepped forward and looked down into the pool. Three large sharks circled below. Of course—Finn's first warning had been that the penalty for failing any area was death. She breathed slowly and looked up at the netting. She'd have to cross like monkey bars, though these would be much more difficult than any monkey bars she'd ever encountered—and it had been quite a few years since she'd tried. The netting would move. She might roll. Once she got to the center between poles, she would sink down, so she would need more effort to cross to the next pole.

With a short yell to amp herself up, Mara reached up and held onto the netting. Changing her mind, she turned around and faced the door. She swung herself down a few feet, then grunted with effort as she brought her legs up to the netting. *There.* She tried not to look down at the sharks, but she could hear the snapping below.

She tilted her head up to look across at the netting ahead. This is how she wanted to be—headfirst so she could see where she went without strain. She continued her climb, left and right, left and right, until she was halfway to the middle pole. She looked ahead to gauge the distance and came face to face with a massive shark. It snapped only a few inches from her face, startling her into nearly letting go of her holds.

She screamed, then shouted, "No! I'm not breakfast!"

Focusing on the netting, she continued toward the middle pole, trying to get to the pole because it, at least, was higher and away from the sharks. She paused here, trying to catch her breath. She could feel the rope digging into her skin. She could feel her feet slipping more the longer they stayed in the same square of the netting.

Groaning in pain and exertion, she continued across the second half of the netting, hoping if she ran through it as fast as she could, her hands wouldn't give way first. She scaled the second half of the netting within ten minutes. When her hands reached the last section of rope, she twisted to the left to look down at the water. The sharks were circling directly under her. She pulled herself up as high as she could.

The sharks grew impatient, jumping up and snapping at her back—one, two, three. Once the third shark snapped, Mara made her move, hoping that it would be a few seconds before one of them made another attempt. She glanced quickly down at the platform ahead and swung her legs down with all her might.

They made contact—but not with the platform. She hit something squishy, jarring her body and making her fall onto the edge of the platform, her legs in the water. Screaming, she kicked her legs and pulled herself forward. Her foot made contact again, propelling her fully onto the platform. Jerking her knees to her chest and inching as far away from the pool as possible, Mara looked back.

A shark burst forward and chomped on the platform. Mara could see its face was already bloody. *A shark. I kicked a shark. I kicked a shark in the face,* she thought, panicking.

"She kicked the shark in the face! Yeah!" someone screamed in the distance.

Panting, trying to catch her breath and trying to calm herself from the realization that, not only had she faced sharks, but she had angered at least one by kicking it in the face for good measure, she noticed dully that the crowd was cheering. The sea elves were cheering her. That was a good sign at least.

Remembering that the guard had told her she wouldn't be timed, Mara stretched out on her back on the platform, careful to remain a safe distance from the shark pool. She lay there for a few moments. slowing her breathing and resting her muscles. Once her breathing had calmed, Mara stretched out her hands and examined them. They were butchered. Both hands were bloody and covered in bubbling blisters.

Nothing she could do about it now. It was time to keep moving. She heaved herself back up to her feet to face the second area of the gauntlet.

Ahead of Mara was another pool, about the size of a small pond. Across this pool was a large door with three indents—one was round, one was square, and one was triangular. Looking around, she couldn't see any way to cross the pool without swimming in it. Finn had told her the second area would require her to find the keys to open the door ahead. The keys could only be in the water.

Looking down, Mara could see the pool was full of jellyfish. Beyond the jellyfish, the water was just clear enough for her to see a round ruby, a square sapphire, and a triangular emerald deep in the pool. They were spread out to the left, right, and center. She exhaled sharply and began to pace back and forth, thinking out loud.

"There's no way to get through without being stung by the jellies, so I'll have to just take that and deal with the pain." Mara hadn't been stung by a jellyfish before and assumed that it was similar to being stung by a bee. She could handle that. She looked down at the water. "If I swim straight for one of the keys and get across to the other side, that will give me time to recuperate before going for the next one—right?" She looked around her, remembering she was alone. "Right."

Counting down from three, she dove into the water and swam toward the center of the pool, deciding to go for the sapphire first. Squinting, trying to see as she swam, Mara grinned as her hand circled around the sapphire key. Immediately, she began feeling sharp stabs of pain. Jellyfish tentacles began to wrap around her arms. One jellyfish floated closer to her and slid its tentacles under her armor and around her torso.

She gasped with the pain, inhaling a mouthful of water. Scrunching her eyes and clutching the sapphire, she kicked forward as hard as she could. She felt the tentacles rip away as she began kicking up toward the surface. Moments later, she burst out of the water near the far end of the pool. Howling with the pain, and coughing up water, she threw the sapphire up onto the platform, grabbed the ledge, and heaved herself up onto it.

She growled and yelled up at the sky, slamming her hand on the platform a few times in frustration. It hurt way more than she could have imagined. She covered her face with her butchered hands. She knew there were fast ways to relieve jellyfish stings, but there wasn't anything she could do about it now. Maybe once she got all three keys, she could just rest before moving on. She rubbed her face and shook her head before flipping to her knees and looking reproachfully into the water again. She dove in.

Mara lay on the platform and stared up at the sky. All three keys were next to her on the platform, but, in the process, it felt like the jellyfish had stung every inch of her body. She was taking her time to get used to the feeling so she could function for the rest of the gauntlet. Finn had told her the next would involve quick thinking and agility. She would have to be alert.

She stretched her limbs and felt the pain ebbing a little, so she rolled over and stood, picking up each of the keys and inserting them in the door. With a click, the door swung open. Mara's jaw dropped.

"Seriously?" she shouted.

Once the door opened, there was another click, and the figures in the room began to move. The whole room ahead of her was filled with rotating posts. Each post had an arm or two sticking out the side and metal spikes covering its entire surface.

Mara glared at the obstacles ahead of her, trying to find some sort of pattern. She could see to the left, there seemed to be a little more space. She might be able to make it through there. Jumping in place for a moment to prepare herself, Mara moved to the left and stepped in between two posts.

She was immediately winded as one arm hit her in the stomach. It bounced her off into another post, which swept her back out of the field again. She groaned and felt her stomach. The chainmail had done its job, keeping the skin from being punctured, but she was sure she'd have an aggressive bruise. Her shoulder and side both had also been protected by the chainmail, but there was a gash up her left forearm. As much as she loved her bracer, she wished the spike had hit the other side, so she would at least have been protected.

Mara reached her right hand up under her left chainmail sleeve, wrapped her fingers around the cloth underneath, and pulled as hard as she could, ripping off her sleeve. She folded the sleeve over, slid it down to her forearm to cover the gash, and switched her bracer onto her left arm to keep the material in place. Examining her handiwork, she shrugged and murmured, "Yep, that'll work."

She looked down at the poles again, and then turned and went back out the door. Keeping an eye on the jellyfish, she swept her right hand into the pool a few times to pull out some large rocks. One at a time, she took the rocks back into the other room and stacked them up against the wall. Then, she hopped up onto the stack and pressed her back against the wall for balance.

She peered out at the posts from her new vantage point, examining the patterns. Every two minutes, a single path was created that went all the way through to the other end. Mara stepped down and counted. When it was time, she stepped into the right side, continuing to count down. At ten seconds, she moved to the left. After another ten seconds, she moved to the right. Right, right, left, center. Her feet landed on the other platform just as one of the arms came around and clipped her back. She did it.

The door to the fourth stage was already open, revealing a spectacle unlike anything Mara had ever imagined. Finn had told her that she would need to remember how they had defeated the kraken to make it through this area—but she hadn't expected it to be literal.

The room was filled with the wooden shape of a kraken. The kraken's body extended through the whole room. On the far side, wooden tentacles climbed up the wall. Mara could barely see the door behind. To the right and left, other tentacles lined the wall horizontally, their suckers represented by open holes in the wall. Mara was sure something was going to shoot out at her from there, but what would cause it? As she stepped into the room, there was a rumbling sound as the room shifted.

Holes opened in the floor and more tentacles rose from the opening, flailing around. She would need to dodge the tentacles to get through to the door—though she still didn't know how to open it. Testing a theory, Mara stepped to the edge of the obstacles and reached out a hand toward a flailing tentacle. Once the tentacle grazed her hand, there was a clang from the wall as an icicle shot out at her and stabbed into the wooden limb where her hand had just been.

"Okay, so it's just like fighting the ice kraken," she said. "How did we defeat the kraken?"

Mara scanned the room. Near the base of the door tentacles, on the lower end of what would be the kraken's head, two wooden eyes were sticking up from the ground. Those eyes would be pressure plates that would open the door—that's what she hoped, anyway.

Looking at the flailing of the tentacles for a few moments, Mara realized these seemed to be missing a pattern. There was no right way. She'd just have to go for it. Moving to the center at the edge of the moving parts, Mara stepped off onto the kraken's head. She tried to dodge all the tentacles on her way, but she was hit a few times. Each time, she flattened herself to the ground until the icicle had been shot, then tried again. Finally, she made it to the kraken's eyes and stomped down on them with both feet. The wall of tentacles rumbled and slid down to reveal an open doorway, and the movement behind her stopped.

The fifth area was a room full of stone pillars at varying heights. Finn had told her she would not make it to the end unless she moved quickly. The pillars themselves were sticking out of steaming, bubbling water. Boiling. She would have to cross the room without falling into the water. Peering across, she couldn't see a doorway. Mara looked all over the room before finally seeing an opening near the top of the wall on the opposite side.

The first two pillars stood in front of her like stepping stones. Not wanting to wait, since Finn had said this area was all about speed, Mara stepped onto the first pillar. Nothing happened. Encouraged, she stepped forward to the next pillar. This one began to rumble and sink into the water as she stood. Releasing an involuntary squeal, she hopped back onto the first pillar.

"Okay, some of them sink," she murmured to herself.

Ahead of her, she could see multiple paths forward—some rose near the top and some lowered. Maybe all but the first pillar would sink. She would just have to climb as fast as she could and hope that the pillars didn't sink too far for her to make it across to the door.

Speed, speed, speed. Mara launched herself forward, over the gap where the second pillar had been, and onto the next highest pillar. As soon as she hit the pillar, it began to slowly sink. Looking at the next highest pillars for a second, she assessed and jumped, trying not to waste time thinking, while at the same time trying not to make an irrevocable mistake because she hadn't thought.

She scrambled to stand on the pillar, looked at the next options, and jumped again. Quickly, she made her way across the room, stumbling more and more the higher she got. The gap between pillars seemed to get wider as the pillars got higher. When she jumped to the last pillar, she misjudged the distance and slipped, hanging onto the edge for dear life.

The pillar sank slowly as she struggled to pull herself up. When she finally made it up to the top, it had fallen a few feet and was too far away from the door for her to make it there. Turning quickly to the side, Mara launched herself at the adjacent pillar. She was making a last-ditch effort to get a little higher. This time, she landed on her belly on the pillar and was able to stand shortly after it began to sink. She jumped at the doorway and made it through.

Mara sat, exhausted and panting, leaning on the doorframe, and trying to catch her breath and rest her spent muscles. Looking out into the next room, she discovered she was on a rock-climbing wall. Once she stepped off the small platform for the doorway, she would have to descend a rock wall. The footholds appeared to be made of different colors of coral—pink, blue, and yellow. Directly below her and out halfway through the room were spikes. She could see a thin pole crossing the sea of spikes. Beyond the pole, before the doorway, was a mud pit.

For this room, Finn had told Mara to remember who the queen was and to not try the easy way—though the way was easy near the end. She wasn't sure what the first part meant, but just jumping out into the mud pit was probably taking the easy way. Perhaps it was shallow mud and that's why it would be easy later? That would definitely shatter her body now—she sat at least three stories in the air.

She would have to scale the wall and cross the spikes. She took some time to rest and stretch before moving on. Once she heard deafening boos all around her, she decided she'd rested long enough. Turning to the edge of the small platform, Mara put a foot down on a blue chunk of coral. Her stomach dropped through her feet as the coral immediately fell off the wall and shattered on the spikes below.

"Okay. No blue then."

She pushed a foot on a yellow chunk. It fell and shattered near the blue one.

"Ah, the queen!" Mara exclaimed, shaking her head and grumbling. She tested her foot on a pink piece. It held. "Obviously it was the queen's hair," she grumbled.

She began to scale the wall, making short work of it once she knew which steps she could use. When she neared the bottom and stepped onto the pole across the spikes, she was relieved to find the pole was completely solid. She stood for a few moments, resting her weight on the wall, so she could steady her legs before trying to cross.

Balance had never been a strong point for her, so she was extra careful crossing the abyss of spikes, inching her way across. About two thirds of the way through, she began to wobble and to over correct herself. She knew she wouldn't make it all the way across like that, so she made a mad dash. She made three big steps and jumped across, face first, into the mud.

She lay there for a moment, expecting something to try to kill her again, but nothing happened. This was just mud. She stood and slowly trudged her way across and into the doorway for the next area.

This room was different. It seemed still and calm. There were a few mossy rocks to one side, a small bank to the other, and a shallow pool in the center. Resting halfway out of this shallow pool was a giant sea turtle with a face more like that of a snapping turtle. It was the size of a bear, but not just any bear—the Great Silver Bear.

Mara cautiously stepped forward, then sat and crossed her legs at the edge of the pool. "I'm not sure if you can understand me, but you remind me of someone."

Who might that be?

"You can understand me!" Mara said excitedly, still trying to keep her voice down and resisting the urge to clap her hands. "You remind me of the Great Silver Bear in Aeunna. You ... you don't seem like you belong here. The Great Silver Bear has a large cave and a forest to roam over. It's not fair for them to have you here just as a game for the elves."

The sea turtle grumbled a little. *I am here for the gauntlet. That is all I have ever known.*

"I mean ... I guess you can't miss what you don't know," Mara said a little mournfully. "What are you here for?"

I ask questions and eat you if you give the wrong answer.

Mara blanched. "Well, I guess I'm ready whenever you'd like to ask your questions," she murmured shakily.

Very well. The sea turtle ambled closer to Mara and looked into her eyes. *Who are the greatest creatures of the sea?*

Mara looked down at her hands, thinking. Was there a right answer? Should she just say sea turtles—because that was what he wanted to hear? "I don't know." She sighed. "I don't know enough about the sea to say who the greatest creatures are—I'm really inexperienced. From what I do know, I'd have to say otters. That's not based on anything important. They're cute, and my dad told me once that they hold hands when they're floating to keep from floating away from each other. I used to hold my little sister's hand in the lazy river because of that. But that's probably not what you want to hear ..."

Hmm ... The sea turtle was silent for a moment before rumbling, *Why are you completing the Serpent's Gauntlet?*

"The short answer is because I was told to. The queen told me I had to complete the gauntlet in order to earn someone to come with me on my trial. I have to get someone to come with me so I can prove I'm the right person to lead the forest dwarves and fulfill a prophecy. I just ... I want to help people," she finished quietly.

Hmm ... The sea turtle considered her for a moment. *Very well. You may pass.* The turtle moved to the side, stepping off a huge pressure switch, and the door behind him opened.

Mara jumped up, startled. "Wait—that's it? I thought I needed to answer your riddles three or something."

No. You must simply answer my questions honestly. You have proven you have the courage to be honest, even in the face of danger. You may pass.

Her jaw dropped. "Uh, thank you! And thank you for your approval, Great Turtle." She stood and headed toward the open door.

Forest dwarf.

"Yes?"

You have been kind. I would like you to know that the most treasured creature of the sea is the angel of the sea.

"Thank you! ... What is the angel of the sea?"

The sea turtle slowly turned around to her. *A mermaid.*

"Wait, wait, wait!" Mara ran up close to the sea turtle. "Mermaids are real?" she exclaimed.

They were. They were lost when the gods left. The sea elves hope that one day they will return. The turtle turned back away from her and settled himself into his shell. *This will help you on your quest. Good ... luck ...*

She knew better than to disturb him. She quietly thanked the sea turtle again and then headed through the next door.

The next room Mara entered appeared to be empty. There were three other doors—one on each wall. An inscription on the floor read, *The angel of the sea will set you free.*

"Thank you, majestic sea turtle!" she whispered.

She looked around at the doors. The whole room was dark. She stepped into the room, and as her feet left the platform, the door behind swung shut. As soon as the door closed, the room was filled with sounds. All sorts of animal sounds erupted from each door. After playing all at once, the doors played one at a time.

To the left, Mara heard a deafening croon that was surely a whale sound. After a moment, the room went silent. Not really sure what else she should do, she walked over to the left door and turned the handle. In the distance, she heard gasping and shushing from the grandstands. She paused.

Stepping to the side, Mara flung the door open and backed against the wall. As soon as the door opened, a great burst of fire exploded out of the opening. Had she been standing in the doorway, she would have been fried. "Alrighty, then ..." she whispered, wide eyed. She closed the door gingerly and tiptoed away.

As soon as the door closed, the door across from the one she came in started making sounds. This was less distinguishable, but it seemed to be from something that roared. After a loud, prolonged roar, all was silent. Mara strode over to the second door, moved to the side, and wrenched it open. The doorway was full of crossbows. As soon as it opened, dozens of bolts shot across the room and buried themselves in the opposite wall.

"Not you then, I guess," Mara muttered, gingerly closing the door again. She walked back to the center of the room and looked down at the inscription on the floor again. No sooner had she looked, sound came from the final door. It was a beautiful song—the most melodious voice Mara had ever heard.

"The angel will set you free. Duh." She slapped a hand on her forehead and strode to the final door. For good measure, she stepped to the side and opened it cautiously like the others. Nothing happened this time. Peering into the doorway, she saw a lit, curved hallway.

As Mara passed through the hallway and opened the door to the ninth area, there was a roar of cheering from the grandstands above. The ninth area was different. There was a round room with a couch, a table with food, a weapons rack, an armor rack, and, to one side, a cabinet, counter, and a chair in which an elderly blue-skinned woman sat.

"Hello," Mara began warmly. "What is this place?"

The old woman tapped her throat silently and pointed to a sign on the wall to Mara's left. *You have thirty minutes in this room to rest before the arena. Allow the crone to attend to your wounds, eat a snack, change to dry armor, and select your weapons for the final challenge.*

"Okay then." Mara turned to the old woman again. "So, you can't speak?"

The old woman shook her head and moved behind the chair, tapping it with one hand.

"You're going to help me with my injuries?"

The old woman nodded.

Mara slowly walked across the room and sat in the chair. The woman circled around to stand in front of her and tilted her head inquiringly. Feeling every movement, Mara pulled off her bracer and torn shirt sleeve to reveal the gash up her left arm. She explained the injury to the crone, and then she told the weathered woman about the jellyfish stings and showed her sliced and blistered hands.

Methodically, the woman moved from injury to injury. The gash in Mara's left arm had been deep enough to warrant stitches, so she screwed up her face and tried to keep it together as the old woman stitched her up. After putting some sort of poultice on the wound, the woman moved on to the jellyfish stings.

About ten minutes later, her injuries tended, and her arm wrapped, Mara stepped into a small closet-like room to strip her soiled clothing and change to something dry. More comfortable for the first time since she left that morning, she strode over to the table with food, grabbed some meat and cheese, and plopped down unceremoniously on the couch.

Once she'd polished off her food and had time to rest on the couch, Mara crossed the room again to select her weapons. Examining the variety available, she decided to go with what made her most comfortable—but she didn't think the battle axe was the best choice. This was a duel, so she wouldn't be using a bow either. She withdrew the supplied sword and tested the weight with a few swings. Additionally, she grabbed two small axes.

A bell sounded in the distance. She heard the crowd roar in unison, "One more minute!"

"One minute, one minute," Mara murmured. Slipping the chainmail shirt and her dragonwolf bracer back on—back on her right arm this time—she slipped the two axes into her belt, grabbed the sword, and headed for the final door.

Mara stood in front of the door, breathing deliberately and trying to calm herself. The crowd around her chanted, *Ten, nine, eight* . . . Mara held the sword in her right hand, and her left enclosed Kip's trinket. Just one more step and she would have everything she needed to complete her Ranger trial. Win this fight. Get everyone home. . . . *five, four, three* . . . Mara let go of the necklace and grabbed the handle.

The bell sounded again. She opened the door and stepped out into the light of the open arena. The arena was simple—just a dirt circle with high walls. There was nothing else in the arena but the ferocious Candiru. Mara expected some kind of bell to signal the start, but Candiru's battle cry told her that was not the case.

Mara squeaked and brought her sword up just in time to catch the downward chop by the queen's champion. She cried out in pain as the movement strained the gash on her forearm. She twisted her sword around and backed away from Candiru. The sea elf began to circle the arena, eyes on Mara, swinging her sword threateningly.

"Boo! Fight!" someone shouted from the stands.

"Come on, little girl, come and get me!" Candiru taunted.

Mara knew there would be taunting in a battle, but she also knew she had to engage to get it over with. She raised her sword and stepped forward—but Candiru charged her instead. Mara twisted her sword to catch another high chop. Candiru quickly swept her sword at Mara's left side, and it caught her in the ribs. Her chainmail was sturdy enough to block the slice, but the momentum was torturous to her ribs.

Howling with pain, Mara was sure she'd heard a crack. Taking advantage of the moment without gridlock, she backed away, gasping, stumbling, and clutching her side.

"You think you can beat ME?" Candiru roared. "A human child? I'm insulted!"

Mara grinned despite herself. That's how she was going to win. "It doesn't matter what I think! Your queen thinks I'm good enough to fight you," she taunted, trying to sound confident and brave.

Candiru roared again and charged her. This time, Mara was ready for it. She stepped quickly to the left, bringing her sword around to catch Candiru's shoulder and slice into the back of her arm.

"You see? I was the first to draw blood! What does that tell you?" Mara shouted.

Before she could taunt any further, Candiru turned and charged her again. This time, she swiped from the side, chopping Mara's sword out of her grip and out of reach. Wasting no time, Candiru whipped her sword back at Mara—now defenseless.

Mara put a hand up—making Candiru cackle madly. She swung at Mara's neck just as Mara's fingers enclosed the stiletto's hilt. She pulled the stiletto out of her hair, catching the sword above her. Mara twisted the stiletto and backed away, out of reach. Thinking quickly, she threw the stiletto past Candiru's ear. The sea elf turned to see where the stiletto landed, giving Mara the time to make a mad dash for her sword.

When Candiru turned to see Mara facing her again, sword at the ready, she swore loudly.

"Yeah!" Mara panted. "Tricked by a human who's only been fighting for a few months. How does it *feel*?" she shouted.

Mara hoped upon hope that the rage tactic would continue to work. When Candiru charged her again, she assumed it had. Mara brought up her sword to block another chop, but the sea elf had another plan. In one swift motion, Candiru pulled one of the axes from Mara's belt and swept it up at her leg as she passed. Mara wasn't ready—the blade of the axe sliced deep into the back of her thigh.

She screamed in pain and turned, limping, to face Candiru again. Candiru had her. The only way Mara would be able to win would be if she took out Candiru quickly—if she waited too long to bandage her wound, she would lose more blood than she could spare. Candiru saw the blood streaming down Mara's leg and cackled, tossing the axe away and raising her sword again.

The axe would do it. As Candiru charged her again, Mara drew her remaining axe with one hand and braced the blade of her sword. As soon as Candiru's sword came down, Mara pulled the axe away, hooked the hilt of the elf's sword with the base of her axe blade, and yanked with all her might. Candiru's sword was ripped out of her hands.

While Candiru looked, startled, in the direction of her sword, Mara slammed into the elf with her shoulder, knocking her to the ground.

Limping forward quickly, she brought the tip of her sword to meet Candiru's throat. That was it. She had won.

Whatever Mara had been expecting to hear from the crowd, the chant, "Kill, kill, kill!" was not it. She looked down at Candiru. Although her expression was defiant, the elf also hung her head in shame. When Mara didn't move, Candiru shouted, "Finish it!"

"I thought I did finish it," Mara began, but Candiru shook her head.

"The gauntlet ends in death. That's the only way to complete it—either I kill you or you kill me," she said simply.

Mara paused. "W-what? That's ridiculous!" The crowd around her booed, but she ignored them, continuing to address Candiru. "You are the queen's champion. The only reason I was able to beat you is because you underestimated me—because I'm an inexperienced human. If you had gone into this ready to fight a seasoned warrior—and not been so angry to fight lowly me—you would have killed me in the first two minutes. I'm not *better* than you."

Mara tossed her sword out of reach and shouted up toward the stands, "I will not kill your champion! That's a waste of a good life and a good fighter." She turned back to Candiru and offered a hand to help the champion up. The elf turned away from her, looking shamefully at the ground.

"Enough!" shouted a voice from the stands. The bell rang again, and Mara looked up to see the queen looking furious. Ula stepped forward and glared down at her, holding up a hand for silence. As soon as the stands went quiet, the queen met Mara's gaze. "Human! You have failed the Serpent's Gauntlet! By refusing to kill my champion, you have proven yourself to be too weak for the test of the sea elves!"

All around the grandstands, the sea elves were cheering and screaming in approval. Mara looked down at the disgraced Candiru and back up to the queen. She tried to speak, but her voice was drowned out by the crowd. All she could even hear herself say was, "It's murder!"

The queen held up a hand again. "Enough! You will be able to stay on our island until you have tended to your wounds. By the time the sun is highest in the sky, you must leave our island. You are no longer welcome. Take her away!"

Guards appeared on either side of Mara and dragged her away, out a side door, down a tunnel, and toward the docks, leaving a trail of blood in their wake.

CHAPTER SIXTEEN

PAIN AND LOSS

Teddy gathered medical supplies from the storeroom of *Harrgalti*. The ship was relatively quiet. Kip and Ashroot had been sent to the village to see what supplies they could scrounge up before the companions left the sea elves' islands for good. The only sound that could be heard throughout the ship was Mara's muffled sobs.

Mara lay on her stomach on her bunk, her face buried in her pillow as she cried. Teddy knelt silently by the bed and cut Mara's pant leg to completely reveal her wound. The first thing he did was add a numbing poultice. As he cleaned the wound and threaded a needle to begin stitching it, Mara sniffled and spoke.

"I can't believe it. I ruined everything. Finn told me the key to the arena was to show no mercy, but I just— I-I couldn't— and then I ruined everything. I failed."

"Had I been in your position, lass, I wouldn't have killed her either," Teddy told her as he pulled the first stitch closed.

She sighed and pounded her head into her pillow a few times. "Well, I guess we both would have failed. That sure makes me feel better," she said miserably.

"There's nothing you can do about it now, Mara."

They sat in silence for a moment before Mara pressed further. "You seem to be very calm about the fact that I failed my Ranger trial—and all of this was for nothing." She twisted around to look at him. His face was taut as he tied another stitch in the back of her leg.

She opened her mouth to speak again, but, just then, there was clamoring above them. Kip and Ashroot appeared on the stairs, their arms full of supplies. Teddy turned around to them and called, "Ah, it's about time you two returned. I was starting to worry you'd gotten lost!"

"Lost on an island? Come on." Kip laughed.

Ashroot took her load wordlessly into the galley. Kip sighed and followed her, looking back briefly at Mara as he passed by. Although Ashroot stayed in the galley, Kip just dropped everything off on the table and came back out to sit on the floor in front of Mara. He reached out and patted her arm, looking into her tearstained eyes.

"I hope you have your dragonwolf carved," she said quietly, looking away.

"Why is that?" he asked her softly.

"Because you'll be going home soon. This is over."

"You were a beast, Mara. You completed so many difficult challenges today. You kicked a shark in the face! You have nothing to be ashamed of," Kip replied, caressing her cheek.

She buried her face in her pillow again. It seemed like Kip and Teddy were proud of her for failing. She had *failed*, though. She had spent almost a year preparing and working toward completing the Ranger trial. She could only do it once, and she'd come so far. How could she have come so far just to fall short? She'd let everyone down, and they didn't seem to care.

"Kip, will you get Mara something else to wear? These pants are shot," Teddy said.

Kip nodded and disappeared into the storeroom. While he was out, Teddy had Mara slide her leg off the bed so he could get an arm around it. He put an ointment along the incision and then wrapped it up. Once he was satisfied, he instructed Mara to sit while he unwrapped the bandage on her left arm, and she asked him why.

"That woman couldn't have been too generous when she was patching you up," he explained.

"Um, there aren't any more pants," Kip announced, popping his head out of the storeroom. "All I can find right now is this." He held up a blue mass.

"That's perfect, Kip, thank you," Teddy replied quickly.

Mara scowled. She knew she had pants in there, but she couldn't go look for them herself. Now, to add insult to injury—literally—she'd have to wear Freya's trial dress. She couldn't focus much on the injustice, as Teddy had just pressed a thumb into her incision. She inhaled sharply and groaned.

"What's the deal, Teddy?" she shouted.

"As I suspected," he replied calmly. "This needs to be cleaned better."

He tended to the arm and wrapped it back up again. Once he had finished, Teddy and Kip helped her stand. They led her into the hold so she could lean on boxes for balance while changing her clothes in relative privacy. Teddy came into the hold once she'd gotten the dress on and helped her back out toward her bunk.

Ashroot emerged from the galley and informed them that they had everything they could get from the sea elves. Teddy agreed that there wouldn't be anything else they would really need, so they should all head up to the deck to prepare to set sail. Mara leaned on the handrail to amble up the stairs.

Once they got to the deck, however, they discovered they had a visitor. Finn stood near the top of the stairs with a large bag in hand.

"Going somewhere?" Kip asked testily.

"Well, yes—I'm coming with you," Finn announced.

Teddy grinned and clasped the elf's arm in his own. "I knew we'd be seeing you! Welcome!"

Finn turned to Mara, who gazed at him in shock. "I don't understand," she said finally.

"You needed a sea elf to come with you," Finn explained. "I'm a sea elf."

"But I failed the trial," she protested.

Teddy held up a hand. "Well, that's not entirely true."

"What?" Mara shouted. "What do you mean by that?"

"You failed the queen's gauntlet—but that wasn't where you needed to succeed," said Teddy. "Your trial is to undertake a predetermined task to earn your companion on the trial. You don't need the queen's approval—you need the companion's approval. If I'm not mistaken, Finn gave his approval when he helped you to prepare for the gauntlet." He turned to Finn. "Right?"

"Mostly," Finn began. "I'd wanted to help you fight the kraken. When my mother declared the gauntlet was your trial, I had to see how that would end. And, well, where my mother saw you sparing Candiru as a weakness, I see it as a strength."

"What?" Mara asked incredulously.

"There was no reason for you to kill her. You won, but you spared her because you weren't going to kill for sport. That's why I'm here." Finn looked around at the others, and then ventured. "I assume that's why everyone is here."

"It's as I said," Ashroot interjected, patting Mara on the leg. "We're all here because we believe in you."

Mara's eyes grew bleary again. She looked around at her companions, unable to express her gratitude. After an awkward moment, she cleared her throat. "Well, shouldn't we get going, then? We've got a long way ahead of us."

"Yes, Boss," Teddy joked.

Finn grinned and followed Ashroot downstairs to dispatch his bag at his bunk. Mara, braced by Kip, limped over behind Teddy to the helm of the ship. As they made their way slowly away from the sea elves' islands, Mara found herself feeling way more optimistic about the journey than she had thus far.

Mara lay in her bunk, feeling the ship rocking around her. It had been a few weeks since they'd sailed away from the sea elves' islands. Finn had spent most of his time on deck with Teddy, so Mara hadn't seen him much since the first day. She shivered, and a hand pressed a cold cloth to her forehead.

Although Teddy had cleaned the gash in her forearm, Mara had some sort of infection from her bout in the gauntlet. The jellyfish stings were healing nicely, though she suspected there would be some light scarring. A few of her ribs had definitely been cracked, but Teddy didn't think any were broken—it would just take time for those to heal.

Her leg and her forearm had to be drained daily, and they were treated and rewrapped twice a day. Ashroot had been making a disgusting herbal tea for her every day to help dull the pain, fight the infection, and lessen her fever. Both wounds were red and aggravated—and they couldn't figure out why. Teddy was coming below deck to change her bandages and avoiding contact otherwise, because he thought her lack of improvement was because of him. His wife may have been the healer for Aeunna, but she hadn't taught him everything she knew, and it wasn't his fault if things were going wrong.

Kip spent most of his time by her side, mopping her brow, keeping her hydrated, getting her to eat. He told her some of the stories he'd told Loli just to pass the time. Now, though, he was telling her what Teddy had planned for the next step.

"There's a cove near the northernmost tip of the mainland. There's a human village in the cove—a village he knows. He's planning for us to sail into the cove so you can get proper medical attention. Hold out for another day or two and we'll get you looked at by a professional, okay?" He patted the cold cloth on her neck briefly before moving it back up to her forehead.

She was clutching the necklace he'd made for her as she drifted off to sleep.

Teddy and Finn stood at the helm of *Harrgalti*. Finn was steering the ship while Teddy looked over a map.

"Are you sure you can trust these people?" Finn asked.

Teddy didn't look up from the map as he replied, "Am I sure I can trust *you*?"

Finn stood silently for a moment. "I have nothing to do with Mara's illness," he replied as delicately as possible.

"Maybe not, but something happened in that gauntlet that she can't shake and I . . . I can't seem to help her."

"These people can?"

"Yes, these people can. They owe Mara's family a debt."

"Why?"

"You'll see when we get there," Teddy snapped.

The men sailed in silence for a while. Teddy was unwilling to offer more information and Finn was hesitant to keep getting shot down. After a few moments, Ashroot emerged from below deck bearing sandwiches. Finn set the pin in wheel and they all sat down to eat together.

"So, when do you think we'll make it to this town?" the bearkin asked.

"It won't be more than an hour or two," Teddy replied, giving Ashroot a reassuring smile.

"And then what?" Finn asked.

Silence.

"Yeah, what's next?" Ashroot asked.

"Well, Ashroot," Teddy began, causing Finn to huff quietly. Teddy ignored this. "We'll sail into the cove and dock in Nimeda's port. I know the healer there, so I'll talk to the village elder about helping Mara, and we'll stay in a guest house while she is taken care of. There's a decent shipbuilder there—though she's nothing like Lir. She should be able to help us get the ship patched well enough to handle the waters of the Dragon's Teeth. We'll stay in Nimeda until Mara and the ship are all healed up, and then we'll head on."

"I do have a suggestion," Finn began.

Teddy ignored him again, but Ashroot asked, "What suggestion?"

"This is Mara's trial, so she cannot be dependent on us. She needs to have practice sailing the way the sea elves do."

Teddy only grunted, but Ashroot replied, "Oh, that makes sense."

Finn continued, "I know, even though I haven't done anything to hurt Mara, you don't trust me, sir, because of what happened to her during the gauntlet. I hope to gain your trust during this journey, but until then we all have to look out for Mara. While we're resting, I want to take her out on the ship and teach her how sea elves sail before we head into more dangerous waters. Is that going to work for you?"

Teddy sighed and stared off into the distance for a moment before replying. "I know you came because you believe in her, and I know you're here to help. I've never had a good experience with a sea elf besides Lir—if you can count Lir—so it's harder for me to see you as someone who doesn't wish ill on outsiders like Mara. I'm convinced your mother's distrust is why Mara is sick—even if my lack of experience in healing arts may have something to do with it—but I can't continue to punish you for my own fears." He met Finn's eyes and stared into their depths. "Once Mara is healed well enough to sail, we will wait at the village until you deem her ready for us to move forward. If she gets worse and not better, I may have to employ some of your mother's tactics," he warned.

Finn cleared his throat uncomfortably. "Well, wouldn't that be interesting," he grumbled.

The two men stared at each other for a moment, unblinking. It was Ashroot who broke the silence. "Okay!" she exclaimed. "I'll go back down and tell Kip and Mara."

She took her sandwich plate with her and disappeared below deck again, leaving Teddy and Finn to finish off their sandwiches and go back to their business in silence. After weeks of Teddy's testiness, Finn only hoped that this village would provide some break and positivity for everyone.

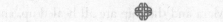

Due to the calm waters and Finn's expertise, they sailed into the cove about a month after leaving the sea elves' island. It was the smallest cove on the mainland, but it was by far the most pleasant on the coast. Port Albatross was a nice town, but because it was a melting pot of adventurers, it also included some unsavory characters.

Nimeda was nestled in the northernmost area of the mainland, and it was kept safe by its seclusion. Further north, still in view of the cove, was the northern island of dragons. Further northwest, if someone stood on the cliffs at the edge of the cove, they could barely see the Dragon's Teeth in the distance. They rarely got visitors because of these two draconian legends looming over, and this worked in their favor. However, this also made them wary of visitors when they did have them.

Ashroot had brought up the leftover cream-colored canvas at Teddy's request. Kip had been coaxed from Mara's side to climb up the rigging and help Finn to wave the canvas, a show of peace to the townspeople. Teddy steered the ship up toward the docks, watching. No guards came, and no ship met them.

As they entered the cove, they could see townspeople lining the docks. One lone elderly woman stood at the end of an open dock with her arms crossed. Teddy could see her as they drew nearer, and he recognized her features.

"Who's that?" Ashroot asked, coming to stand at Teddy's elbow.

"That there is the village elder of this town—Inola. We met a long, long time ago, in a similar situation." Seeing the apprehension on Ashroot's face, he added, "She was kind to us then. I'm sure she still will be now."

After smiling reassuringly at Ashroot, Teddy turned back to the docks and sighed deeply. The woman had long salt and pepper hair. Her face was wrinkled with age and hardened with something else. She wore a long, red dress and leaned slightly on a tall walking stick topped with a metal ball.

"Boys—drop the canvas," Teddy ordered, not turning. "Finn, get us docked here."

As Finn took over the wheel, Teddy strode to the edge of the ship nearest to the dock, straightening his vest as he did. When he reached the edge and lay a steadying hand on the bulwark, the village elder was only a ship's length away. Teddy waved awkwardly with the hand not clutching the ship. Unsmiling, the woman waved back with the hand not holding her walking stick.

Once the ship had drifted near enough for her to speak, the woman addressed Teddy with an aged voice, shaking her head. "Tederen, Tederen . . . What terrible event causes you to darken our doors?"

"The usual kind," Teddy replied, smiling politely.

"Who needs my help this time?" she asked, placing a hand on her hip.

Teddy paused, his smile fading. "Mara needs your help. Mara—the daughter of Toren and Kenda."

"What?" the woman whispered, incredulity in her voice.

"Yes. She's below deck. She's had a feverish injury for a month now and I can't seem to help her. Our ship is also in need of repair . . ."

The woman was waving her hand dismissively. It wasn't like Queen Ula had waved, but rather the movement one makes when they've been overcome and are begging for quiet. She turned around to the villagers as she waved. "Micco! Go to the healing hut and get a traveling bed, quickly! Isi, please gather your apprentices to assess the damage of their ship. Fala and Nadie, head to the hut and prepare a bed and supplies. Gad, please take your children and prepare the visitor's home. The rest of you, please return to your business," she finished, finally.

As soon as Finn had the ship near enough, Kip laid out the plank for the woman to board. She strode up the ramp as soon as it had been laid and met Teddy at the top. "Inola, how——" he began.

"Where is she?" Inola asked quickly.

"Below deck. She . . ." Teddy trailed off. As soon as he'd said, "below," the sour woman had turned away from him and rushed to the stairs.

She emerged mere seconds later, charging toward Teddy. She brought her walking stick up and rapped him hard on the head before shouting, "How could you let *your niece* get in that condition? What's wrong with you?" She bonked him again.

Teddy was spared the need to respond as Micco appeared at the top of the ramp, holding a stretcher. Huffing once more at Teddy and brandishing her stick in a final threat, Inola beckoned wordlessly to Micco, who followed her down the stairs.

Mara floated in and out of consciousness. Dimly, she knew that she was moving. It wasn't the rocking of the ship but something else. She opened her eyes, but everything was still cloudy. She could see Teddy behind her, apparently carrying at least part of what she was laying on. His voice was loud. He was arguing with an old woman as they walked. They were passing building after building.

Mara looked over and was shocked nearly out of her state. It was her dad. How could her dad be here? Why here? Something was different about him. She thrashed a little, trying to get a better look. He was grey. He didn't look right—he looked young. That was him though. It was definitely him. By some magic, he'd made it back to her.

She tried calling out to him. "Dad! Dad, I'm here!" It came out as a raspy whisper.

The stretcher stopped. The old woman put a hand on her face. She was trying to draw Mara's eyes away. Mara reluctantly looked at the woman, ready to tell her to go away, but the woman placed her hands on either side of Mara's face. She was saying something in earnest—but Mara couldn't make out what it was.

The woman looked familiar somehow. She knew she hadn't met her before, but she felt like she'd met someone like her. The woman kissed Mara's forehead and tucked her blanket around her, covering her shoulders and effectively swaddling her. Then, the woman disappeared, and the bed kept moving. Her father faded out of view and Mara sank back into darkness.

Mara woke a few times over the next week, but she never really understood what was going on. To prevent her from injuring herself by trying to understand what was happening around her, Inola had kept her sedated until her injuries had finally begun to heal. She had spent a full twelve hours once the traveling bed had made it into the healing hut trying to stabilize her.

The gashes from the gauntlet had both gotten infected, but the larger issue was something worse entirely. Inola had asked Teddy where Mara got the injuries and how, and then she told him that they were lucky to have come to Nimeda. Inola had treated injuries of the type before.

In an effort to weed out the imperfect from those who completed the gauntlet, it seems Queen Ula had tipped various elements of the gauntlet with a slow-acting poison. It was meant so the victim would suffer for weeks before death, and it was a surprise that Mara had been able to survive the poison for a full month.

When Teddy had turned on Finn after hearing this news, Inola placed herself firmly between them. Finn tried to explain he hadn't known, but Inola told Teddy that none of them had ever known. She only realized that it was the same poison after so many sea elves had come into her care, sailing in the north waters. It was meant to be a final punishment. To Inola's knowledge, the only people who knew about the poison were the queen, the one who'd done the poisoning, and the victims Inola had saved—who would never have returned home after such a disgrace.

If they were going to save Mara, they had to act quickly. They'd gone right with the herbal teas. Inola suspected that was how Mara had survived as long as she had. They just needed to tweak the concoction and make

Mara drink every half hour for the first two days, then every hour until the poison left the body.

That was the easy part. In addition, Inola would need to keep Mara sedated for a few hours to properly clean the wounds. She needed her assistants to hold Mara down for the job. Before they began, the villagers had to forcibly remove Mara's companions. Everyone wanted to remain at her side. Once the healers had finally convinced the companions to leave, they had to take them away to the guest house, because the first time Mara screamed in pain, Teddy and Kip both tried to force their way back in.

Because guests were so rare in Nimeda, rather than an inn, they had decided to leave a house ready and vacant for any visitor they had. There were two bedrooms, so once Mara was healed, there would be one bedroom for her and Ashroot and one for the men—but no one felt like resting. Ashroot took advantage of the fully stocked kitchen to stress cook. Finn was writing a letter to his mother about what he had discovered. Kip and Teddy paced. When they got sick of pacing, they got wooden practice swords from the first villager they could find and sparred in front of the house instead.

Meanwhile, properly cleaning the wounds was a grueling task. To remove the residue of the poison—besides the diluted poison that was in her bloodstream—they wouldn't be able to just rinse with alcohol or apply poultice. The wounds had to be scrubbed. Inola removed the blue dress Mara wore and changed her into a simple dress from the healing hut—something like a hospital gown.

They needed to start with the older wound first, so Inola unwrapped Mara's arm and delicately reopened her incision. This was the first time Mara screamed and thrashed, causing her companions to be banished to the guest house. Inola poured her own rinse over the wound first to remove as much poultice and infection as she could do easily. Next was the scrubbing. She removed some of the dying flesh and then used a special small sponge to scour the inside of the wound.

The rinsing and scouring process continued until Inola was satisfied that the source of the poison was gone. She then added her own, simpler ointment and stitched up the incision with the precision and sterilization of a professional. After the woman added a pain-numbing poultice to the skin around the incision and wrapped it up, Mara's first wound was finally ready to begin healing.

Inola completed the same process for Mara's leg. Because Teddy had cleaned the wound immediately—rather than waiting through over half of the gauntlet before it was lightly patched up—the leg gash was in better shape. The process was a little easier, though, due to the size, took the same amount of time to clean and cover.

After listening to Mara's breathing when placed on her side for the leg wound to be tended to, Inola knew the two gashes weren't the only worry. An examination of Mara's side showed that Teddy had been wrong about the ribs. A few of them were, indeed, simply cracked, and had healed well enough on their own. However, two ribs had severely fractured and were pressing into Mara's lung. Those could only be repaired with surgery.

Luckily, transportation from Earth had once been common among the settlers of this village. It was common enough that the healers in the town learned how to perform operations that were common necessities among warriors—such as repairing fractured ribs. A few hours and a dozen stitches later, Mara had finally been completely patched up. All they could do was give her the scheduled doses of herbal tea and wait for her body to work out the poison and begin to heal.

Nearly collapsing with the fatigue the many hours of surgery had caused, Inola made her way to the guest house to tell Teddy. The end of the operation had an immediate effect on everyone. Inola had ordered Kip and Teddy to rest and leave the first few days, at least, to the professionals. This was her order, not as healer, but as village elder, so they had to obey. Her apprentices took turns watching Mara and making sure she got her tea.

Finn sent his letter, by borrowed messenger hawk, to his mother. Then, as if by magic, they all fell into bed, able to relax for the first time in a long time.

CHAPTER SEVENTEEN

FAMILY

Mara stood in the Nimeda town square wearing a loose red skirt and yellow tank. Teddy had braided her hair and Kip had given her a magnificent crutch. It was relatively simple, but he'd told her that carving the knotted patterns on her crutch had kept him occupied while she had been recovering.

She bent her leg a few times. The ache was immense, but the numbing poultice was doing its job. Her leg was healing nicely, and she could put some weight on it. Inola had told her that it would be another week or two before her leg and arm were healed enough for her to use properly, albeit delicately. Her ribs were a different story. She'd still have trouble breathing deeply for a couple months, but Inola had assured her it would go back to normal.

Ah, Inola. Mara was anxious to find out just how she knew the woman. She had been tight-lipped whenever Mara had woken, telling her that all would be answered when Mara was well enough to walk around and function without sedation. The time had come, and when Kip had come to give her the magnificent crutch and take her for a short walk, Inola told Kip that here was where they would meet.

Sinking down into a chair Kip had brought, Mara stared at the image before her. There, in the center of town stood a tall man, life-sized, carved from a material much like marble. He held a sword in his right hand, its tip resting on one foot. His eyes were kind, he held one hand out in front of him as if he was gesturing to an unseen friend, and his mouth spread wide in a grin.

The greatest feature though, Mara told Kip, as her eyes filled with tears, "My dad. That's my dad."

"Really?" Kip asked. "I thought your dad was a forest dwarf."

"He was, he was, but . . ." she blubbered and made some incomprehensible noises while gesturing to the statue.

As Kip tried to dry Mara's tears and calm her enough that she could explain, Inola appeared behind them. "Yes," she said. "That is Toren . . . Mara's father."

"How do you know him? Why is he immortalized in the middle of your town? What—" Kip began, but Inola held up a hand.

"These are answers for Mara," she explained. "And I have been waiting to speak to one of Toren's children for a very long time, so could you please give us this moment alone?"

It was a request but based on the look in her eyes—and the fact that she was the village elder—Kip knew it was more of an order. He tipped his head in acknowledgement, gave Mara a soft squeeze on the shoulder, and left without another word. Inola had a chair of her own and pulled it up next to Mara's, settling herself in it with a low sigh.

"How did you know my dad?" Mara asked quietly.

"My, that is a long story." Inola sighed. Seeing the expression on Mara's face, she placed a hand on Mara's shoulder and quickly added, "But it's one you need to know. First, however, tell me what you know about your father's Ranger trial."

With an aggravated sigh, Mara recounted the tale as Teddy had told it to her, leaving out the heavier judgments of her mother. She stared at the ground as she told it, trying to make herself remember all the details and prevent herself from being distracted. ". . . but then he went to Earth with my mother, so he wasn't Ranger for long," she finished.

"Maybe not, but he was a good one while he was there."

"How do you know that?" Mara pressed.

"Well, let's go back to his trial. The first thing he wanted to do to protect the people in the village was to get them to evacuate. He wanted them to move to a safer town."

"I didn't know that."

"No, you wouldn't. If he had been successful in convincing the people to evacuate, he would have failed his trial. He had to save the village as it was, not the people as they could be somewhere else. But ... he wanted to make sure we were out of harm's way before he faced a god, and he was willing to fail his trial to ensure we survived."

"Wait," Mara stared at Inola for a moment. "We?"

"Yes." Inola sighed. "We. Many of the people did take Toren's advice. We came to this cove because he loved it. He told us that it was a beautiful, safe place, and that watching the dragons fly in the distance was a magical experience. He said we would always be protected because Aeola had blessed this land with a special grove—sgiath trees."

"Sgiath trees? What are those?"

"They're all around us." Inola gestured to the land wrapping around the cove. "You cannot tell from here, but when you've more strength you can go see them up close. They're gnarled, bulbous, grey trees that grow a reddish moss that makes them look like rusted iron. Their leaves are great shield-like spades—this is why they're called sgiath trees. Sgiath means shield. Aeola is the goddess of protection, and she has blessed these trees to remain evergreen, always steadfast protecting us. Here, we would surely be safe, but ..."

She sighed again, this time a weighty sound full of sorrow. "My lifemate and I decided to come here and to bring with us however many villagers wanted to go. The village split in half one day, and we packed up for the new life Toren made for us—but my lifemate had one more thing left to do before he would join us here."

Inola sat quietly for a moment, softly sniffling and remembering something quite painful. Finally, Mara placed a hand on the old woman's shoulder and asked, "What did he need to do?"

The woman took a deep breath, steadying herself. "He volunteered to help Toren complete his trial by going with him into the lair and facing the traps. As you know, he didn't make it back out again."

Mara stared at Inola, finally realizing how she knew the woman's face. "No ..." she gasped. "No way!" Inola met her gaze and Mara managed, "You're my *grandmother*, aren't you?"

Inola nodded and whispered, "Yes, my dear Mara. I'm your grandmother, and I have waited twenty years to hold you in my arms."

As Inola reached out, standing. Mara stood shakily and hugged her grandmother with all her might.

Mara spent a lot of her time in Nimeda with Inola. After the second week, her wounds had healed well enough for her stitches to be removed, but Inola still monitored her to make sure everything was healing nicely. They frequently took walks around the town.

Inola asked Mara about her life, wanting to catch up all the years she had missed. Mara told her grandmother about her sisters, lingering more on Kara. "I just wish I had the chance to say goodbye," she said. "Mom and Dad knew, and Sara probably wouldn't care all that much, but Kara and I just ... *lost* each other. I miss her." Mara twisted the pink bracelet from her sister around her wrist.

Her grandmother hugged her. "You don't talk much about Kenda. I understand," she began, "but she was completely different when I knew her. We took her father's death differently."

"Yeah," Mara grumbled. "You *built* a village and she tore one apart."

"It's not so simple as that."

Mara snorted, so Inola asked her to pause and sit for a moment. They settled on a bench near the docks, overlooking the cove. Inola sighed before beginning, "Based on what you've said, you never wanted for anything—except maybe your mother's love."

Mara shrugged and nodded. "We always had food on the table, and we were able to do the things we wanted to do."

"Well, your mother didn't have that. Our village was dangerous. We barely got by, and a lot of times, your mother went without. We all did. We decided to try this new village because we wanted to be able to give her the opportunities she never had—but she got tired of waiting. She saw a way out and she took it. Your mother did have many flaws, I won't deny that, but she didn't do what she did out of malice or selfishness—it was survival."

Mara sat quietly for a moment, then ventured, "Well that doesn't really explain why she treated me the way she did. Or my dad. And sometimes Kara."

"It does though, Mara," Inola explained—as if to a small child. "You liked that game you told me about. Dragons and Defense."

"DUNGEONS & DRAGONS," Mara murmured.

"Yes, that. You liked things that reminded her of where she'd come from. *You* reminded her of where she'd come from. She pushed you away because she didn't want to remember the fear of Modoc or the uncertainty of her life there. I'm not condoning what she did, by any means, and I do regret I was absent from so much of your life—because we would have had a talk many years ago and I would have put a stop to it—but you've wasted enough energy being mad at her. You should focus on what you have. Family is not measured by time together or blood ties. You've found a new family since coming to Ambergrove. That is as clear as the water in the cove, after seeing how your companions acted when you were ill."

Inola nodded toward the crystalline blue waters ahead of them, so clear Mara could see the colorful fish swimming below. She thought about what Inola may have seen. Ashroot had been stress cooking, sure. Finn had been consulting with the town's shipmaster, focusing on repairing *Harrgalti*.

She absently caressed the necklace Kip had given her. She was no longer walking with the crutch, except on her worst days, but Kip had been ever-present. Ashroot had told her that Kip and Teddy had to be thrown out of the healing hut. She could only imagine what sort of trouble Kip had gotten into since they arrived in Nimeda.

Teddy was surely the greatest example. As with Inola, as soon as Mara had met Teddy, she felt an overwhelming connection to him. There was an immediate bond, and not just because he was her only relative—he certainly wasn't anymore—but he'd also been so protective of her, and he'd taught her so much. He also greatly resembled her dad.

"I was appalled when I'd seen what condition Tederen brought you to me in, but your friend Kip explained what you had been through one of the many times he haunted my door. Tederen has done his best to take care of you, and he's done almost as well as a grandmother would—in the area of warm clothes, supplies, and food, anyway. I'm hopeless in battle, no matter how much I love you."

Mara chuckled. "The way Teddy talked about your reunion, you did as much damage as you could with that stick of yours!"

"This is true. I do somewhat regret that. I was operating on past hurts." Inola's face fell.

"What *did* happen when you saw each other last? I got the impression he really didn't want to stop here."

"Ah." Inola looked awkwardly at her hands. "Well, that's a story . . ."

She proceeded to tell Mara about her first time meeting Teddy. Teddy was worried about Toren's survival through the trial, and once Mara's grandfather and Toren had left, Teddy had made a few offhand comments about her grandfather not being good enough protection. He thought Toren would die because of the human, but in the end, Dakota had actually saved Toren's life. Inola did not accept Teddy's apology.

The next time she had seen Teddy, it was when he had come to beg a favor. Toren had decided to go to Earth with Kenda, and Teddy wanted Inola to convince her daughter to stay. She refused out of anger at Teddy, so he told her that whatever happened to Aeunna without Toren—and whatever happened to them on Earth—was on her head.

"So, when Tederen showed up in my village after so many years, and he'd brought you in such condition, I couldn't help but be angry. We'd put so much on each other. But, after a few days, and talking to your friend, Kip, about your journey, your uncle and I had a little heart-to-heart. He's a good one, that Kip." Inola finished, looking down at Mara's hand, which was still absently caressing the necklace Kip had made.

"Yes . . . Yes, he is," Mara replied.

Mara panted as she reached her destination, collapsing on the ground. She lay at the crest of a cliff overlooking the cove. She'd been at Nimeda for nearly a month and was doing her best to build up her strength. She climbed up to the cliff at least once a day, and she'd been sparring with Ashroot so she could slowly get used to the movements to fight again.

She was winded from the effort of the climb, and her leg had begun to cramp where her thigh was still healing. She massaged her thigh through her pants. The people in Nimeda were more traditional, it seemed. They had been appalled at the idea of Mara wearing pants, just as they had been appalled that she had been fighting. In the end, she was able to get some pants specially tailored by one of the younger seamstresses in the town.

Generously, the woman had made some extra shirts and pants for Mara, so she wouldn't run out as quickly the next time she was injured and her clothes ruined. The town seemed to exclusively use red material, as that was the easiest for them to make with local dyes, but Mara was still able to get a few garments in earthy tones. She wore some of those now.

After a moment massaging her leg, Mara stood again and looked out over the water. Finn was below, sailing *Harrgalti* around the cove. He'd created a complicated obstacle course for her, trying to replicate a more hazardous setting in the cove. All he had to do before Mara's lessons began was test the ship himself to make sure it had been repaired to his satisfaction.

From that distance, the ship looked good as new. They had even found blue sails to replace the one Ashroot had made. It was Finn's idea to keep that one tucked away as a spare—and to use if they wanted to strike fear in their enemies when they approached. As she watched, Finn sailed the ship gracefully around his obstacles and out into the open water. Way off in the distance, Mara could see the Dragon's Teeth. They were so close to their goal. Part of the reason she climbed up to the edge of the cliff every day was so she could look out at their final obstacle.

She heard rustling behind her. "You're a little late today, aren't you Ash?" Mara asked, still staring across the waters.

"Oh, I don't know. I think I made good time," said a man's voice.

Mara turned to see Kip, reddening. "Oh, sorry. I was expecting Ashroot."

"That I figured, since you called me Ash." Kip chuckled. "Ashroot and Teddy had a talk and decided you were ready for a step up, so I'm here to practice with you instead while she assists Finn. Do you want to get started?"

Mara nodded and headed back down the crest a little to where Kip stood. They had been focusing on swordplay since that took the most leg movement and arm strength combined. Kip worked slowly with Mara, but he used more force with his strikes than Ashroot had to give. He also danced away so she had to come after him. No mercy.

They worked for a long time. The sun had moved noticeably in the sky by the time Kip called for the end of the training. "Marvelous job, Mara. Really." Kip panted.

Mara stuck her sword in the ground and began massaging her arm. "Thanks, Kip. I think I'm doing better—getting stronger." She grimaced as she touched a tender spot.

"Come. Sit," Kip ordered, steering Mara to the edge of the cliff and helping her to sit down with her legs dangling over the cliff face.

He sat to her left and pulled a small container out of his pocket. As he opened it up, Mara smelled the familiar odor of the pain-numbing poultice. Kip wordlessly reached a hand out for hers. She reached out her left arm and laid her hand, palm up, into his. As he began to massage the poultice into her scarred arm, Kip ventured a question.

"Do you miss your father?"

"Yes, I do," Mara replied automatically. "Of course, I do. It's been harder being here—with my grandmother, with Teddy, going past the statue every day .... It's been so long since I've seen him."

"So ..." Kip began slowly, "What is it you miss doing with him the most?"

Mara thought for a moment, and then laughed.

"What?" Kip asked.

"Oh, it's stupid."

"Tell me," Kip pressed, pausing the massage and resting his hand in hers.

Mara's face reddened, and she looked out across the water. "I know that every day is like playing D&D here, but I loved to play D&D with my dad and with Kara. He introduced us to our first campaign with a story about a gnome and a dwarf getting kidnapped by giants. I loved that story, and I loved that game."

A single tear streamed down her cheek. Kip reached up and wiped the tear away, his hand lingering on her cheek. She looked into his warm, brown eyes and smiled. Someone cleared his throat behind them, causing Kip to jerk his hand away and Mara to turn toward the noise. Finn stood a few feet away.

The elf cleared his throat again. "Mara, the ship is ready. It's time for you to practice sailing like a sea elf," he announced.

Kip stood, helping Mara to her feet before turning to Finn. "She just finished swordplay. Inola will want her to rest and do that tomorrow," he said sternly.

"Very well," Finn conceded. "Ashroot is ready for us all to come for lunch, so ... whenever you're done with ...this," he finished awkwardly.

Finn turned without another word and headed back down toward the village. Mara followed, grabbing her sword, trying not to look back at Kip, sure that his face was as flushed as hers felt.

Chapter Eighteen

Obstacles and Ornaments

Bright and early the following morning, Finn led Mara and Ashroot toward *Harrgalti*. Kip told Mara that they would be training the full day—as long as she was doing well—so Ashroot came along to prepare meals for them through the day and to fish for supper in the open waters.

"You'll be sailing all day. I'm going to explain to you what to do, but you need to do everything yourself. Clear?" Finn called.

"Yes, Finn." Mara yawned.

Once they boarded the ship, Ashroot went straight below deck. Mara assumed she was heading to her bunk. Finn drew up the anchor, pulled back the plank, and instructed Mara to head out into open water first.

"I want to see how you fare in the calm waters before we try with obstacles," Finn explained. "Don't worry. I'm here to help you as you need it, so ask me whatever you need to."

Mara nodded silently, focusing on steering the ship away from the docks without hitting other ships. Once she made it to open water, she was comfortable. Teddy had shown her how to sail when they'd first set out, and she'd done some sailing among the small icebergs in the south, so it came to her easily enough—even after a few months. Once she got out into the open water, she called to Finn.

"What's going to happen to you because you came with me?"

"What do you mean?"

"Well, because the queen banished me from the island hoping I would die, and then you came with me anyway. What will you do when this is over?

Will you be able to just go home?" When Finn did not reply, she continued, "Do you want to?"

He walked up beside her. "I don't know what I want. I never heard back from my mother after your grandmother told us about the poison. I sent her a letter and the hawk returned without it. For a long time, I've felt like I didn't belong. How could my mother be so heartless as to decide a scratch in the gauntlet should mean death? We sea elves have always been more brutal than we need to be. The only reason I would ever return would be to see if I, as king, could change them."

"That would be nice! Your people are amazing—so much of their majesty is wasted because they don't trust anyone. I spent quite a lot of time the past few weeks reading Marlin's history of the sea elves," she explained.

"That's good to hear!" Finn replied in surprise. "It's good for you to learn as much as you can about us. That should help you when you sail as well. Now ..."

Finn began to quiz Mara, asking her about different elements of the ship and presenting various hypotheticals. After an hour or so, Finn was satisfied in her ability to sail in clear waters. Ashroot called them below deck to eat a brunch. While they ate biscuits and gravy, Finn rolled out a detailed map.

"This is what I want you to use to practice," he explained. "I've set up obstacles all through the mouth of the cove. The villagers should have set up the rest of it by now, so the next test is with these."

Finn took some time to go over the full map, telling Mara that she would not be able to look at it again. There were floating buoys to create an obstacle course that was meant to mimic the treachery of the Dragon's Teeth. This would allow her to go through obstacles without being thrashed around by waves. The path twisted around and would require quick thinking to navigate as it got smaller and smaller. Once she finished her brunch, they headed back up to try the course.

Mara squealed quite a few times as she tried to navigate the course. Finn had made it so it would be very difficult for her to damage the ship—or anything else—while she tried to learn.

"Stay calm," he murmured. "You've got this. Just think about what you're doing and go through the motions—you can't hurt anything."

"Okay, okay, okay, okay."

"That's three more 'okays' than I would believe is actually okay!" Finn exclaimed. When Mara laughed, he continued, "There it is! Now go!"

Mara bumped into the buoys a few times, but overall, she did well. Finn had her turn around and complete the course again the opposite way, adding an additional obstacle. He made her go through the course backwards and forwards three times each before he was satisfied, and he had her sail back out into the open water again before they stopped for an early lunch.

For their lunch, Ashroot had cooked a few lobsters she'd caught during the course. As was customary, she'd also included fruits, vegetables, and cheese. They'd made it most of the way through their meal before anyone spoke. Finally, getting full and stretching back into her chair, Mara asked, "So what's the next test?"

Finn had just popped half a lobster tail into his mouth, so he chewed for a moment and held up a finger before swallowing and replying, "I've gone to the north and spoken with some of the water dragons above."

"*What?*" Mara and Ashroot shouted.

"Yes. Dragons."

"Wow …" Mara sat up in her chair. "What did they say?"

"They are going to create obstacles for you in the north. The trade is that if you injure a dragon, they get to eat us."

"That seems fair," Ashroot said quietly.

The obstacles the dragons had created were simply themselves. There were some rocks jutting out near the southern tip of their island where waves tended to crash. Two water dragons would allow Mara to sail around the rocks while they splashed around in the water to create unpredictability.

As Mara neared the area Finn had mentioned, she felt rather than saw the dragons swimming on either side of the ship. The ship was pulled side to side, making it harder for her to steer. After a few little splashes, one of the dragons burst out of the water and perched on the deck in front of her.

Mara gasped. The dragon was much smaller than she had expected to see, but also way more magnificent. It was sleek with violet scales like fish scales glimmering all over its body. It had four clawed legs, but the tail was like a whale's fin and the wings were like a flying fish's fins more than like actual wings. Mara suspected they were more for swimming than flying but could be used to glide just like flying fish did. Finally, it had a sleek, salamander-like snout with large gills fanning its head.

The emerald eyes bored into Mara as it asked, *You are the dwarf who needs our assistance?*

"Yes," she replied. "Thank you so much for any help you provide. Finn told me what you had planned. I promise I will do my best, and I am deeply grateful."

I am sure you will. My mate swims at the back of your ship. We will push you around obstacles three times, as your companion has requested of us. If you harm us, we will eat you. Do you understand?

Mara nodded wordlessly. With a nod of acknowledgement toward Finn, the dragon dove back into the water and the thrashing began. The first time Mara was guided into the rocks, she was too nervous and slammed the starboard side into a rock. Squealing, she overcorrected and hit a rock on the port side.

"Calm down!" Finn shouted.

Helpful. After another scrape into the rocks, Mara righted herself, thankful she'd hit rocks and not a dragon. Her second pass went better— she hit a rock, but only the one. Her third pass was flawless. Mara sailed between jagged rocks, steered around to weave through the hazards, and avoided the dragons as they splashed to veer the ship off course. When she emerged into the open water after her final pass, all was calm.

Both dragons glided out of the water and landed on the ship this time. The violet dragon's mate was its opposite, with a sleek, emerald green body and violet eyes. They both stretched their mouths into frightening grins, showing their pearly teeth, which were perfect white with a rainbow glint.

The green dragon spoke. *You have done well, dwarf. Your chances of survival if you sail through the dragon's teeth are . . . moderate.*

Moderate was not good. "Oh. Um, I'm sorry that I did so poorly," Mara said, glancing at Finn and back to the dragons.

You misunderstand, the violet dragon said. *Only the most experienced have high chances of survival. For a dwarf, you have done the best that can be expected. If you allow your fear to overcome you, you will fail.*

The green dragon added, *If you sail with a purpose and do not let yourself be defeated, you will not be.*

"But, what does that even mean?" Mara asked.

The dragons slowly shook their heads. The green one said, *We have done all we will to assist you. We will answer no more questions. Our bond has ended.*

Sea elf, said the purple dragon. *Please provide us our payment.*

Mara looked back at Finn, confused. He nodded to the dragons and beckoned Mara to a large wrapped bundle on the edge of the deck. He whipped the canvas off to reveal a netted cage full of hundreds of crabs with bound pincers. They slid the cage out into the center of the ship as the dragons shrieked with pleasure. One dragon floated down to either side of the cage and clutched it in its magnificent claws.

Good luck, the dragons said, before lightly tipping their heads to Mara, then to Finn, and taking the cage of crabs away with them. Once they disappeared, Mara turned to Finn. "Crabs? Why crabs?" she asked.

Finn laughed for a while before answering, "Dragons are magnificent creatures, but it's hard for them to sneak up on prey that's in the sand. The water dragons love crabs—they're their favorite food—but they are unable to catch them on their own."

"Wow," Mara replied. Meeting Finn's eyes, they both burst into laughter. Finn ran up to Mara and hugged her, picking her up into the air and twirling her around as he shouted with joy.

"You did it, Mara! Amazing job! Now let's head back to Nimeda before nightfall," he said, giving Mara a final squeeze before taking the helm himself.

As they entered the cove, Mara could see bright lights strung from the docks, through the town, and up into the forest near the cliffs. She turned around to Finn to see that he and Ashroot stood together, smiling.

"What is this?" she asked.

Finn just threw his hands in the air noncommittally before busying himself with the docking. Ashroot hopped over and hugged Mara, saying, "Oh, I thought for sure you would question us taking you out all day today!"

"Wait, what?" Mara asked again.

"Nothing, nothing. Come on," Ashroot replied, grabbing Mara's hand and pulling her off onto the docks as soon as Finn was ready.

Mara walked apprehensively through the town, following Ashroot and the strung lights. They walked past the center of town, where Toren's statue glowed with wrapped garlands, and they walked up through brightly lit trees to a grove near where Mara had sat with Kip the day before. Gathered in the clearing were Inola and Teddy—and the whole town. There were tables laden with food, with wooden crates stacked next to them, and a boar was roasting nearby on a spit.

Looking around, Mara saw Kip emerge from the darkness of the forest, holding a circlet made of leaves and delicate, colored flowers. He grinned as he placed it on Mara's head and said, "Happy birthday, Dragonwolf."

Kip had steered Mara to a center table—she was too bleary-eyed to get there on her own. She'd coasted through the meal, not really understanding her surroundings. The boar was tasty, but the conversations continued around her as she just smiled and ate. She'd been thinking about how nice this was, sure, but she was also remembering her last birthday. She couldn't believe she had been there for an entire year.

She loved her family on Earth, and she thought she would dwell on the loss of them, but how could she dwell on what she had lost when there was so much she had gained? She missed them—she would always miss Kara and her dad—but she'd made great friends who'd done wonderful things for her here. She'd accomplished so much. She thought about that last magnificent cake, with the dragon curled around it, and wondered if there would be a cake today. If there were, they surely had a better reference to make a dragon—since she'd seen dragons earlier that day. In a year, she'd gone from seeing dragons in movies and D&D to seeing dragons just a few feet away. It was unreal.

Mara dimly realized there was a bell sounding, and it briefly reminded her of the gauntlet. She felt a twinge of pain in her arm before looking around and seeing a new arrival standing at the highest point of the clearing.

"Salali?" Mara exclaimed.

The traveler Mara had met in Port Albatross stood there, clearly an important guest. Salali grinned at Mara and announced, "Yes, hello again, Mara! Nimeda is my hometown. I didn't know who you were when I met you so many months ago, but I'm glad to be able to assist the daughter of Toren. I've considered what you said. I am here today to tell a story for your birthday—and I do believe you know this one."

Mara looked up at Kip, who was sitting across from her, and he grinned and mouthed, "Happy birthday."

"Now then," Salali began, clearing her throat. "Tonight's tale is one that many of you may know—a bedtime tale once told around the realm. This is the tale of Gaetan, Brim, and Golos, and it begins like they always do." She took a deep breath. "Once upon a time, an old dwarf named Brim lived in a hill. His neighbors hated to see him walk by, because they were not friends. His neighbors were the gnomes. The gnomes believed the hills were theirs and theirs alone, so they frequently tried to get the dwarf to leave the hill. None of their plans ever worked—but they always made the dwarf very angry.

"Finally, the dwarf had enough of their schemes and decided he wanted to get rid of all the gnomes instead. There were so many more gnomes, so what was he to do? Well, he traveled far to find another hill dweller—Golos the giant. Golos the giant was known for his hatred of gnomes, so he was happy to come deal with Brim's problem. Brim, excited to finally have the hill to himself, didn't ask the giant to explain how he would get rid of the gnomes. That was one of many mistakes, for hill giants are crafty and often underestimated.

"Golos was happy to get the gnomes out of the hill because he wanted it for himself. The giant stomped over to the gnome village and destroyed all their homes—but he didn't stop there. Much to the dwarf's despair, Golos destroyed his home, too. Suddenly, Brim and all the gnomes found themselves lost on lesser hills. After days and days trying to figure out what to do, they finally decided that they would have to work together to get their homes back.

"Learning his lesson from the giant, Brim made sure the gnomish elder drew up a contract. They agreed to live together once they'd gotten rid of the giant, and they agreed to never fight over territory again. The gnomes agreed that the dwarf had a right to live where he lived, and they wouldn't try to drive him out anymore. The dwarf agreed to use his expertise to help them all get their homes back.

"Finally, once they had signed contracts and prepared, Gaetan was sent to be the gnomish representative on the quest, and he and Brim left for their old home." At this point, Salali took a deep breath and spoke very fast. "So the dwarf and the gnome traveled the land, fighting all manner of monsters, and blah blah blah, until finally they made it to the hill. They had an epic battle with the giant, involving trickery and teamwork, and they got their home back. They all lived happily ever after. The end."

Some of the townspeople were looking around and murmuring, so Salali asked, in mock confusion, "What? You don't like that ending? Something missing?"

Mara knew what was missing. She'd heard her dad tell this story before, and she smiled warmly.

Salali continued, "Near each table is a box. Someone move that box to the table please." One person from each table—Kip at Mara's—placed the crate on the surface.

"Now, inside that box is a group effort birthday present for dear Mara," Salali announced. "Thanks to Nadie, who was also born on Earth, we had enough information to construct the basic version of a popular Earth game called ... *what was it called again?* ... DUNGEONS & DRAGONS!" Salali thanked the short woman, Nadie, who stood next to her and had apparently answered her question.

Nadie stepped forward and explained the basic rules to the group, telling each table they'd be playing together simultaneously with one tablemate as the Dungeon Master. Once all the groups had completed the short campaign, they would have some final surprises before the party was over. "For now, though, let the campaigning begin!" she called.

Mara played the short game with Inola, Teddy, Finn, Kip, and Ashroot. Teddy played the role of Dungeon Master, which made Mara smile, since that was the role her dad played when he told her this story. Mara played Brim, and the others played gnomes. They enjoyed the game—though Finn was upset about the lack of realism. He figured since he'd stabbed something in the face, it should be dead. Hit points were ridiculous to him. However, with any frustration from realism or from the finesse required to replace the standard dice set with other objects, they also had a lot of fun. The forest was filled with laughter.

Finally, once everyone had completed their game, Inola stood to address her village, bringing Ashroot with her. "This marvelous young lady," she began, "has blessed us with a creation from Aeunna. I will only warn you once—the anamberry has the power to kill in high doses. Eat only the amount you are given. Understood?"

There was a murmur of assent throughout the forest.

Inola turned to her granddaughter. "Mara, I have sixteen years of birthdays to make up. I believe the best way to do that is to pass along a precious gift I was given long ago. The night my lifemate died, during the completion of a Ranger trial, the goddess Aeun came to me and she gave me a gift—this." She held up a leather necklace with an emerald leaf hanging from it. "Aeun told me this precious gift would not give back what I lost but would be for what I found. I found you, Mara. My wonderful granddaughter, after seventeen years apart. So—this is for you. Come here."

Mara stood, blinded again with tears, and walked up to her grandmother. As Inola slipped the necklace over her head to rest next to Kip's, she said, "You're going soon to meet Aeun. Tell her I have given you my gift and she'll grace you with her favor." With that, she pulled Mara into a tight hug, kissing her on the forehead before turning back to the group, one arm still around her.

"In honor of Mara's seventeenth birthday, Ashroot has made seventeen different anamberry desserts. They are waiting for us down at the statue of Toren in the village. Please follow our guest of honor and make your way down there before you head home for the night."

She steered Mara forward, and then Kip slid his hand into Mara's and led her through the forest for the final piece of the most wonderful birthday celebration.

The following morning, Mara woke up with a grin and a full belly. Her arm and leg still ached, more now that she had slept off a full day of rigorous sailing, but she was content. She gently caressed the two trinkets around her neck, one in each hand. She couldn't believe Kip had become such a wonderful friend. He had listened to her wants—though probably sent by her grandmother—and he had ensured she had a great birthday, even if she had forgotten it. Her grandmother, not knowing the value of her gift, just knowing it had been the gift of a *goddess*, had handed Mara perhaps the most valuable thing she'd ever owned.

She hoped it would come in handy when she finally made it to Aeun. Grunting with effort, Mara stood and began what had become a morning routine. She bared her leg and rubbed some of the pain-numbing poultice on it, stretching the muscles and massaging into the meat of her leg. Inola had told Mara to do this for a few months at least once a day, whether there was pain or not. It would prevent scar tissue from knotting up and causing her problems later.

As she began to massage the poultice into her ribs, much more delicately, as they would take many months to properly heal, Ashroot stirred. "Morning, Mara," the bearkin said sleepily, stretching and rolling to sit up in her bed.

"Morning, Ash." Mara turned awkwardly away from her friend. She was grateful that people in Ambergrove still wore bras and underwear, but she still felt weird standing in them around someone—even Ashroot. She patted her leg and discovered the poultice had dried, so she slipped on a pair of brown pants.

"Are you ready for today, Mara?" Ashroot asked quietly.

Mara patted her ribs and decided the poultice was dry enough for her to wear a loose shirt. She slipped a raspberry colored shirt on and sat back on her bed, looking over at Ashroot as she began rubbing the poultice into her arm, which always took the longest. "What do you mean?" she asked.

"Don't you know?" Ashroot asked awkwardly.

"Apparently not—ah—are you going to tell me?" Mara grimaced as she rubbed a particularly painful spot on her arm.

As Ashroot opened her mouth to reply, there was a knock on their door. Finn opened it, stuck his nose in, and announced, "Are you girls packing? The ship is ready to go whenever you have your things together." He closed the door without another word.

"Oh," Mara said quietly. "I forgot that passing Finn's little sailing test meant it was time for us to set sail again." She stared at her arm while she massaged the ointment in.

"You'll miss her—I know," Ashroot began, guessing the cause for her friend's long face, "but she'll still be here when we come back through. And now that you know where she is, you can come visit her when this is all over. It'll be okay."

Ashroot walked over and patted Mara on the shoulder reassuringly, and then they both began to pack.

It seemed the whole town had gathered for their departure. Finn had been taking charge of the loading while Kip carted supplies to the ship, Ashroot was picking out fresh foods to bring along, and Teddy was securing loose ends and making sure nothing was forgotten. Mara sat with her grandmother, trying to be strong.

"What you have to do is so important, Mara," Inola reasoned.

"I know."

"And you know what? Now that I know you're here, I'm not letting you get away. Once you finish what you need to do, come back here and see me. You'll always have family."

"I don't get how I was so happy last night ... but I'm so sad this morning," Mara blubbered.

"You have a hard road ahead of you, and you worry—that's not a bad thing." Inola embraced her in a hug with the warmth of seventeen years of grandma goodbyes.

Teddy found them like that awhile later and told Mara it was time to go.

"Chin up, Dragonwolf," Inola said with a watery smile, kissing Mara on the forehead.

With a final goodbye, Mara turned and allowed Teddy to steer her away. They strode past the villagers who'd lined the streets to see them off. Mara paused at the statue of her father. It was life size. And it was the closest she would ever get to him again. Mara stepped up to the statue and embraced it, quietly promising her dad that she would do him proud.

Finn steered the ship away from the cove and toward their final destination. Teddy had planned for Mara to continue working with Kip for most of the journey to the Dragon's Teeth. They weren't sure what they would be up against, but she would need to be ready to fight, just in case.

Although they could see the Dragon's Teeth from the overlook in the village, they weren't as near as they seemed. After over a week at sea, they still had a long way to go. Teddy and Finn took turns at the helm. When they weren't sailing the ship, they were fishing with Ashroot. Although they'd been able to get a lot of supplies before leaving town, they wanted to preserve them as long as possible—so they'd been having a lot of fish.

Kip and Mara spent a lot of time together, sparring. Occasionally, Mara fought with Finn or Teddy instead for the varied practice. Finn joked she needed to practice with someone more her size, which infuriated Kip. Time passed quickly, and they enjoyed spending it together. Mara learned more about Finn and his people while they stayed up together cleaning fish. They all took turns keeping watch at night. Teddy was usually by himself now that there were five of them—but switching shifts gave everyone a chance to get to know each other better.

Mara was standing at the helm during an early morning watch with Finn, when he whistled for her attention and told her to slip the wheel pin in place and come to the bow. When Mara met him at the bow, she blanched. They'd made it. It had taken a couple weeks already, but Mara was sure she would have more time. It was no use. There, not fifty yards away, were the jagged shards that would decide their fate.

CHAPTER NINETEEN

THE DRAGON'S TEETH

"What are you talking about?" Mara shrieked.

Teddy, Kip, and Ashroot had come up to the deck and were alarmed at Mara's behavior. Finn raising his hands to calm her down, as if she were a petulant child, just made her more irrational.

"What's the problem?" Teddy asked.

Finn spoke first, in a measured voice. "I was trying to explain to Mara that, since we've reached the Dragon's Teeth, she—"

"He said I'm the one who has to sail the ship through *that*!" Mara interrupted, flinging a hand out to point at the waves crashing into jagged rocks not too far away.

To her surprise, no one else seemed to see this as news. Ashroot looked nervously at the ground and Kip looked anywhere but at her, but Teddy just shrugged and gave her a look as if to say that was the obvious conclusion. Seeing her anger rising, Teddy cleared his throat and explained, "We came on this journey to help you, Mara—not to complete it for you. Finn was always here to give you the skills to make it through yourself."

"*What?*" she shouted again. "I'm not ready for this! Are you all really prepared to put your lives in my hands?"

There was an uncomfortable silence before Finn said, "We've already done that, Mara. Each and every one of us left to follow you, and we know that we're not all going to make it through. We're here anyway—because of you." She looked around and saw the others nodding in agreement.

"I need a minute." Mara disappeared below deck without another word.

Teddy was the one to come check on Mara awhile later. He found her sitting on her bunk, staring at items on her bed. First was the dragonwolf bracer, second was her dad's cuff, and third was the token of Aeun.

"What's troubling you, lass?" he asked.

She lingered on the items before answering. "I don't know if I can do this, Teddy. For each of the trials, it was just my life at stake. When we were in the south, we were all fighting together. Now, it's just me. You're all depending on me, and if I do one thing wrong, you all die—and I'm responsible!" She slammed a fist on the mattress.

Teddy sank onto her bunk. "Look at me," he ordered. She glanced up miserably, and he continued, "We *chose* to be here. Every one of us. You chose to take on the trials to be the Ranger and the rest of us *chose* to come along. If something happens to us, it won't be because *you* made a choice, but because *we* did."

Mara nodded slowly and picked up her bracer, tracing the wings of the dragonwolf. "Okay, Teddy" she murmured.

"Good." Teddy patted Mara's leg. "Why don't you gather up all your trinkets and come up top, so you can show us what you're made of?"

Mara sniffled and breathed deeply, trying to calm herself and dry her tears before heading back up. She wiped her eyes and patted her cheeks, and then ascended the stairs. She hoped that she looked like a hero. The dragonwolf bracer was strapped to her right forearm. Her necklaces—tokens of fondness—framed her first token from Ambergrove—the deep claw marks from the Great Silver Bear. The cuff from her dad, which had been passed down through her family, rested next to the token of friendship from her sister.

Her face set, without a glance toward her companions, Mara strode to the helm and spun the wheel in the direction of the jagged rocks. Waves crashed into the massive rocks, forcing their own current like the water dragons had done. Mara followed the current in at the widest point. She breathed deliberately, trying to focus. As they passed the first jagged rocks, they glided easily into the jaws of the Dragon's Teeth.

There, Mara saw additional obstacles she hadn't planned for. Dozens of ruined ships stuck out of the water, but *Harrgalti* was moving too fast to contend with them. Knowing the ships would do less damage than the rocks, she erred on the side of the wreckage as Little Red continued through them. She twisted the wheel to the left and glided past another rock before skidding the ship across a rowboat and smashing the rowboat into a nearby ship.

As she sailed around jagged rock after jagged rock, trying not to catch anything else, she could see it—through a mass of wrecked ships were two stony teeth with a clear opening. She took a deep breath and clenched her fists on the wheel. There was a reason there were so many wrecked ships through here. They'd seen the end in sight and had rushed for it. Navigating as slowly as the current would allow, Mara began to sing a shanty, hoping that would lighten the load and help her through.

Although the others had not spoken to her, no doubt to prevent distraction, once Mara began to sing, they sang along. Teddy and Finn both seemed to know the song, and they sang loudly. Kip and Ashroot had trouble. Kip just fumbled a beat behind, and Ashroot decided to vocalize instead—poorly, as one would expect from a bear. Mara was heartened. They were together, and they would make it through together.

She made her way around the ships—right, left, right, right, left—until the ship was directed right at the opening. The final row of teeth. Extending the final line of the chorus and shouting the words rather than singing, Mara made a final beeline for the opening, and the ship burst through and away from the danger with the force of the crashing waves.

She could hear shouting and cheering behind her as she looked out on the stilling water and the formations of islands in the distance, but she still clutched the wheel. Finn dropped the anchor, and the ship came to a stop in the calm center of clear water. They'd done it. They'd made it through, and the isles of the gods were ahead.

Suddenly, Mara was swept off her feet and the wheel wrenched out of her hand. Kip, despite being two thirds her height, had picked her up like a bag of feed and was twirling her around in circles. As she spun, she got glimpses of Ashroot jumping up and down, Teddy grinning, and Finn rushing to the abandoned helm.

They would still have a few days of sailing left before they made it to the islands, hopefully unscathed. Mara suggested they take a day to celebrate and reassess before moving forward. Teddy and Finn worked on minor repairs for the ship, and Ashroot holed up below deck to prepare a fancy dinner.

Mara and Kip were below deck, cutting up spare pants. The water was so clear and beautiful, Mara wanted to blow off some steam with a little swim. She cut one of her pairs of red pants into shorts, grabbed a red tank top, and changed her clothes in the storeroom. When she came back out, Kip was pulling off his shirt. He turned around to face her wearing massacred black pants.

She laughed at the sight of him and ran past him up the stairs. Kip chased her and caught up with her right at the top of the stairs, picking her up again and hauling her over his shoulder. In a few great bounds, he jumped overboard, taking her with him. Then, they did something Mara hadn't done in a long time—they played.

Ashroot called everyone down for their meal a few hours later. As they filed into the galley, they met a magnificent sight. Ashroot had brought a small boar from Nimeda and roasted most of it, leaving it in the center of the table full of fixins. There were mashed potatoes. There were large rolls. There were bacon-wrapped shrimp.

"This is amazing, Ash!" Finn exclaimed as he sat.

The others murmured their agreement as they took their seats. Teddy reached for a shrimp and Ashroot rapped his hand with a big wooden ladle.

"Not yet!" she commanded, as he stuffed his poor knuckles in his mouth. "... I have something I'd like to say," she added quietly.

Teddy folded his hands on the table and said, "Go ahead, Ashroot."

"I know this has been a long journey, even for those who came in later. Finn, I appreciate how you have helped me with fish and deep-sea creatures. Kip, you have also helped me by teaching me how to be more brave. Teddy, you have been good and fair—fatherly when I've been without my own." She kept her head down as she spoke, but she nodded in each direction in turn. "Mara, when I met you, I knew I'd be willing to go to the end of the world with you. Now, here we are. I don't know what the next few days will bring, but I made this meal for you all to show you how much I appreciate having you ... as family," she finished, in a near whisper.

"Me too, Ash," Mara said, resting a hand on Ashroot's paw.

"I have a question," Mara began, approaching Teddy a few days later. "Which is the right one?"

She stretched the map in front of him on the deck. There were dozens of islands ahead of them, each spanning about a quarter mile. There were no labels on the map—just the general shape. The islands formed a dotted triskelion. She handed the map to Teddy, who peered down at it a moment before answering.

"No one actually knows," he said.

"Wonderful! That's great. Well, do you have a guess or anything?"

Teddy traced the islands with a finger. "There's one island for each god or goddess. That's all I know. I'm not sure at this point which to suggest."

Kip walked up to where they stood at the bow, calling, "Finn wants to know which island we're going to go to."

Mara looked at Teddy, who shrugged. She sighed and said, "The first one, I guess!"

It was in this way they found themselves dropping anchor by one of the islands in the center of the triskelion. It was warm and green. The island was covered in trees, so their chances were good. Ashroot and Finn stayed behind to watch the ship as Teddy, Mara, and Kip headed onto the island.

They weren't on the island very long before they came across a small stone cottage with a mossy roof. On the porch, leaning back in a large rocking chair, was a giant, tanned man with dirty blond hair and dirty brown clothes. As soon as she saw him, Mara began to back away, knowing this was the wrong god and not wanting to anger him.

"Who enters my domain?" he asked with a rumbling voice, eyes closed.

Mara paused and sighed deeply before stepping forward. "My name is Mara. I'm on a Ranger trial and am seeking Aeun. We've come to the wrong place, sir."

The god's eyes snapped open. He sat up and looked at Mara, and then his eyes settled behind her. "That would make you Kip?" he asked, pointing to the gnome.

Startled, Kip nodded.

"Good, good. That's good," the god rumbled. "I am Baerk, god of the earth. We will have reason to meet, but not quite yet," he told Kip. As Kip stammered, Baerk turned to Mara. "Following your heart has led you this far, miss Mara. Return to your ship and steer it wherever your heart takes you. That will lead you to Aeun," Baerk told her kindly.

"Thank you so much!" Mara replied, bowing deeply, not sure what else to do to show respect, and very much confused about the whole interaction.

"Right-o. Best be on your way, I think. You have a very long journey ahead of you before we meet again, and you need to get going. Farewell, Dragonwolf." With that, Baerk turned and strode into his home, closing the door without another word.

They'd been dismissed. They made their way back to the ship in silence—no doubt each trying to process what the god had said.

Once they reached the ship, Mara made her way to the helm as Kip and Teddy explained some of what had happened on the island to Finn and Ashroot. She unrolled the map, assessing before closing her eyes and holding onto the emerald leaf token with one hand. Slowly, she placed a finger on the map and opened her eyes. Her finger rested on a heart-shaped island at the tip of the whorl nearest to the forbidden lands. She gazed at it for a moment, nodded, and told the others she was ready to try again.

She sailed the ship this time. She went south, below Baerk's island and between two others—so she could approach the new island from the north and avoid the forbidden lands. From there, it was a straight shot. It only took a few hours for the chosen island to be in sight. Mara sailed in between the mounds of the heart shape, directing the ship into a small cove.

As soon as she passed into the territory of this island, however, a thick mist fell. Mara's necklace began to glow, there was a flash, and everything went dark.

Mara awoke in a soft hammock made of leaves. She sat up quickly and looked around, causing the hammock to shake and throw her to the ground. Someone behind her laughed melodiously. Mara turned. She was in a beautiful forest near a clear pond. There were woodland creatures drinking from the pool, sampling the grass, and just bathing in the sun. Behind Mara stood a beautiful woman.

She was tall, with reddish brown skin the color of Aeunna tree bark. She had twinkling green eyes and poofy, green hair that framed her face like leaves on a tree. She wore a long, white dress with leaves and delicate creatures embroidered all around it. As she walked toward Mara, the hem of her dress rustled the ground and stirred up butterflies.

"You have come a long way, Mara Green," the woman said. She extended a hand to help Mara up. Mara took it apprehensively and stood.

"You ... Are you Aeun?" she asked timidly.

The goddess nodded and smiled at Mara. "I am she, the mother of nature, and the matron goddess of the forest dwarves."

"So ... I've completed my trial?" Mara exclaimed.

"Hmm ..." Aeun shook her head. "Not quite, I'm afraid. You were to come here so I could instruct you further. You completed each trial to gain your companions. You have done well—they will be your dearest friends and your solemn responsibility while you undertake the task I have set for you."

"What?" Mara asked derisively. "I earned a token from the Great Silver Bear. I saved Kip's family and got his help to sail through the Ice Mountains. We defeated the *ice kraken*. I completed the Serpent's Gauntlet of the sea elves—and was poisoned by the crazy queen. *And* I sailed through the Dragon's Teeth! I don't know how I made it here, so how am I going to go do something else?"

Aeun looked Mara over patiently, shaking her head. Mara looked down, chastened, and clasped her hands before blurting an apology.

"I understand your apprehension, Mara, but I would not have chosen you for this task if I didn't believe you could complete it. You have spent the past year preparing yourself, gaining experience sailing, fighting, surviving, learning the people, and finding loyal friends along the way. This was all necessary and will help you in your next endeavor."

"I'm sorry—I am. I know that the forest dwarves believed I was some chosen successor, so I knew there would be something big coming up. What is it I need to do?" Mara asked, as humbly as possible.

"Come with me." Aeun guided her to the edge of the pool and knelt down. Mara knelt beside her as the goddess swept a hand over the pool. Ambergrove appeared on the surface of the pool like a geographical map, gliding from the isles of the gods to the forbidden lands. "Long ago, travelers from Earth settled in this land. At that time, it was called Lesser Earth." A bustling city materialized, and the images continued to shift as Aeun told the tale. "In the early days, the people lived in harmony. They brought their science from Earth and used it to better lives. Then, after a while, Toren stuck his hand in."

"Toren?" Mara asked.

"God of chaos, after whom your grandmother named your father. He reminded the humans of the other things their land possessed in large quantity. Famine, war, debt, greed. The greed of the people, driven by chaos, corrupted the cities. They developed currency and hoarded goods. They fought over their possessions. People sat in large homes and feasted on more than they could ever eat—while others begged in the gutter and went days without food. It brought all Ambergrove down low. The greed and chaos seeped into all lands, and the other lands began to fight needlessly. Finally, the gods banded together against Toren. We tried to use our magic to remove science from Ambergrove. We banished the people from the cities back to Earth, removing even Ambergrove's magic in the process. It was no use—the darkness had already taken root.

"All through Ambergrove, dissention ran rampant. Race fought race and people stopped trying to help each other. To limit the spread, we forbade all from entering the old cities. The races separated to their own lands and have remained thus for centuries. In the recent century, however, people have been making their way to the forbidden lands to follow a new leader—someone who enjoys chaos and wants to see it continue.

"We cannot stick our hands in any further. We've done all we can. My task for you is to travel into the forbidden lands, find the source of this darkness, and stamp it out. Renew the land from the ruined cities to something beautiful this world can be proud of. Set the example for others—so we might spend the next few centuries repairing our world and one day emerge anew."

Mara hadn't realized Aeun was finished. She was trying to process all the goddess had said. The task before her seemed impossible. Complicated. Unbelievably dangerous. "So ..." Mara began apprehensively. "So—you've given me the history of the land and what the future should be. What exactly is my trial? What am I supposed to do here?"

Aeun smiled at her and rested a finger under her chin, raising her head gently. "You will travel to the forbidden lands, work to cleanse the land of the darkness that holds it, and defeat the new leader. If you are able to rid the land of the evil that holds it, you will prove yourself to all, and you will open the door for other brave adventurers to mend our world."

Mara nodded blankly. "Makes sense, makes sense ..."

Aeun laughed a laugh that was more like a song, causing birds to flit down into her hair as she said, "You will understand in time, Mara. Rest now. You must rejoin your friends soon."

Mara awoke sometime later feeling refreshed. She felt more confident—though she had to swallow the fear of failure and the fear of what would happen to the others if she failed. She stirred more slowly this time, stepping lightly out of her hammock and wandering around the pool in search of Aeun.

She finally found Aeun on the southern edge of the island, staring out over the water toward the forbidden lands. Mara blinked and rubbed her eyes. The land itself seemed to be dampened under a dark gloom. Aeun's dress whipped out behind her and her hair rustled dramatically as Mara approached and stopped beside her.

"It looks bad over there," Mara whispered.

"That it is, but your heart can bring light to it—if you're ready to undertake the task." The goddess looked down at her.

Mara stood silently for a moment before taking a deep breath. "I am," she said. "I have to be."

"Good answer!" Aeun exclaimed, patting Mara on the shoulder and turning to walk back through the forest.

When Mara just stood staring, the goddess turned briefly and reached out a hand, beckoning for her to follow. They walked in silence all the way across to the small cove. Mara clutched her necklaces as they walked, trying to feel some sense of security about the task ahead. She nearly walked into Aeun as the goddess stopped at the edge of the cove.

"What have you got there?" Aeun asked her, pointing down at her hands.

"Oh, this?" Mara asked, opening her hands to reveal her necklaces.

Aeun reached out and clasped the necklaces. Looking at the necklace from Kip, she grinned and nodded approvingly. When she held the emerald leaf, Aeun's eyes widened. "Hmm," she began, looking into Mara's eyes. "I see you have something for me."

"Oh? ... Oh! Right! This was from my grandmother, Inola. She said you gave her this token after my grandfather was killed during my dad's Ranger trial." Mara sputtered.

"Indeed," Aeun replied, straightening. "She gave this to you?"

"For my birthday this year—since it's the first time I've met her," Mara explained.

"Hmm ..." Aeun closed her fist around the emerald and it disappeared. She grasped Mara's right hand and turned it so the dragonwolf on her bracer was facing upward. "What do you know of the dragonwolf?" she asked sharply.

Mara laughed heartily. "I made that up when I was little. My dad thought it was funny, so he made it my Ranger symbol."

"Is that so?" Aeun asked mischievously, snapping her fingers.

Something howled from the forest behind them. Mara turned and saw a giant wolf the size of a draft horse—only it wasn't a wolf. As it approached, it stretched out broad wings. There was a scuffle underneath the creature as three dragonwolf pups tussled at their mother's feet.

"What?" Mara exclaimed. "H-how are they—"

"You dreamt of the dragonwolf when you were small, Mara—not because you had imagined it, but because here is where you have always belonged. The dragonwolves are among many creatures that have disappeared from the world. When the world fell into chaos, I brought the dragonwolves to the isles of the gods for their protection. They are so blindingly loyal, the servants of chaos clamored to have them for their own—to use them against each other."

"So that's how Kip has been able to carve a dragonwolf for Loli all this time," Mara marveled. "They're *real*."

Mara had never been sensible when it came to puppies. Now, seeing adorable puppies she thought she'd made up, she just had to pet one. It seemed the puppies had the same idea. As she approached them, the puppies paused their tussling to tackle her instead. Mara squeaked and laughed as she rolled on the ground with them, the puppies struggling to lick her. Their mother grew impatient and barked at her young, so, with a last look at Mara, they lumbered back toward their mother.

All but one. The smallest of the puppies—barely the size of a terrier—paused a few feet away from Mara and whined. It had soft terra cotta fur that poofed out and made it look twice its actual size. Its wings were small—too small for it to fly, but enough for a glide and hop, like a fledgling owl. It approached Mara again in this way, looking back at its mother. Mara looked at the mother, too, as the fierce wolf stared into her eyes. Finally, the mother tipped her head and retreated into the woods. The young pup yipped and jumped into Mara's lap, licking every bit of her face it could reach—to Mara's joy.

"It is decided," Aeun declared behind her.

Mara stood and held the puppy in her arms, turning toward Aeun. "What's decided?"

"I have accepted the token returned. The mother wolf has deemed you worthy. Her young pup has chosen you."

"Wait, wait …" Mara looked down into the bright blue eyes of the young pup. "You mean it's mine?"

"She. And yes—she is yours." Aeun replied, smiling warmly. "Now— I think your friends have been waiting long enough."

Mara nodded to the goddess, scritching the pup's chin as she did. "Thank you for everything."

"Until we meet again, dragonwolves," Aeun said, nodding to Mara and snapping her fingers.

Mara stood on the deck of *Harrgalti*. As soon as they appeared, the dragonwolf pup squeaked and hid in the closest corner. Mara looked around. Her companions all stood on the deck, frozen. As she looked at them, she thought she heard a snap, and she saw a flash of green light as her friends came back to life.

"Mara! You made it!" Teddy shouted, running over to her and hugging her.

"How did you know? You were frozen." Mara said.

"Ashroot told us," Finn explained. "She met the goddess, too, and got something her da had asked her for. Aeun snapped her back here and froze us all soon after she returned."

Mara just stared at them with her mouth open for a moment before congratulating Ashroot and hugging Teddy.

"So, how did it go? What did she say?" Kip asked.

"Let's go to the table and talk," Mara suggested.

They all gathered around the table in the galley so Mara could explain. She told her friends the story of the old cities—a story the rest of them had heard before—though it seemed some details had been omitted. She told of the future the goddess had painted and the task Mara was set. They all listened quietly while she explained and sat quietly after she finished.

"I-I know it's a lot to ask," Mara began. "You've come with me this far. You risked your lives to make it through the Dragon's Teeth. I won't think any less of you if you want to go home now." She looked down at the table and picked at her nails, not ready for their answers.

The others began to talk over each other. Mara looked up as they quieted and stared at each other. Teddy nodded and looked to her. "We're here for the long haul, Mara. Our fight isn't over until yours is."

Mara smiled as she looked at her uncle. She met each of her friends' eyes in turn as she said, "You mean it? You're all with me?"

Nod after nod met Mara's eyes. She smiled as she looked at the last nod—Kip's. "I have to have the best, fullest dragonwolf story to tell Loli," he told her with a soft smile.

As he said "dragonwolf," there was a yip and a clatter behind them. With all her might, the dragonwolf pup jumped and glided, landing clumsily on the table. Ashroot squeaked and fell back in her chair. Finn stood and backed into a fighting stance, brandishing a loose fork. Teddy and Kip just laughed as the pup yipped and jumped into Mara's arms, licking her face.

"It seems we're all ready!" Teddy laughed, reaching out a hand to pet the pup.

Ashroot and Finn, realizing there was no danger, laughed and came to pet the pup as well. Yipping and wagging her tail happily, the puppy rolled onto her belly on the table, enjoying the attention she got from her new friends. Mara smiled. They may have a long road ahead of them, but today was good. They were together, they were happy, and they had been victorious. Fear was for tomorrow, but the journey was far from over, and one among this happy band would not make it home.

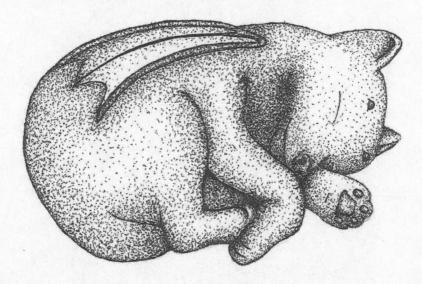

9 781665 502030

CPSIA information can be obtained
at www.ICGtesting.com
Printed in the USA
BVHW042154280223
659432BV00009B/91

9 781665 502030